THE WAR OF LIGHT

THE COMPENDIUM TRILOGY

C. D. TAVENOR

LEGACY OF LIGHT

HAMMER OF MARIPES

My love, you cannot leave. You will fail.

It is for that reason I must leave. Even if I fail, I will have failed knowing I did more than nothing.

We are at peace. They do not threaten us.

If we are to move beyond "peace," we must do more than simply wait. We must unite. I must follow the commands of our Lord of Light.

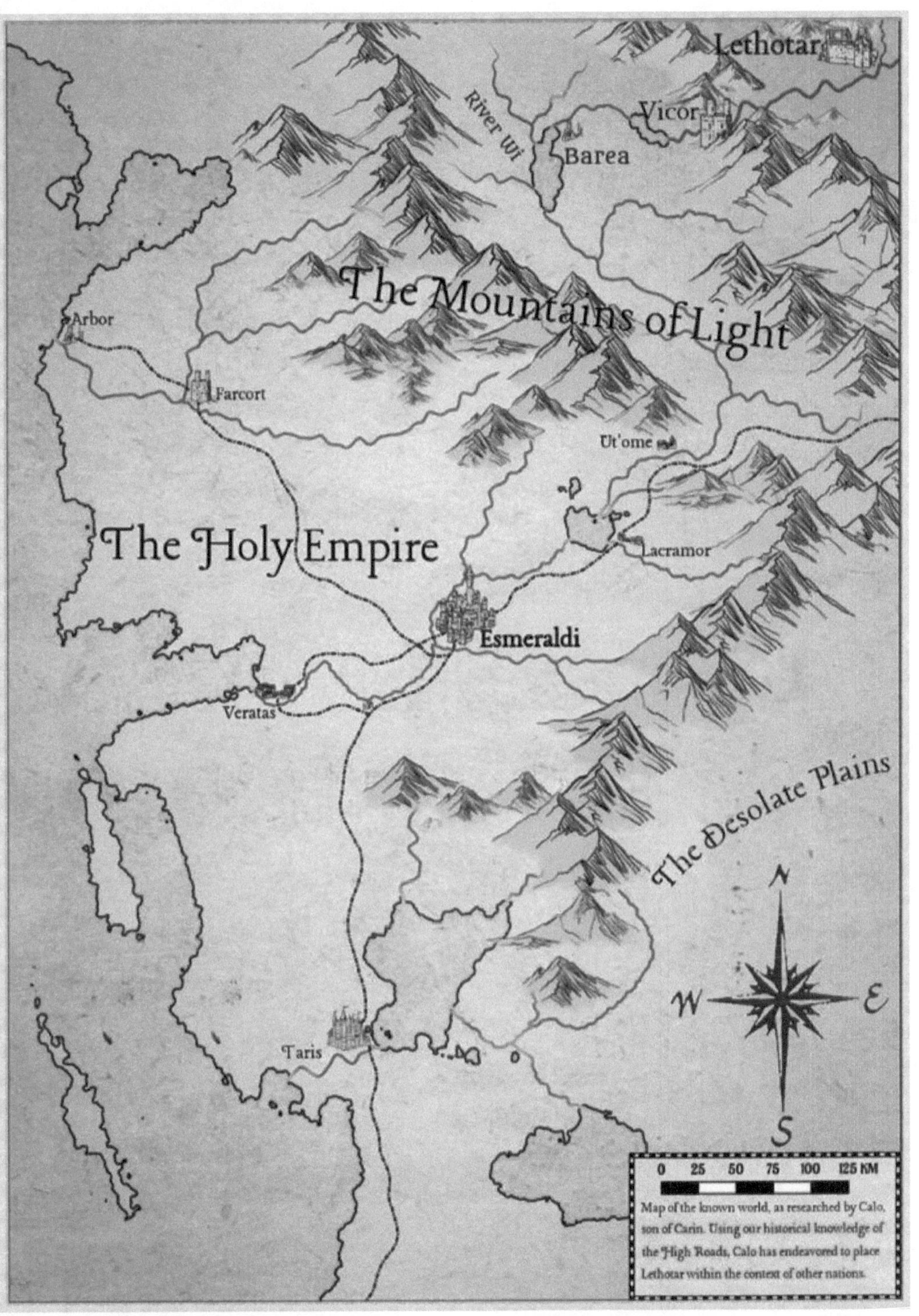
Lethotar
Vicor
Barea
River Wi
The Mountains of Light
Arbor
Farcort
Ut'ome
The Holy Empire
Lacramor
Esmeraldi
Veratas
The Desolate Plains
Taris
N
W
E
S
0 25 50 75 100 125 KM
Map of the known world, as researched by Calo,
son of Carin. Using our historical knowledge of
the High Roads, Calo has endeavored to place
Lethotar within the context of other nations.

I

"All rise for her Majesty, Empress Emelia II, Her Excellency of the Ten Kingdoms, Matron of the Holy Empire, Anchor of the . . ."

The Voice drones on, listing the many titles of the woman seated in the ornate throne. As I look up the dozens of marbled stairs toward the Empress, her piercing eyes meet mine. I refuse to look away until the Voice says, "Maripes, Envoy of Lethotar, kneel before the Empress."

I obey without question—my task is not one of political or religious opposition. My shins hit the stone, and I stare at the steps at eye level. Just a few seconds pass before a woman's voice speaks with rough edges and harsh tones. The Empress. And her Voice says, "Envoy of Lethotar, you may speak."

I raise my gaze to look upon her once again. "Your Majesty, Matron of the Holy Empire, Empress Emelia II"—three titles, as instructed—"I am Maripes, Son of Peras and Amar." Two signifiers, both informal. After my first sentence, the Voice begins translating. "I come on behalf of the people of Lethotar and the Clans of the Three Valleys. I come offering you my talents—in exchange for free trade between our peoples."

As my lips emit the word trade, the Empress's eyes widen. So she understands . . . does her court know? "I supplicate myself before your throne, your Excellency, and humbly request you consider my proposal."

She shifts toward her Voice, standing a few steps down from the throne. She speaks again, and he delivers her response. "Maripes, we shall consider your words. What talents do you offer?"

I hold back the grin aching to stretch from ear to ear. A few of my counterparts back home didn't expect I would even make it this far. "Your Majesty, while as the great Empress of your people, everything within your domain is yours by right, I have knowledge, and in the words of your Holy Scriptures, 'knowledge is the foundation of all power.' " My hand trembles, and I form a fist to stop the shaking. "Therefore, I offer you the gift of sunsteel and the power of moonstone." There it is again. The flicker in her eyes. "I will teach *your* people the secret of *our* people, in exchange for passage along the High Roads."

Murmurs rumble throughout the hall. The Court of the Holy Empire certainly hadn't expected those words to leave my lips. Sunsteel. Moonstone. Every relic of their people, formed from metals they couldn't smelt . . . and I offered the knowledge to reforge their history—if they pay a small price.

"Why would you offer such a gift?" says the Empress through her Voice. Her eyes narrow, their green tinge peaking beneath her long, dark eyelashes. Her powder-white skin contrasts with the dark, woven up-do forming her headdress. "Why give us such knowledge?"

"Because, your Excellency, we are the People of Light. We give to you that which we can give, so that you may see our way of peace."

The translator stumbles over the phrase "People of Light," and I can't recognize the term he uses in its stead. It didn't sound derogatory, but I'm certain he failed to translate properly. In any case, Empress Emelia nods, raises her left hand as if to shush the already frozen crowd, and stands.

"By decree of my station," she says, "Maripes, Envoy of Lethotar, shall find safety within our walls." I predict the meaning of her words before the translation arrives, given the gasps rising behind me. "You shall treat him as you would a member of the royal family until my Office declares otherwise. Maripes, my Guard shall escort you to your quarters for the duration of your stay in Esmeraldi."

I bow my head, and with the flick of her hand, she ushers me away from her throne as if I was the least important meeting of her day—entirely possible, given the line of other diplomats and bureaucrats behind me. Standing, I turn in stride, my grey wool cloak sticking to my sweaty skin.

My steel boots click against the tiled floor, and the eyes of a hundred paleskins watch my march. No—not paleskins. I can't think in such terms here, especially if I expect to break down their walls too. The people of the Holy Empire watch me. Still, their lingering stares tell me all I need to know. Their hate runs deep, and they wish me dead just for speaking in their presence.

Reaching the end of the cavernous throne room, I sigh, two armed guards wielding pikes approaching. I hold out my hands, expecting the return of the shackles used in the morning, but they shake their heads. They mutter something in their strange language, and I nod as if I understand. They push open the great oak doors, sunlight streaming in, and I follow the soldiers into the city.

Esmeraldi is beautiful. Nothing like Lethotar, of course, but since the day I was "escorted" inside, I've marveled at its architecture and splendor. While my people—the People of Light—build in harmony with the land, the Holy Empire has constructed a metropolis honoring the ingenuity of its citizens. Spiraling cathedrals scale the clouds, and towering mansions declare the opulence of their owners. It simultaneously sickens and awes.

For the second time today, I follow the two stoic guardsmen down what I've come to call as the Main, except instead of left, toward the military prison I've called home, we turn right, toward the Palace. So the Empress wasn't kidding—she's honoring me as one of her own. I may have a greater chance than I thought.

As in the throne room, Esmeraldian eyes dart toward me with every step. I presume the Empress permits me to wear my formal attire because she wants her people to recognize the foreigner walking amongst them. In some ways, it's a perverse statement of power: "I am your Empress; you are safe, even when one of your greatest enemies walks our streets." As if my skin and height didn't already reveal my origin, a wool cloak, black tunic, and armored, steel boots signaled my presence from a block away. Only a fool wears such attire in summer heat this far south . . . unless you're one of *them* from *beyond the mountains.*

In any case, as the guards lead me through the iron gates of the Imperial Palace and into the gardens beyond, the crowds conspicuously trailing behind exhale confusion. Let them wonder. If all goes as planned, they'll see more of my people by the end of the year, including inside the Palace. I'm here to forge an alliance, not threaten war.

The Palace Gardens are a world of their own; exotic flowers, drooping trees, and vibrant bushes of all shapes and sizes spread in waves outward. Encased by a ten-meter sandstone wall, it's shameful the royal family keeps these treasures from its people. Yet another cultural disconnect to overcome, I suppose.

We reach the immense pillars adorning the outer walls of the Palace, and without pause, we step beneath, through a giant iron door, and into a red, carpeted hallway with pristine, white walls. We wind in and out of bizarrely decorated rooms until we reach a staircase winding upward in a corkscrew. After passing three doors, we enter a long hallway with windows on the right side and wooden doors on the left. Reaching the fifth door, one guard steps to the side while the other opens it, ushers me through, and closes it with haste.

Inside is a bed, a desk, an oil lamp, and . . . my bags. Curious. More curious than I'd expected. For my belongings to already be here, the Empress would have needed to order their delivery from the prison hours ago. She'd already made her decision before I said my piece. She's playing a game high above my head, and I need to catch up quickly.

Unsure whether I'm a prisoner inside this room—though I heard no feet retreating away from the door, the guards standing outside may as easily be for my protection as to keep an eye on me—I sit at the desk and organize the contents of my bags. No need to leave without being called for. I place my clothes in the drawers, and upon the wooden surface, I place pens, inks, and papers. It's the first time I've had access to these tools in over four weeks. Dipping a pen in an inkwell, I write, just in case they permit a letter sent to the border and onto my family.

To my love, Vona, and my son, Mono,

I have arrived in Esmeraldi. I wish you were here with me, and at the same time, it is absolutely necessary that you remained home. I believe I have an opportunity; a window has opened, and I must seize it. The Empress granted me audience today, and she wishes to speak with me further.

I love you both, and know that in giving away the gifts of the People of Light, I will bring honor to you both, to the Three Valleys, and to Lethotar.

All my soul is yours,

Maripes, your servant in life and death.

<h1>II</h1>

Moonlight streams through the small, grated window inset into the door, and moments before my mind drifts to sleep, a soft knock raps on the wood. Approaching the door, I look through the gap in attempt to see my visitor.

No one.

Lifting the latch, I pull the door toward me, revealing a short, scraggly-haired boy wearing red silks. Looking up at me with wide-eyes, he motions for me to follow. The two guards are nowhere to be found. Brave boy, considering I'm at least three times his size.

It could be a trap . . . or, it could be an opportunity. Through the open windows, a cool evening breeze chills my calves. I nod, grab my cloak, and follow the child. He leads me away from the stairwell and further down the hall. At the end, we turn left, away from the windows, heading into the center of the Palace. Around another turn, we head up a set of emerald-carpeted stairs, reaching a long hallway. Standing at attention at the far end, I see two royal guardsmen, though most likely not my previous entourage. They flank a purple archway, hands on the hilts of their swords.

Their eyes through helmet slits narrowed with every step I take, and I eventually reach the end of the intimidating hall. The boy says a few words I can't decipher at all, and they nod, reaching in sync to open the oak double-doors.

It isn't worth hesitating, so I proceed underneath the arch and through the open threshold. Inside, a young woman sits in a red wingback chair, her legs crossed beneath a shimmery silk dress. I barely recognize her without the makeup. She motions for me to sit in the chair across from her, next to a table holding a bottle of red wine and crystal goblets.

I lean slowly into the cushioned chair, and its warmth envelops. It's beyond soft, an evasive comfort these past few months. The woman reaches forward, picks up a glass, and sips the wine. I follow suit, its wooden flavor drying my tongue.

"How are your accommodations?" she says. Her accent is choppy, but the grammar and pronunciation flawless. So the Empress *can* understand and speak our tongue, too.

"Pleasant, your Majesty," I say, bowing my head. "You are too kind."

"Oh, Maripes, cut the act. When we speak privately, there is no need for political platitudes. I am Emelia, and you are my *guest*." She takes another sip of the wine. "Now tell me. Don't hold back. Why are you in my city?"

A trick? Her words, designed to lower my guard. Clever. "I have been nothing but honest with your people, and with you. We wish nothing but peace between our peoples."

"But you must have a catch. You know what our religion teaches of your people. You call yourselves the People of Light, yet our Holy Church says otherwise. The Inquisition wanted me to kill you on the spot."

"And why didn't you?" Unconsciously, my fingers tense against the velvet armrest.

"Because I know you are not *accursed*, as my people believe." She watches my eyes, but I don't flicker. "History is much more complicated than any wish to accept. Our people, your people, we are of the same blood when it boils down to the core."

"How . . . enlightened of you." Her words could be truth, but they could also be weapons honed to ensure I give my knowledge. "If the Empress of the Holy Empire denies the teachings of her Church, what happens?"

"I think you already know the answer to that," she says. "So the question for us to resolve—how do we come to an arrangement without the Inquisition destroying us both and igniting a holy war?"

I swallow. Her words ring of truth, and if this is the opportunity, the window into the future to stave off the inevitable, I *must* take it. "We show them I am true to my word. We show them I am not evil, and that my people are not evil. We can't tell them. But proof; visual proof; it can go a long way in the minds of people."

"You don't know my people." She lets out a loose sigh, almost a laugh. "But I agree. We must keep up appearances for now, but know this: I am on your side."

"Why?" I can't help myself.

"That is a story for another day, Maripes. Tomorrow, you will show me the power of your hammer. You are dismissed."

Exiting her quarters, I walk back down the long hallway alone. As I near the steps leading toward the floor with my quarters, a man rounds the corner below and leans against the wall, eyes on me. He watches until I reach the bottom step.

"Welcome to the capital," he says. "I see you're already making waves."

Another who knows my language? Curious. "Can I help you?"

"I just wanted to see the Empress's pet creature."

Intentional antagonism. Don't engage. "Here I am in the flesh."

"She's using you, you know. They're all going to use you in some way."

I turn right, striding away from the man.

"I can help you," he adds. "I can be an ally for you in this place. You need friends. More than you know."

I twist in stride, pointing a finger in the man's face. He's closer behind me than I expected, and I tower over him by at least half a meter. "You don't know what I need, man. The Empress has welcomed me into her home, and that is enough for me."

"Do you know what her father did?"

"Am I speaking with her father?"

"If you ever get the chance, ask her about her father. And the Border Wars."

He takes a step away, out from under my reach. Backpedaling slowly, he turns and walks in the direction from whence he'd come. The cloak he wears is dark, with a red tinge to its embroidery. I wonder if the Empress knows the Inquisition walks her halls this late at night. Regardless . . .

Snakes in the grass with every step I take.

◆ ◆ ◆

The next morning, the small boy meets me at the door. I'm dressed not in my regal cloak, but in my smithing garb—brown pants, a black smock, dark goggles looped over my head. He looks me up and down, almost as if some of his fear has faded, then motions for me to follow.

Sun streams in from the east, reflecting off the child's blonde hair. In the daylight, he looks more official than I'd previously thought. His silk vest is green today, and he wears black, leather pants. His features remind me vaguely of . . . the Empress. Her son? Must be.

Lost in my thoughts, it doesn't take long for us to arrive at the entrance to the palace. Three carriages await, and the boy leads me to the third before he skips over to the first, presumably the Empress's car. Squeezing inside the carriage, my head bumps the top. I'm completely out of my element, save for the hammer resting in my lap. And they know it.

After a few minutes, the carriages roll forward without a word. Exiting the palace grounds, I embrace the opportunity to sit in silence. I don't even look out the window to observe the city.

The letter to my wife and son sits unsent in my room. I'll need to breach the topic to either the Empress or one of her advisors today. My thoughts continuously drift to them. It took far too long to make it here. Our original timeline hoped I'd be on the way back to the Three Valleys by now. Mono's on the border somewhere, acting as a scout for our people. It's his life at stake. If I fail, he's one of the first to die.

And Vona . . . she was insistent my mission was a fool's errand, but understood why I'm the only one who could try. She should have traveled with me. A human statement, perhaps; to see two partners in the world, and not just the beast I am to them.

The carriages roll to a stop, the door opening within moments. I look up, sliding haphazardly to the ground. No *Maripes-sized* carriages in Esmeraldi—a shame.   The sun blazing through the clouds, we stand on a bluff cleverly situated within the metropolis, overlooking a river below. Placed atop the cliff: a forge, complete with an anvil, smelter, and other tools necessary to smelt sunsteel and moonstone. However, the forge looks completely untouched for generations.

It's a relic of bygone era. They know this place was once used to make artifacts of great power, but they've forgotten the methods. It looks similar to the forge in Lethotar—my forge. We found it, just like they found this one. On the other hand, perhaps "found" is the wrong word; for the forges have always been where they've been, waiting for hands to work them. At least, according to our legends. I don't know what stories the people of the Empire tell about them.

"The Empress wishes to see your power," says the Voice, stepping out of the first carriage. Behind him, the Empress gingerly steps onto the rock, followed by the boy. "You shall step forth to the forge, take the bars of sunsteel and moonstone, and craft a sword."

I nod, bowing my head toward them. Approaching the forge, the bars laid out for me I instantly recognize. They're from the smelters in Vicor. It's as we've suspected—they have agents somewhere in the Three Valleys, smuggling the metals out. Yet they should have their own sources of the ores . . . of course. They don't even know how to transform it from the ore into the metal.

I set the hammer beside the forge and stoke the coals to heat it to the appropriate temperature. Just like back home, an unknown fuel source ignites, heats, and prepares the forge in mere seconds. Into the cauldron, I place the sunsteel metals, and even more quickly, they melt.

I'm too focused, and it takes a second for me to notice the ring of royalty surrounding. I look up as the metal liquefies, noting the Empress in her ornate regalia, her son, the Voice, and . . . the man from last night. In the Inquisitorial robe. Who are you? As if recognizing the question in my eyes, he winks. Beyond him, other faces have gathered: members of the court; other important persons I've not yet met.

Once the metal reaches the necessary consistency, I carry the cauldron to a large, marblite slab. Pouring the contents straight onto the white, nearly translucent stone, it spills into a perfect circle. With my hands, I begin to knead the liquid like dough.

The second my fingers touch molten sunsteel, gasps ring through the crowd. I hear the curses, words even I can recognize without knowledge of their language. Empress Emelia mutters something indecipherable, and her Voice says, "Silence, if you do not have the stomach for this, then leave."

Powerful words. Nevertheless, she's right. If they don't want to recognize what's necessary to achieve a welding of sunsteel and moonstone, they should absolutely leave.

They believe the molten material is hot, too hot to touch. It is hot . . . but my skin does not burn. It's a magic I can't explain, though that doesn't mean there isn't an explanation. Yet their belief—or lack thereof—is part of the problem. I knead; it bends. It yields to my touch. It forms a long, flat, thickened beam—the start of the blade. Walking back to my hammer, I lift it onto my shoulder, and return to the formless weapon.

Before using the hammer, however, I set it on the marblite, the tool's shaft toward the sky. From my belt, I pull a knife. On the back of my hand, a healed scar I know well awaits the blade. Slicing it open, droplets of blood stream onto the mallet, the slab, and the sunsteel, cooling into a golden ripple of untamed potential.

"Demon!" The word knocks me out of my space. It's the inquisitor man, taking a step forward to turn and face the entourage. Some friend he claims to be. "Blood magic? Do you not see his game? He intends to murder us here." Somehow, I can understand his words, but he's not speaking my language.

The Empress raises her hand before he says another word. "High Inquisitor, if you cannot accept what is necessary for Maripes to show us his work, please leave."

There it is again. A strange moment, her words clear as day, but it's now faded. Their words continue, but I lack the knowledge to ascertain their meaning. Blood still dripping onto the slab before me, I chance a glance toward the clouds.

"So, Lord of Light," I whisper under my breath. "You grace me with your presence on this day." An important moment, revealing the nature of the dark-cloaked man.

Satisfied with the sacrifice of blood, I wrap a line of cloth around my hand. The pain persists, but it's numb pain, pain I've experienced a thousand times before. In both hands, I take my tool, swing it over my shoulder, and bring it down upon the caking metal.

Like thunder, the crash of the moonstone mallet against the sunsteel thrashes through the air, a sound like no other. Over and over again it swings, working the formless into the formed. Imperceptible fractures form in my mind, and as they shatter, I use them to bend the blade into its final shape. Hours pass; to me, they are seconds. They are nothing. This is who I am. I am Maripes, hammer of the People of Light.

It's over. A sunsteel blade—lacking a moonstone hilt, but ready for one—rests upon the marblite. I look up, and only the Empress and her Voice, her son, and the High Inquisitor remain.

Sweat glistens on my skin. At some point, I removed the smock, revealing my hairless, darkened chest. Gingerly, the blade in hand, I walk toward them. When I'm five or so meters away, I kneel, lifting the blade. "As you requested, Empress Emelia, a blade of sunsteel. If you wish a hilt of moonstone, I shall need to work by night, but I can prepare the entire weapon for you."

No words. Her Voice has communicated the message to her, but no words from anyone.

Then: a sound from the boy. I look up, and he's smiling. His eyes gleam with anticipation, recognizing the blade and its beauty.

He wants it. He craves it.

And it is his. "Your Majesty, I offer this blade as a token to your son, a weapon worthy of an heir to the throne of Esmeraldi."

The Empress lifts three fingers to her lips, her eyes squinting. Before she can speak, the High Inquisitor rumbles some guttural phrase toward the Voice, who looks to his liege for affirmation. She nods.

"High Inquisitor Trallius says the Church will need to inspect the weapon before the boy touches it," says the Voice. "To ensure it is safe in his hands."

Still unable to read the oscillating intentions of the High Inquisitor, I stand and bow. "Then I will remain here through nightfall, finish the weapon, and return it to the palace, where the High Inquisitor can retrieve it for safekeeping."

III

It's well past midnight when I finish, my only companions the two Royal guardsmen left to watch my work and act as an escort. By the end, I've merged both sunsteel and moonstone into a final, forged blade. I wrap it in white silk. The carriages have long since departed, so we walk through the dark city in silence.

At night, Esmeraldi reminds me of Lethotar. Stars in the sky, clouds wisping in front of the moon, the night looks almost the same here. Pity our peoples couldn't see each other similarly.

Leaving the bluff, we walk along wide, cobblestone streets. Around us, mansions of the wealthy tower, surrounded by ironclad fences and lush gardens, declaring their opulence. All is quiet. The palace looms in the background, and—

Out of the shadows, ten men holding axes, swords, and clubs. I look to the flanking Royal guards, their eyes shaded by helmets. Is the empress so foolish as to let an ambush like this happen? Something else is at play.

"Run!" The Guards know one word in my language, but it's all I needed to hear. They kick into a sprint, and I follow suit. The crowd forming around us converges.

My longer stride quickly outpaces the royal soldiers, even with a hammer roped to my back and the sword in my hands. Glancing over my shoulder, I watch one of the guardsmen fall to the ground, raising his arms in defiance. The mob gnashes and slashes, breaking through his shield and mutilating his arms.

I stop, for the crowd nears the second guard. He motions with his arms for me to flee, and I shake my head.

"Run!" he screams again. I comply. Those two men, loyal to their Empress even for a man they know as accursed. Even as I flee, a stray thought bounces around in my mind—what could possibly generate such obedience to their sovereign?

Reaching the steps of the palace, I rush inside. High Inquisitor Trallius waits, three sycophants in tow. "Welcome back, Maripes. Where is your guard?"

Apparently, he has no qualms speaking my language in front of his servants. "We were attacked. In the streets. Not far from here."

With his left hand, he beckons the black-robed men out the door. Without question, they exit. "I'm sure it's just a misunderstanding. My men will handle it. Give me the blade, return to your quarters. Everything will be all right."

I step forward, handing him the weapon.

He uncovers it. "A beautiful blade. Well done."

"What game are *you* playing?" I can't help myself. He's an enigma. "Do you think I'm a demon, or are you something more than just the High Inquisitor?"

"I am who you think I am, Maripes. I am the guardian of the people of the Holy Empire, and their faith, and I will ensure they remain untainted by evil. You've made the right step toward ending this conflict, let's see if you can follow through."

His answer satisfying, I take leave and head to my room, after one last look out the door. Those guards . . . I didn't even know their names. They deserved better.

Before reaching my quarters, the blond boy—the prince—stops me on the stairs. Motioning with his tiny hand, he points toward the gardens out a window. Without waiting for my response, he walks away. Looking out the window, I see the Empress seated on a marble bench beneath two culipa trees, their blue blossoms glowing in the night.

The night is not yet over; my host desires more time.

Even with my long strides, I can't keep up; the boy skips ahead down the hall and into the private palace gardens. Once I reach the exit, he's waiting for me by the edge of an immaculately trimmed hedge. The path to his mother is visible. I pass by the boy, my boots crunching the small pebbles along the path. Empress Emelia lifts her eyes. She's reading.

"Thank you, my son," she says. "Please, rest. Get your sleep. You've had a long day." He sprints back toward the palace. "Thank you for joining me, Maripes. I heard what happened in the streets. This will result in . . . problems."

News travels fast here, apparently. "If you need to imprison me while the matter is investigated, I understand."

"No, no, none of that. It won't come to that. But with my guards not making it back to the palace . . . the story will be told by the hooligans."

"The High Inquisitor sent his men to help," I reply. "Perhaps they made it in time to rescue one of your guards."

"We shall see." Her eyes mist, as if a deeper thought lies beneath the surface. "I apologize for Trallius's behavior. My brother . . . he is zealous in his convictions, but he rarely follows his words with meaningful action."

Brother. The politics of Esmeraldi click into place. Her brother is the High Inquisitor . . . which means they both were once potential heirs to the throne. Questions linger. What motivations might a brother wish to keep secret from his sister? His words: *When you get a chance, ask about her father.* I hold my tongue.

"Of course, he does believe you are evil," she says. "He's certain of it. Nothing will ever change his mind."

"Except you."

"No, not even me."

"Then if *you* can't convince the High Inquisitor, what am *I* doing here? Your Holy Church is the glue of your empire."

She sighs, closing the book in her lap. "I appreciate your blunt and straight-forward approach to all of this, but it's all much more subtle than you can possibly imagine. There's a battle for the soul of the Empire occurring every day, and it's not necessarily between my brother and me, even if superficially it may appear as such. It's inside the heart and soul of every one of my citizens. We live in opulence, we live in splendor, yet we have oppressed people living on the streets of every city. They are in pain, and they see the wealth of their overlords; people like me. And in reaction, some lash out . . . latching onto hate toward people like you. Still others . . . they're finding new philosophies to explore."

"You're the Empress," I say. "Is it not easy for you to break down these barriers? Give to the needy? Heal the sick?"

"From where does my power come, Maripes?"

"Your religion proclaims your family as the perpetual and eternal ruling class of the Holy Empire."

"Yet without the support of the Lords, the Guilds, and the Generals, I am nothing. So where does my power come from?"

"Those who benefit from you remaining in power."

"Precisely."

"So what is the battle? Where do my people enter the picture?"

She smiles. "If I establish an exclusive deal between your people and the Throne; where the Throne becomes the exclusive source of sunsteel and moonstone, then I have a new card to play."

"And you think it's enough to break the cycle of power crippling your people."

"That's the hope."

I lean against the tree, and she turns on the bench to face me more directly. I say, "What happened to your father?"

Her eyes flash. "My brother told you to ask, didn't he." It isn't a question.

"He did."

"Sit beside me."

I sit.

"My father was an evil man," she adds.

"My father fought in the Border Wars," I say, "thirty years ago. I've heard the stories."

"What do you know of the stories we tell, here in the Empire?"

"I can't imagine they're kind to my people."

"They are not, and they are false, at least generally so. Anyway, when I was a child . . ."

INTERJECTION

Emelia walked through the forest, tears in her eyes. Her father wouldn't let her play outside? Then she'd just run amongst the trees. Their army was entrenched for miles around—what could go wrong? Besides, she was twelve. She could take care of herself.

Skipping along a deer path, she came across a darkened patch of dirt. Crouching, she sniffed it, the faint scent of iron on the air, like the medical tent in camp. Blood. Maybe an animal was wounded nearby. Looking into the brush, she saw red droplets on leaves of ferns and mossy roots. Striking off the trail, a moan rose from the other side of a juniper trunk.

Furtively, Emelia stepped around the tree and came face to face with . . . one of the enemy. Adorned in golden plate armor, his greyish skin almost looked green. Sickly. Blood seeped from a wound in his shoulder. Her eyes widened, for his eyes darted toward her. He grimaced, unable to lift his hands.

"Help." The word was in Emelia's language. Her father had taught her the basics of the enemy's vernacular, though, and she doubted this warrior knew more than a few of the Empire's words.

She said, "Let me go get help."

"No." In their language this time.

"You're dying."

He said something unintelligible. Pointing at a pouch on his hip, he said, "Medicine. In there."

Emelia nodded, rushing to his side. In the bag, she found herbs, bandages, and vials of swirling, multi-colored liquids. Holding each up, one at a time, he pointed at the third vial and the bandages. "Open." Words in her tongue, this time. "Put on bandage."

She nodded, dumping the fluid onto the cloth. Holding out the soaked wrapping, he took it from her, pressing it against the gash. He sighed, as if instant comfort enveloped him. Streams of steam floated into the sky.

"Thank you," he said. "You not bad, like they say. Some of you. Some of you good."

Her mouth hung open, unsure of what to say. She started to back away when a screech echoed through the branches above. With a glance back toward the wounded soldier, she noticed his widened eyes. Fear.

"Caracrow." He stumbled to his feet, picking up an axe she'd not previously noticed. "Will eat you. Be ready."

She rushed to his side, leaning against the tree. Shadows flirted with the ground, every sound in the forest having ceased. It was as if everything waited to see what the creature would do.

Without warning, a darkness descended from high above. Black feathers, crimson beak, emerald eyes, golden talons. The Caracrow dove. It was bigger than she imagined any bird could be; like a lion, its aggression was present just in its sheer bulk and power.

The accursed one guarding her—he was ready. Even seriously wounded, he lifted his axe in both hands. The creature screeched. He swung his axe with grace, as if it were a feather floating on the air. The blade connected with the creature's neck, but its momentum carried into the soldier, and both man and beast crashed into the undergrowth. Her terror-induced paralysis lifted, Emelia hopped to the rescue, pushing the mutilated creature off her patient-turned hero.

"That was amazing!" she said. "A brilliant move." The creatures brown blood dripped onto her dress, but she didn't care. "I'm sure my father will give you safety, I—"

"Father?"

"Yes, my father. The Emperor?"

His eyes shifted, from fear, to pain, to resignation, to . . . something else. Then again to pain. "You leave. Leave me. Your father no help me."

"Why not—"

An arrow whizzed into her hero's leg, and Emelia screamed.

IV

"I never learned his name," says the Empress. "But my father executed him on the spot. Well, not immediately. They dragged him back to camp, interrogated him, and made me watch as the Inquisitors ignited him in a blazing inferno. Burned at the stake."

"And did you tell Maripes that soldier's mission?" The voice of the High Inquisitor, in the garden. Shuffling noises come from all around—I'm certain not just the Empress's brother joins us.

"Does the mission matter?" I say. "War is war. Amidst war, each side has its terrible moments. Come join us, Trallius. Let me tell you of the horror I witnessed as a child. Perpetrated by *your* people."

"Maripes, he's not supposed to be here," whispers Emelia. "Be on your guard."

I nod, and out of the bushes, Trallius trots, his cloak fluttering in the midnight breeze. There's a crunch behind me, and I spare a glance over my shoulder. Three of the High Inquisitors' minions emerge from deeper in the garden . . . alongside the thralls from the street brawl.

"Neither are they," I say, pointing over my shoulder.

Empress Emelia rises from the bench, and I follow suit, but she motions for me to sit back down. "Trallius, what do I owe the pleasure of your presence in my private garden? You are supposed to tread here by invitation only."

"Dear sister, I'm here to protect you from this beast."

He's purposely choosing to speak in my language, I note. He wants me to hear his words . . . and he doesn't want his followers to know what we say, perhaps? Alternatively, he doesn't care.

"He's not a beast," says Emelia.

"Fine. Accursed one. Demon. Whatever you want to call him; I'm not sure the exact word in this vile language. But tell him—why was your *friend* in the forest that day?"

"It doesn't matter. As Maripes said, war is war."

"So he has corrupted your thoughts? Can we trust you as our Empress?"

Trallius slides his hand to his side and pulls a sword from his hip. My sword. The sword built for the prince. My hand slides to the hammer looped across my back before I realize my mistake.

Trallius shouts a command in their language, and Emelia's gaze darts toward me. "What are you doing?" The foes close in around us.

"He means to harm you," I say. "He thinks you intend to kill me."

"No, he means to harm *you*," she says. "He cannot touch me."

"You're wrong." I slide the hammer from its sling, resting it in my hands. Trallius approaches, and I circle, the sycophants approaching from under the trees.

"Give it up, Maripes," Trallius says. "Your people are liars and cheats. You send wolves in sheep's clothing to us, but you have only one thought on your mind. You wish to topple our Empire."

"Trallius, stop," Emelia orders, still in my language. "Maripes is harmless."

"Just like the soldier in the woods? The one sent to assassinate both of us in our sleep?"

Before either of us can reply, the parties converge. I swing with my hammer, but it's easily blocked by one of the lesser inquisitors. I'm too tired from building the sword all day. They grab my arms, knock the hammer to the ground, and push me to my knees.

Emelia steps back, holding her hands out. She stumbles away from me, and Trallius stalks toward her, blade in hand.

"You see, Maripes, it's pretty simple. I have the weapon you made. You are in the Empress's garden." He pushes Emelia toward a hedge. "I found you here, the blade still wedged in her stomach."

"Trally, what are you—"

The sunsteel blade darts forward, slicing with terrible beauty. Piercing her dress, she lets out a gasp and falls to her knees some ten meters from me. Her eyes are filled with pity and sadness.

"I tried to save your people," she mutters, her words barely audible. "I tried."

◆ ◆ ◆

My thoughts drift in and out of consciousness. Images of Vona, back home, and Mono, scouting in the borderlands. A stray memory hits; it shatters my resolve. Mono is marrying Ero in the spring. I never could have imagined a more perfect man for my son, and I'd miss their wedding. I never even had the opportunity to mail my letter.

The hours pass, the beatings continue, and days and weeks blur together in icy, burning pain. I don't know how much time passes, but suddenly . . . light blinds my eyes. I'm shoved into an arena, an executioner's block in the center. Inquisitors guide me forward, and I comply. I'm long past opposing the inevitable.

On a dais set off from the jeering crowds, the High Inquisitor stands tall, a golden scepter in his hand. Next to him, the prince watches, anger in his eyes. The boy couldn't be more than ten or eleven, but at his hip, the sword I made for him rests. I can see it now; a boy told by his uncle to use the weapon to enact vengeance against an evil enemy. A boy, now the holder of the throne . . . yet for the next half-decade, his uncle will rule as regent. He will certainly bring war to my people. He'll have his opportunity to destroy us, the so-called *accursed*.

I step onto the wooden platform. I failed. Emelia hadn't failed—I had. I wasn't vigilant. I wasn't ready for the games played by the imperial tyrants of an empire crushing its people, and my own, under its heel.

I can't understand any of the words echoing throughout the stadium. Of course, the High Inquisitor doesn't have a reason to translate his words for me anymore. He's won. The people are on his side. Though . . . I wonder. I remember the teachings of our priests: *In the final hour of our people, The Lord of Light will return.*

"Lord," I whisper. "I have forsaken your truth. I have failed our people. History descends toward our darkest hour. We are the People of Light, your humble servants. Join them, and rend our enemies as they strike our lands." The executioner pushes me to my knees, and I lean my head onto a stone block stained with dried blood. "With my life, accept this prayer, and may Mono, and my love, Vona, find peace and safety in your arms."

With a whistle, the blade descends.

LEGION OF MONO

If only they'd known us as something more than simply accursed. For we are so much more.

Lethotar
Caris Valley
As it was known, prior to battle upon the Bridge of our Lord

V

Incense wisps through the air. Plated in gold, the shrine flickers in the dancing candlelight, spraying shadows on the sandstone walls of the room. Kneeling before the shrine, facing west toward the setting sun, I pray.

"My lord, have you forsaken us after all this time?" My left fist flexes. "We are the last bastion of our people, yet you have not stepped onto the battlefield to protect us from their endless hosts. Without end, they pour through the passes, yet you have not brought upon them disasters to halt their slaughter. Where are you?"

I prostrate myself on the floor, spreading my arms wide, palms facing the ceiling. Breathing in, the smoke-filled air rushes into my lungs. I savor the flavor, the bitterness of the incense scratching the inside of my throat.

"Today, we face our enemy on the greatest of battlefields. On your battlefield. I ask for a sign. I ask that you bring us victory." My eyes close, my mind envisioning the future I know I'll never see. "I ask that you smite our foes so that our children can live in peace, as we once lived in peace before the enemy arrived at our gates. Lord of Light, hear my prayer."

Propping myself up onto my knees, I swing both arms against my chest, pounding my pectoral muscles. Satisfied with my prayer, I stand. "Ero," I call through the door, "I am ready to begin."

The door opens, and my husband enters, carrying a pitcher of oil and a basket of rags. His spindly elbows dangle at his sides in his unassuming grey tunic. Those arms hold our family together, even as I leave for battle after battle, breaking his heart. Even in this final hour, he doesn't object, not once.

And the rose! A single rose from his garden rests in the basket.

"You look beautiful today," Ero says.

"You always look beautiful," I say in return. "Is Ermo asleep?"

"She is. She believes you said farewell last night, but also believes you will return by the end of the week."

"I *will* return by the end of the week."

It's most likely a lie, but he won't push the issue. We can't afford to lose hope, even to each other, even if we both know the Holy Empire cracked our resolve years ago.

I slip out of my white tunic and strip my loose cloth pants, standing naked before my spouse. As much as I love him, though, it's not a romantic ritual. All across Lethotar, my soldiers join me, all embracing the Spirit of Rejuvenation.

I bow my head, and Ero approaches with a pitcher of oil. The golden liquid drips into the creases of my neck, down the muscles of my grey-green shoulders, and into rivets and crevices, forming vertical streams and pools. The coolness of the liquid invigorates me, my skin glows.

As the final drop of oil leaves the pitcher, my husband sets it before the shrine to our Lord. From the basket, he takes the rags, gently smoothing the oil into a sheen across my entire body. His touch comforts me. It reminds me: I am loved.

After each rag absorbs the oil, Ero says three words. *In death, life.*

My love places each used rag in the empty oil pitcher. When the final rag lands, he circles me twice with a still burning stick of incense before it follows the rags. The sealed pitcher ignites, and flames lick the air just above its rim.

"In death, life," I say. I try to smile, but I can't lift my cheeks. The pain overpowers me.

Still without clothes, I walk toward the closet near the back of the room. Before I reach it, Ero squeezes my bicep. Turning me, my husband holds the rose in his other hand. I don't say a word, and Ero places the rose, sheared of its thorns, between the gold ring looping through ear cartilage and my bony head.

I pull Ero into a tight hug, kissing him on the forehead. "I will return to you and Ermo."

"Yet you will not, if it is your duty to die."

I close my eyes, knowing my husband speaks the truth. He always speaks the truth. "I will only die if it means you have died also."

Ero kisses me on the lips and leaves the room. Even if I see him before I leave, it's our final moment together. Before hell arrives, before the soldiers of the Holy Empire arrive to obliterate us, he accepts my duty one last time. I cherish the moment in my heart. The rose means more than Ero can ever know.

I return to the closet, opening the door. In the center, neatly folded in an open drawer, leather underclothes lie ready. I slip into them, buttoning the shirt and tying the belt. Above the drawer, my hand-forged armor hangs, gleaming brilliantly in the candlelight.

It's time to face my fate, and the fate of my enemies, on the battlefield. I step into my armor, ready for war. This responsibility will break my bones.

I remember the battle of two weeks ago vividly, at the Gates of Vicor. The fortress guarding the only viable mountain pass into the Caris Valley withheld the probes of the paleskin armies for two years—until they arrived with overwhelming force. We lost Commander Tathias, and the Second, Third, and Fourth Legions. They held the line—we escaped to hold another line for a few days more. I remain the sole surviving commander of our military.

Satisfied my armor is ready, I grab my spear from its stand. I walk into the living room of our small abode. Ero sits near the fire. Ermo must have awoken, for she's bundled in my husband's arms, snoring. Ero's asleep too, so I approach them quietly, lean down, and kiss them both on their foreheads. I reach the door, look back at my family one final time, and whisper, "If only we could have done more to save you."

Entering the evening air, I look down toward the war camp slowly forming outside the city gates. I'm both terrified and looking forward to our final stand. Their army has entered the Caris Valley; they've given us no other choice. The forward scouts arrived two nights ago, informing the Council that "the enemy approaches with a thousand swords, a thousand bows, and a thousand horses."

So just one week after our retreat to Lethotar, just one week after I reunited with my family, just one week after my Ermo's fifth birthday, I once more step toward the battlefield.

◆ ◆ ◆

They first arrived in the night.

Fifteen years ago, on my second tour along the slopes of Mount Wistir, Zet and I tracked paleskins we *thought* were just smugglers, infecting our frontier villages with their scummy drugs and drinks. Instead, we found so much more.

Sliding down a rocky slope, we followed their hour-old trail. Reaching the bottom, I looked back just in time to watch Zet stumble into a boulder.

"You're making too much noise," I hissed.

"Oh hush," Zet replied. "They're probably trembling in their boots, knowing we're on their trail."

We continued, the path leveling off and into the forest adorning the mountain. After another few kilometers, a branch snapped. I took my spear from my back, Zet unsheathed a dagger, and three seconds later, two paleskins zipped out from behind a grove of pine trees, intent on attack.

We were ready, however. I whipped my spear toward the first vagabond, and it sliced him in the chest. Zet threw his blade, the steel digging into the second enemy's skull. Just like that, the battle ended. We approached our victims.

They wore grey cloaks with red trim, belted at the waist with a black and gold clasp. Lying next to my foe, a book written in a language I couldn't read splayed across the moss. Hanging from a gold chain from his neck, contrasting against the blood dripping from his chest, I noticed a silver triangular pendant. The man coughed, his eyes staring with terror up at me as his life drifted toward the abyss.

"These aren't smugglers, Zet," I said. "This one's an Inquisitor of the Holy Empire." At the sound of my words, the assailant trembled even as life slipped from his grasp. "They aren't supposed to come near our border, though, based on the peace established after the Border Wars."

I glanced at my fellow scout. He slid his weapon out of its target, tilted his head toward the sky, and sniffed. "I smell smoke," he said.

The scent registered inside my nostrils, too. "That's no ordinary smoke," I said. "We must hurry."

Leaving our enemy to rot in the woods, we sprinted into the underbrush to the north. For three more kilometers, our run took us in and out of old-growth forest, beneath the great veliper trees and cresting redwoods. At last, we reached the ridge overlooking the frontier town of Ut'ome.

Except it was engulfed in apocalyptic fire. Surrounding the small village, we could see the banners of the Holy Empire, our supposed new ally in this world. Hundreds if not thousands of troops watched the flames eviscerating the bodies of our people piled in the center of the village.

"My father failed," I said. "They've chosen total annihilation."

I dropped to my knees on the ridge, but Zet placed his hand on my shoulder. "Mono, we don't have time to mourn. You know all too well they'll do anything to acquire what it is they desire. We must return to the Three Valleys. We must warn our people."

VI

I call my spear *Flame of Maripes*, the weapon given by my father when I graduated from the Academy of War. Crafted from sunsteel and moonstone, the fire of his soul always burns in my hands when I fight. His presence is by my side as I approach our war camp outside Lethotar, our Fortress of Light. As the tents come into view, I stare longingly back up the streets of the only true home I've ever known. Oblivion will not claim the final refuge of my people. Except—I know it will.

Built into the sheer rock face of Mount Intir, the streets run zigzag across the rocky face and deep into the ground. I know those tunnels well—I helped dig some of them. My eyes halt on one outcropping, behind which my house nestles. Where my family rests. Ermo's hardly a baby anymore, but she'll always be a tiny bundle of joy in my heart. Lethotar could crumble to the ground, but if Ero and Ermo are safe, I'll have succeeded in my duty as a husband and a father.

Beneath the cliffs, the city spreads atop the slopes and foothills of the mountain, roads and bridges crisscrossing from hill to hill and stream to stream, forming an intricate network of agriculture, commerce, and life. The first night I met Ero, when we were still children, we created a makeshift raft, placed it in one of the aqueducts, and foolishly believed we could sail out of the city and into the river.

It sank in three minutes, the beams drifting apart.

The memory almost forces me to return home. My feet twitch, but my head involuntarily tilts toward the war camp, my duty. I turn away from the visage of Lethotar and its environmental majesty. Below my vantage point, the rolling hills surrounding our capital intermingle with patches of farmland and forest. Beyond the outskirts of hamlets and villages, the valley spreads. In the distance, a snaking gap in the trees forms the path of the Caris River, flowing out of Lethotar and toward the Chasm, where we'll make our final stand.

Death rests on the faces of my brothers and sisters in arms inside the camp. Like me, Zet stares longingly back at Lethotar, holding his war hammer over his shoulder, his massive shield on his back. It's nearly impossible for me to believe we've been by each other's side for every day of this war. As I step into the center of camp, he looks up. He nudges my fellow Masters, and they call for their troops to drop their work—their commander has arrived.

Though I want to flee back to the arms of my husband, my feet somehow pull me onto the stump in the middle of the camp.

"All rise for the words of the Master of the Spear, Mono, son of Maripes, Commander of the Fifth Legion of Lethotar," says Wikar, my first lieutenant, standing dutifully below me. "His words are law, and we will follow them to the letter, to our last breath."

The first ritual words before each battle. Today, they hold truth I've never heard before. I place a hand on Wikar's shoulder, his muscles loosening at my touch. Inhaling sharply, my attention turns toward my soldiers.

"My brothers and sisters," I say, "today, we fight for the freedom of our people. For fifteen years, we have fought this enemy, and we have had many victories, but we have also had many defeats." I internally sigh—I can give them more hope than that. Those words are weak. "Our true victory? Not once, *not once* have our people wavered. Not once have we given up in the face of overwhelming odds. Even as we march to war today, our people continue their lives in Lethotar. They prepare for what is to come, they prepare for their flight into the caves, into the deep, into the world beyond our own."

My eyes turn toward Reata, my Master of the Bow. She's glancing from soldier to soldier, but she subtly nods, acknowledging the truth in my words. I add, "Yet even as they prepare, they live. They go to school. They worship our Lord. They love. They argue and fight, and they believe in us."

I pound my spear twice into the stump, and my troops reply

with a guttural hurrah. "We play our part in history. This supposed Holy Empire may wish to erase us from *their* history, but tomorrow, we will ensure *all* who face us, face our blades, face our spears, face our arrows, face our hammers—we will ensure they know and remember us for the rest of their lives. Lives we shall shorten considerably, throwing them deep into the pits and rocks of the Chasm!"

It's not a perfect speech, but it's the best I can do. We all know our duty. I see it in Reata's eyes, in Zet's toothy grin, in Yero's crooked stance, my Bearer of the Shield. "We will fight with honor, we will win with honor, and we will die with honor. However the Lord wills the outcome of today's battle, we embrace it with open arms."

I roar my battle cry, a deep inhuman shout into the evening sky. The Fifth Legion joins, their voices cascading and creating a crescendo of five hundred soldiers prepared for war. I find hope in knowing our loved ones can hear the sound from their homes, even deep in the cliff-side streets of the city.

"We face them at the Bridge of our Lord." My spear points northward. "Every last one of us will fall before our enemy crosses the Chasm. For Lethotar, for the Lord of Light, for the love we protect behind these walls, we will fight forever!"

When I was a child, I often traveled with my mother, Vona. She'd married Maripes to cement an alliance between the Woodland and Iron clans, and her people lived in the treetops above the River Wi, their forest cities sometimes spanning kilometers above the rushing waters.

I loved visiting those trees, swinging from house to house on vines or clomping across rope bridges spanning hundreds of meters. My favorite memory? Hiking with mother to observe the bolog. We would enter the cherry groves managed by her *pa*, and, lumbering amongst the tree trunks, we always found one or two of the creatures.

"Why don't they eat us?" I asked, our silent footsteps rounding the edge of a massive auburn redwood.

"That's a good question, my son," she replied. "The bolog do not eat us because we do not threaten them. It's that simple. We have a symbiotic relationship with them. We provide them food, we provide them safe shelter amongst our groves, and in return, they protect our flocks, our crops, our lands from pestilence."

We trotted down the trail, arriving at a clearing. Leaning against a tree was a particularly large bolog, its scaly arms and legs the width of the trunks nearby. I was no larger than its chest. Full-grown bolog grew to six or seven meters in height, but this one was nearly fifteen or sixteen meters tall. Thick, grey skin covered its arms and legs, its stomach and neck a patchy white. Its back, armored like stone, reminded me of the turtles that swam in the creeks of Lethotar.

Unfazed by the massive creature, my mother walked straight to it, handing it the dead rabbit clipped to her belt.

"Thik," she said, "I've brought you lunch."

The bolog peered down at us, a strange smile crossing its face. It grunted, but it reached out its massive hand. With two fingers, it took the corpse dangling from Vona's outstretched arm. In one gulp, it swallowed the snack whole. It pushed against the tree, and I could hear the branches high above creak from the strain.

"They are harmless," said my mother. "Our friends."

VII

I step onto the bridge, its metallic sheen reflecting the moonlight high above. My three captains walk by my side, and in the distance, the war horns of our enemy reverberate, though they've not yet arrived at the canyon. Kilometers below, the river flows as it has always flowed. To the west and east, the gorge expands in glory.

It is our final line of defense. The bridge is the only way to cross the river, and the Council decreed: we, the Fifth Legion, will hold our ground, ensuring not a single enemy makes it to the walls of our home. Its solid form symbolizes our dauntless resolve, one single piece of metal cast across the three kilometers of the Chasm, the narrowest section of the canyon. We will fight fathoms above the river for days—weeks, if necessary. We will fight for our families, for our freedom, and for the soldier beside us.

"Has a battle ever occurred on this bridge?" asks Zet. "I scoured the histories, but I found nothing."

"Neither did I," says Reata.

"Yero?" I ask.

"There is one tale, though it comes from legends before our Confederation formed." Yero scratches his cheek. "And it's from before this bridge existed. I think it applies. We all know it well."

I nod, clasping Zet on the shoulder. "We do, but you should remind us. We must remember who fights with us today." I try to smile, more for my own sake than their own, but my lips can't move.

Yero scans the breadth of the canyon. "Our Lord of Light stood on this side of the gorge, facing down his enemies, the demons of Hell. He smote them with lightning. Upon their deaths, he molded this bridge from sunsteel, connecting Lethotar to the other kingdoms. Before long, the people of Lethotar became the people of the Three Valleys; the People of Light."

"I thought that was an apocryphal legend," Reata says. "More importantly, I thought he used moonstone."

I give my Master of the Bow a sideways look. "More importantly? I don't think it's time to argue dogmatic semantics. The story has power. Use it in your soul."

"If the Lord stands with us today, where—"

A trumpet sounds from the other side of the gorge, cutting her words into pieces. I turn toward the noise, looking for signs of our enemy. To reach us, they must cross all three kilometers of the bridge. *To reach Lethotar*, they must meet us in battle. We'll face them in the center of the expanse above the Caris, forcing them to fight on our terms. At its widest, the bridge can hold fifteen soldiers at a time. We have the advantage.

"I do not expect them to attack tonight," I say. "It would be quite foolhardy of them to assault this position while we have the cover of darkness. But . . . we will be ready."

I pull *Flame of Maripes* from my back, holding it to my side. The shaft rests on the sunsteel of the bridge, and a tiny jolt runs up my arm as the two identical metals touch. "Bearer of the Shield, you will follow my men and me in pairs to the center of the bridge. *They will not break us.*" I don't look at my captains; I continue to stare across the void toward our unseen enemy. "Master of the Blade, your men will hold in reserve behind the Master of the Bow, until I give the command to charge. Master of the Bow, you will stay out of range of their archers—we know our arrows reach further. Otherwise, give them hell from the sky. We will make them face us on the ground, where we will win."

The words taste like ash in my mouth. We've all stepped foot onto this bridge to die for our families. We will not win. Strategy and tactics don't matter anymore. I turn to face my troops one final time, doom beginning to overwhelm reason. Thoughts of the Lord of Light surge from my subconscious soul in attempt to give hope, but he can't breach the shadows clouding my mind. Even still, I prepare to speak the remaining rites of war, the passage heard before every battle for the last fifteen years.

I don't believe it anymore. My brothers and sisters probably don't either. For the first time, though, I'm the one who will utter the verses. I glance at my spear, moonlight brilliantly reflecting off the ever-sharp spear point at my weapon's tip. If only my father could *actually* fight by my side today. Raising the weapon to the sky and inhaling the cool night air, fear evacuates my heart.

Somehow.

"Fifth Legion!" I cry. "We are the bastion of hope for our people. We are the last bulwark, the final defense. We stand, we fight, we die. Yet we still live!"

I can see the eyes of every soldier; they glint with starlight, terrified and brave. Even those I can't see, I know their eyes. I know all five hundred men and women standing before me. I've trained them, I've sparred with them, I've raised them since they were babes. I close my eyes.

"I declare to you the words of our Lord of Light!" Raising *Flame of Maripes* further into the sky, I point its shaft toward the Moon. "In the final hour of our people, I will return to fight by your side. I will stand beside you, before you, above you, beneath you, and behind you. When all hope has lost, regain it, for I will smite the stones that block your path, rend the rivers that oppose you, and return peace to the land of our people."

"So says our Lord," my soldiers reply in unison. "We fight for him as he fought for us; we fight for our love as he fought for us. We fight for Lethotar as he fought for us!"

I roar, turning to face the far side of the bridge. I cannot see its composition, yet an army slowly steps onto the battlefield. Marching in columns, they're like copper and iron toys ready for us to cast into the icy depths below.

"Perhaps you are wrong, brother," says Yero. "Perhaps they attack tonight."

"Better now than later."

INTERJECTION

"Why I have no grandpa?"

"He left a long time ago, my Ermo."

"But why?"

"I don't know the best way to tell you."

"You can tell truth."

"I don't know if you're ready."

"I ready."

"Grandpa died fighting the Empire."

"So how?"

"You know my spear?"

"The *Flame of Maripes*."

"I named it after him, because of how he died."

"Why?"

"They wanted our moonstone and sunsteel weapons. They can't make them, you see. They have no sources, and they don't know how to bend the metals."

"Why not?"

"I don't know. However, your Grandpa could, and he offered to teach them. He proposed a trade between our peoples. We'd trade moonstone and sunsteel, and they'd give us free passage through their lands. Open their borders. Let our people interact and learn from them. Even travel to the southern nations or beyond, across the seas and deserts leading to distant lands."

"What Grandpa do?"

"Grandpa taught them, and after they believed he'd taught enough, they killed him."

"But Grandpa fought back?"

"Oh Ermo, how he fought. He didn't tell them a single thing."

"I think I know now. He stood up to them. Like a bully."

"He was a flame until the end, my Ermo, and he died doing what he loved. Helping people. He tried to stall the inevitable. But

he didn't realize he faced a truly impossible task."
"Do you face an impossible task, father?"

> *How could I lie to my daughter? How could I tell her I don't know what actually happened to my father, that no one does? That one day, he left on his mission, and we never heard from him again? Just . . . the next we knew, the Holy Empire arrived and ignited the war anew. We knew he failed. We just didn't know why.*

VIII

The bridge rumbles. It shouldn't rumble. The enemy troops don't put that much force in their steps. *We* don't put that much force into our steps.

Something is wrong.

"Master of the Bow, what do you see?" I say, squinting.

"I cannot see *that* well in the dark, Commander, but I see an impending charge, just like you." Reata pulls out her spyglass, staring through the long ocular tube. Her eyes widen. "Probably two kilometers out still."

"Composition?"

"Unknown. Wait. It's not horses. They're not charging with cavalry. I think I see—no."

She hands me the spyglass. I almost don't want to look, but the instrument rises to my eye, and I peer through the lens. It focuses, and in the dim light, I can see a dozen or so beasts charging across the bridge. Larger than anything the Empire has ever fielded, I can't believe what I see.

"The bolog." The spyglass drops, shattering at my feet. "They've tamed the bolog."

Stifled gasps explode behind me, and I chastise my stupidity. Fear had dripped into my words.

"Tamed them?" Yero's exasperated breaths are behind me. "Not tamed. They must have starved them."

"Is there a difference at the moment?" Broken glass crunches beneath my boot, and I face my Master of the Blade. "They are now our enemy, whatever has happened to them."

"Yes, in fact there is." Yero crosses his arms. "It means they don't care what they attack. The bolog starve. Let's give them something else to eat, in addition to us."

I nod, understanding and recognizing the plan. "We charge." I face all three of my Masters at once, the enemy at my back.

Zet and Reata both bare their teeth. "Yes," they say in unison. "We charge."

Yero shakes his head. "Not exactly what I had in mind."

"We know bolog, Yero." My legs pivot, knees bent, spear pointed toward our enemy. "They do not. Do you not remember our days as children, do you not remember playing *spook the bolog*?"

Their grins burn the back of my neck as they recognize the truth in my words. I hear Yero pull his greatsword from its harness on his back, signaling his agreement with the plan.

"Shieldbearers!" I shout, preparing our cadence. "Spearmen! Archers! And Blades!"

Zet lowers his massive shield in front of me. Behind us, the unsheathing of blades, the clink of weapons hitting steel, the twanging of bowstrings, it all crashes through the night's stillness. Five hundred legionnaires prepare to charge. Our finest hour.

"One hundred twenty paces!" I bellow the words, and a metronome ticks inside my mind.

Two steps.

Per second.

Our charge begins, *Maripes* in my left hand as I jog.

Two steps.

Per second.

Zet's stride perfectly matches mine.

Two steps.

Per second.

Wikar marches beside me. Yero and Reata have returned to their companies. We each command one hundred and twenty-four men, each ready to die today.

Two steps.

Per second.

Our eternal stampede shakes the bridge. Ahead, we see the bolog, immense globs of saliva dripping from their mouths. Massive scars lace their stomachs.

Two steps.

Per second.

Not only did the Empire starve them, it tortured them. Once peaceful creatures reduced to beasts. Tears well in my eyes. If only I could give them Ero's rose. They were more than mere carnivores.

Two steps.

Per second.

Crunch. Crunch. Crunch.

Tiny, stray pebbles crack beneath my feet.

Rumble. Rumble. Rumble.

The mighty steps of the bolog shake the entire bridge, but it holds strong. They're just fifty meters from us, so it's time for phase two to begin.

"Two hundred paces! War cry!"

Our march transitions into a full sprint, and our five hundred voices roar. No context nor substance emanates from it, for the roar is that of anger, that of strength, that of fear, that of love. The bolog understand; the bolog stop. The bolog cower, and the bolog run—back to their torturous masters.

"One hundred sixty paces!" As we slow, the bolog pull ahead on their reverse rampage. In less than a minute, they smash into the troops hidden behind their initial charge.

"As I suspected," I utter through my labored breaths. "They hoped. To mask. Their own attack. They will. Pay."

Zet replies with a simple grunt.

I run a few numbers in my head, counting the number of strides taken over the duration of our charge. Six minutes have passed—we're nearing the center of the expanse. Perfect.

"Hold!" Five paces later, we halt our march. "Turtle!"

Shields rise, spears ready, and soldiers crouch. A shieldbearer behind me shadows us with his immense arms. From the outside, we've created our impenetrable cocoon.

"Volley!"

I don't need to look over my shoulder to trust Reata's heard my words. The beautiful crescendo of bowstrings resounds, and through the slit between Yero's shield and the next scale of our chrysalis, chaos unfolds. The bolog smash their arms into the supposed *Holy* Empire's soldiers, and one of them even picks a soldier up, throwing him over the edge. At the same time, a dozen or so spearmen rush a bolog, pierce its flesh, and push it to its death below. Arrows descend upon the scene, and I hear the cries of pain as arrows pierce the Empire's ranks. No bolog falls to the volley, for their armored shells protect them from the attack. They don't even care, the pieces of wood glancing off their backs like annoying gnats.

"Bows, range!"

My archers begin their retreat, and by counting the paces through vibrations, I feel them halt after fifty. They release another volley, and our projectiles descend upon the enemy once more. Another fifty paces. Another volley.

"Halt!" Reata's words are distant, but I agree with her unilateral command, unable to provide it from my current position.

Minutes pass. The Empire defeats the last bolog, shoving it over the side of the bridge and into the Chasm below. As if on a timer, a distant twang shrills through the crisp air. The Empire's archers have targeted us with their own arrows, but we're ready. We've been ready. Arrows bounce soundly off our shields, clattering harmlessly through the cracks.

"Twenty paces!"

We push forward, the turtle remaining in formation until another assault commences.

"Halt!"

The gaps close. The arrows pepper our turtle. No casualties.

"Thirty paces!"

We've closed the gap to twenty meters, and a line of enemy spearmen faces us. Unlike the Legion, the Empire uses leather shields held individually by each foot soldier. They're mobile, but our weapons can pierce straight through their flimsy shields. They might as well not even use them.

"I can see the whites of the damn paleskins' eyes," Zet mutters.

"Let's get this over with already."

"Patience, my friend," I say. "You'll have your chance."

Another twang. Followed by another. And another. And another. Reata issues new commands, and more arrows fly into the helpless soldiers even as they raise their shields. At the same time, arrows from the Empire's own bows rain down upon our formation in constant waves. They're finally learning. I order our march to cease, lest arrows slip through the gaps that form during our slow shuffle.

"So we let them throw away all their shots?" Wikar asks from beside me.

"Indeed." I sigh. "We can wait, at least until they adjust. We've waited a long time for this day. Let's wait a little longer."

For a time, we crouch beneath the incessant rain of cedar and copper. The rhythm becomes a melody in the dark, pounding uselessly against our steel. I stare toward our enemy, and they slowly back away from us. We'll lose our advantage if they retreat too far.

Through the slit, I witness a new sight emerge. Red light arcs above the battlefield, traveling a steady course straight for our position.

"What new devilry is this?" Wikar exclaims.

"I don't know." I clench my hand around the shaft of my spear. "Do you trust me?"

"Don't ask that question."

I let out an involuntary chuckle. "Hammer!"

In swift transition, Zet charges forward, shield straight ahead yet at a slight angle above his head to deflect any incoming arrows. I follow in stride beneath the massive hulk of metal, and by my side, Wikar and his own shieldbearer join the sprint. Behind us, everyone falls in step, and we, the Hammer of Lethotar, lash at the Empire's troops. We collide even as my Legion cries in anguish behind me, experiencing the pain and torment of whatever the accursed imperial Inquisitors have beset upon us.

Now the real battle begins.

I leap into the fray, *Flame of Maripes* striking out from behind

Zet's shield. It slices open the cheek of one foe, and, while pulling the moonstone blade back, I whip it to the side, slicing the face of another paleskin. They bleed a much lighter red, but it's still red.

"To arms!" I cry, but I know Yero has already begun his charge. My Master of the Blade ached for his weapon to strike at these bastards, and now that the battle's started outright, his swordsmen can join the fight. The archers of the Empire will cease their fire, lest they kill their own men. Reata, too, will cease her fire, at least until she puts troops further along the bridge in range.

A spear juts toward my neck, but I step back, out of its reach. Every time I enter battle with the paleskins, I marvel at their diminutive size. At least a head shorter than us, they've only managed to win this war because of their sheer numbers. When the people of the Three Valleys field five thousand soldiers, the Empire brings twenty thousand. When we field two thousand, the Empire charges with ten thousand. They always bring enough to overpower, but never so much that it's a massacre. They know how many soldiers they need to win, and how many they can sustainably feed. Their strategy has intelligence, and I pity its use to obliterate my people. In another life, perhaps I could have shared a bottle of cherry wine, fresh from the grove, with the enemy's commander.

I strike out with *Flame* above Zet's planted shield, this time in a wide arc. The blade slices through three spearmen, sending them sprawling to the ground. Even as I take down these opponents, I look to my left. A spear has pierced Wikar's neck; the lieutenant falls. A new spearman steps forward to take his place, yet the future is clear. Even as we kill our enemy, we fall, and we can only fall so many times.

Shouts emanate from the Empire's troops, and the spearmen retreat a few dozen meters to reorganize their battle line. For a moment, I question the tactic, but their reasoning doesn't take long to reveal itself.

Marching forward through their ranks, the telltale armor of their knights clinks like coins in a purse. Finally, a battle worth our mettle. A few seconds later, I feel the pitter-patter of raindrops strike the sunsteel beneath my feet, my helmet, my hands. My ear twitches, feeling the leafy touch of the rose given by my husband. It still rests there, unmoved. A night truly worth remembering.

◆ ◆ ◆

I was fourteen, sitting by the fire, my mother and father lounging under blankets beside me.

"You know the legend of our Lord, yes, my son?" Maripes said.

"Of course, father," I replied.

"But do you know the truth behind the legend?"

"I don't think I understand."

Maripes stood and walked to the mantle above the fireplace. He grabbed a massive rock and gingerly placed it on the ground in front of me. "Moonstone. You know I work it. You know I use it. Do you know why it is holy to our people?"

I furled my brow. "I don't, father."

"Most don't know this part of our story," said Vona. "Moonstone is holy to our people for it was given to us by the Lord as a gift. Its true power comes from him, for he used it to destroy our enemies in the War before Time."

"What can it do?"

Maripes laughed, sitting down next to me again. "That's the thing; no one knows all it can do. I know what I can do *with it*, but I don't know what it can do."

"What's the difference?"

Vona raised her eyebrows. "Only the Lord knows."

IX

Seventy-five of our people have fallen. By my estimates, we've killed five hundred enemies. Not enough.

Thunder cracks above us, lightning tingling inside my spear each time its crash rattles the sky. Since their arrival on the battlefield, I've killed five knights, piercing their armor between the neck and chest. Yero died three hours ago, but Zet still stands by my side, having dropped his shield in favor of his war hammer. The pouring rain drenches our skin, but the sun will soon rise. I await its growing warmth.

We may hold the line, yet we face an endless throng of paleskin Imperial soldiers. The battle lulls, for both sides tire of fighting, even as our enemy brings fresh troops to the line. It's late. We all desire sleep. Nevertheless, Zet and I step forward. I know they can't understand me, but I will speak regardless, hoping my words strike fear in their minds.

"You have fought bravely, but you have seen your brothers fall," I say. I've always found it ridiculous that the Holy Empire refuses to let women fight. "Why throw your lives away? You have no chance. We are the harbinger of your death."

The soldiers take steps back, pointing their spears at me even as fifteen meters separate us. They murmur in their strange language—short, guttural sounds, like crackling ice.

"I am Mono, son of Maripes, bane of your existence." I pound my chest with my gauntlet, the iron on iron clang echoing through the rain. "I have slain hundreds, if not thousands of your kin over these fifteen long years, do you have anyone who can face me?"

I don't expect a response, but a soldier in white and gray chainmail armor steps forward. He holds an ornate sword in hand, and through the eye-slits of his helmet, I see pale blue eyes and blonde hair. The blade's made of sunsteel—must be one of their few artifacts from a time before time. A *hero*. However, he will not die a hero as long as I stand. I will strike this puny paleskin down, for I too, am a hero for my people.

"You are the *accursed ones*, the ones who scourge this earth," the man says, and to my surprise, it's in my own language. "We will cleanse the world of your filth, and claim this land as foretold in the prophecies. Just like we cleansed the world of Maripes."

"My father was a great man."

"He died for his crimes. It was a magnificent day."

The soldier enters a combat stance, and I lower *Flame*, ready for this ridiculous duel. Zet takes a few steps backward, and behind me, my troops begin their chant.

"Mono, Mono, Mono, Mono."

"I don't know how you know our language," I say, "but in this final hour, you gain one measure of respect in my mind." I don't know why I say it, but it seems the right thing to do. I'm trying to ignore his comments regarding my father, but . . .

"I neither need nor desire respect from you." The soldier lunges, his sword held in both hands. His sword—it glistens. It's sunsteel. Curious.

I bend my knees, stepping to the side to catch the swordsman off guard and use his momentum against him. As if expecting the counter, the swordsman twirls, bringing his blade in an arc toward me. I parry the attack with the sunsteel shaft of my spear, pushing the sword away. As the identical metals clash, the *hero*'s eyes widen, as if he hadn't expected the power of my weapon.

"I am Mono." I whip my weapon toward the man's head, but he ducks. Another thunder crack emanates from the heavens. "My father was Maripes!" I jab with my moonstone spear point, but my opponent parries. "Your people murdered him in *cold blood*." A decade's worth of spite lacing my words, I kick the chest of the paleskin, flinging him backward.

"Your people have murdered throughout your entire existence!" cries the *hero*, water dripping from his helmet. "One crime does not outweigh an eternity of evil. And your father committed the greatest crime of all."

"We are the people of Light; we fight for love and life, not death."

"Liar!"

The swordsman somersaults backward just out of my reach. A tactical mistake, putting his back to me, but I fail to take advantage of the acrobatic folly. Instead, I position my right shoulder forward, my left hand on the back half my *Flame*. I will defeat this boy; the war will continue. It's taken too long already. The silly paleskin pulls his fist out of a pouch at his hip; it's not clear what he holds. In one hand, his sword dangles at his side. The other conceals a secret.

"Don't play tricks with me," I say.

He charges. While closing the gap, the boy throws the contents of his hand into the air, a fine dust cloud descending. Even the pouring rain cannot clear it, and the particles crash into my eyes.

He has no honor.

Darkness envelops me, mixed with flashes of white light, eyes burning as if acid drenches my pupils. Before I comprehend my circumstance, inferno pain flares, a blade crashing into my collarbone.

The faces of Ero and Ermo drift across my clouded vision, safely at home. My bones echo the cries of my men, seeing their commander fall. As if they've always been there, my parents watch from above. A voice says, "Look to the east."

Forcing my neck to bend through the cloudy darkness, I see white. Beautiful light, but it's not sunlight. The sun hasn't yet peeked over the mountaintops. A mighty hand much more powerful than my own strikes out from the rain clouds above, and, raising my weapon in defiance, power surges through my soul. It travels to my toes, to my fingertips, to the tip of my spear along its shaft. The core of this newfound source of strength forms where the sunsteel of my weapon meets its moonstone pike.

Even as blood drips down my chest, I heave *Flame of Maripes* with both hands, arcing it in a powerful sweep. The energy surging through my body clears my vision, and in icy clarity, the paleskin steps back, already preparing his killing blow. He's not yet realized my transformation, for only I see the truth only in my mind.

My spear, my father's spear, my Lord's spear slices straight through the hero's helmet, onward through his neck, and partway through his shoulder before it finds air again. The blade continues its path until it connects with the sunsteel of the Bridge of our Lord, the very bridge laid in place by my Lord of Light. It's my bridge now. A shock wave crackles and shatters, and as I drop to my knees, the surface below me fractures. Releasing *Flame*, I fall face forward to the ground. The sunsteel breaks, the expanse welcoming me.

It also welcomes my enemy.

As I fall, I twirl in the air, watching half a bridge crumble with me. Hundreds—no—thousands of paleskins cry in terror as they plummet to their deaths, but I smile, for I look toward our side of the bridge. My troops are alive, halfway across the massive causeway, where their enemy cannot reach them. Can never reach them. My final moment of life is one of happiness and joy. For drifting before my eyes, I, Mono, see Ero's rose. I've saved him. Ermo. My Legion. My people.

Ero tills the soil of his garden. Ermo plays in the dirt, building mounds into castles. She's so beautiful, and Ero wishes Mono could've seen what she'd look like once grown. Their daughter deserves a better life.

"Dad, what's father doing right now?" Ermo says.

Ero looks to the sky, seeing the sun reach mid-day. The night's rain clouds have already disappeared. If Mono's predictions about the battle are correct, then they'd be commencing the fight just about now.

"Well, I imagine he's telling his troops the Prophecy, their Rite of War, as he calls it."

"The one he recites every night?"

Ero digs at the soil with the hoe. "Yes, you know how it goes." Satisfied, he drops a seed into the new hole.

Looking up from her dirt castles, she says, "In the final hour of our people, I will return to fight by your side. I will stand beside you, before you, above you, beneath you, and behind you. When all hope has lost, regain it, for I will smite the stones that block your path, rend the rivers that oppose you, and return peace to the land of our people."

Ero smiles. "You'll make a wonderful teacher someday. Do you know the next verse?"

"No, father never said it."

"It's not a verse for the warriors. It's a verse for the people."

"What's it say?"

Resting the hoe against the side of the house, Ero sits in the dirt next to his daughter. "So says our Lord. We fight for him as he fought for us. We fight for our love as he fought for us. We fight for Lethotar as he fought for us." He pauses. "This is the part most forget: And when I return to your side, my sacrifice will usher in a new age. A Daughter of the Lord will rise to the throne, and *no longer will the world know us as the accursed ones. No longer will they know us as the orcs.* They will know us as the People of Light, our true form. The People of Peace. *The People of Love.*"

"I don't get it." She returns to her dirt castles.

Drumbeats resound through the streets far below their cliffside home, and Ero recognizes their meaning. Their double meaning. Their Commander has fallen, but the Fifth Legion returns, victorious. He looks toward his daughter. Their daughter. The Lord of Light's daughter. "Love, I've never understood until today."

THUNDER OF ERMO

*You **will** usher in a new age.*

For whom?

The Gates of Vicor
As we believe them to appear,
following the fall of the Legions.

X

I walk along the bridge, suffocated by the entourage of priests, soldiers, and clan leaders. The upcoming coronation is dumb. Unnecessary. They've decided my fate; why have an entire ceremony devoted to telling me who I am?

My father, Ero, is on my left. I remember his words from the morning: "In the end, it's your choice. You must accept the mantle; otherwise, your power is meaningless." Here's the problem no one seems to understand.

I don't want power.

I want freedom.

After hours upon hours of agonizing walking without purpose, we reach the Edge. Just a few meters away, the fractured bridge disappears, kilometers of empty expanse expanding below. A few hundred meters away, the remainders of the northern section of the bridge remain—beyond, forsaken land.

We halt, and my dad's hands rest on my shoulders. High Priest Reano turns to face me, his back to the Edge. "Step forward, Ermo, daughter of Ero, daughter of Mono, daughter of our Lord of Light."

I step forward.

"Do you accept the task laid at your feet, established by scripture and brought forth through prophecy by the actions of your father?"

Right to the point, then. It's been ten years since my father died, and they're certainly brushing past the details to get on with their ritual. No consideration for what I want. "I accept the task," I say.

"And what is your task?"

They want me to say . . . they want me to declare a task to bring restitution to our people. To propose a world where we no longer cower behind the Chasm, our sole source of protection from the

Holy Empire. They desire a declaration of my divinity, the heralded daughter of the Lord of Light ready to step into her role as savior.

"My task . . ." I look up and behind, at my father.

"I am the beacon of light . . ." he whispers.

I thought I had a choice. Instead, even my father—my *father*—is pushing me toward an unwanted fate.

"My task . . ."

"I am the Daughter of Light," he adds.

"My task?" I step out from under my father's entrapping hands. "My task? My task? I will find my own way."

I dart beneath the outstretched hands of the High Priest, not bothering to catch his glance of surprise. Stepping toward the Edge, the expanse welcomes me. A decade ago, my father broke this bridge, fracturing our connection to the world beyond. A voice groans in my soul, telling me to jump.

Do it.

What am I thinking? I'll die. There's no question.

Jump.

No. This is insane.

You wanted a different destiny. I've opened a path for you.

I jump.

◆ ◆ ◆

I never knew my mother. Or, I suppose, I should call her my aunt. She died when I was only a few months old. In the middle of the war, she died not from useless slaughter, but from the common pox. Her death was preventable. The nectar of the yellowbrush bush cures the ailment instantly.

Except by the time she contracted the disease, the Holy Empire controlled the cliffs where the yellowbrush grow. She died. Within three weeks. Ero, her brother, and his husband, Mono, became my fathers. I remember loving Mono. A long time ago, when I was a small child, I remember his touch, his gentle grasp, even though I rarely saw him.

The war with the Holy Empire tore my family apart too many times. I hate everything they stand for. Yet . . . I am not the vessel my people believe me to be. I am not the weapon to destroy the Holy Empire. The prophecy was wrong; I cannot finish what my father started above the Chasm, ten years ago.

◆ ◆ ◆

Wind rushes past my ears. I hear screams, but they're not my own. They're from above—from the Edge. As for me, I'm at peace. Somehow. Straight as an arrow, my body dives toward the rushing river kilometers below.

I have no fear. Strange. An indecipherable voice reverberates in my skull, its words echoing and pulsating and—

Ermo, my daughter, remember—follow the light.

A voice from my past—Mono. My father. Is he with me? No, that's silly. He's dead; I'm probably hallucinating.

From above, the Chasm makes the river look so small. As I near the torrent, it grows, revealing a dark expanse larger than I could have thought possible.

How could I be so stupid? I jumped from a bridge into a gorge kilometers deep, assuredly leading to my death. Nothing can save me now.

Follow the light.

I see no light. Only waves. Only darkness.

Follow the light.

"Stop telling me to follow the light!"

They're the words I want to leave my mouth, but at the speed I'm falling, nothing escapes my lungs. My vision begins to blacken. Blur. Spots dance.

Child, follow my voice. I am the light.

I can't. This is it. The end.

Before I hit the water, my mind slips into the void.

INTERJECTION

Darkness surrounds. I'm outside time, beyond all experience yet experiencing everything at once. A faint sensation of murky wetness envelops me, but I can't tell if it's water . . . or something new. If I've entered the world of the dead, it's different than I expected. Though, I don't know what I expected. To meet my father, perhaps? To face the Creator, or The Lord of Light?

I try to lift my hands, but it's like sliding through molasses. Nothing moves. Eyes. Toes. Fingers. Ears. Nothing moves.

Opening my mouth, a wet warmth floods my throat. I choke. The darkness rushes, not just around, but *into me*, it's trying to destroy me, make me its own.

Follow.

I can't. I have no strength. All will left my soul when I leapt off the Edge, stupidly defying my father and the other elders. I should have listened.

No. Follow.

The damned voice won't stop. It's probably death taunting, telling a story to trick me into letting go. Embracing hell.

No. Look. I am here.

Breaking through the darkness, a spark of white emerges. It's tiny, no more than a single star striking through an otherwise cloudy sky. Yet, it is there. For me.

My daughter, I am here.

"Where?" To my surprise, words leave my mouth, foggy mist escaping purple lips.

You took the first step on your own. You can take the next, too. Follow the light.

I focus. With a guttural scream, my limbs break free of their invisible bonds. My fingers grasp in the darkness, and I fall to my knees, but the light doesn't waver. My hands find something solid—metallic. Grasping it, I don't let my eyes break from the light.

You are the light. They were the light. They are the light. You are all the light. Will be the light.

The light grows. No—it's not growing. I'm getting closer to it. Ripples of blue and grey flutter beneath the white. The light takes form. The sun, shining through waves of water. Mind, soul, and body thrust me back into the world of living, and in my hands, I hold a spear. It's . . . the spear is *pulling* me toward the light. Or am I telling the spear to draw me upward? Crashing through river's surface, my body explodes in pain.

XI

Something wet licks my cheek. It's coarse, and rough, and it's . . . a tongue.

Eyes fluttering open, I'm greeted with the floppy smile of a water-wolf. The mongrel-brown creature lazily stares, as if I should expect it to be there. With my left hand, I push its snout away, and then the memories flood my perceptions.

I'm pretty sure I died. At least . . . it was something like death. It's impossible to survive a three-kilometer fall, but here I am, lying . . . somewhere.

Every inch of my body aches. I remember bone-crushing pain from the fall, but it's fading, replaced with a dull throb, like I've gone for a long run and now I'm recovering the next day.

Sand surrounds me, and a few meters away, the Caris River flows. Sitting on my haunches, I look up and down its banks, but in neither direction are the walls of the Chasm. I must have floated kilometers down river before washing ashore, reaching the wider portions of the canyon.

Next to me, sticking straight up, is a long, metallic shaft. At its end, an ornately curved blade forms a spear-point, almost like a pike. The weapon is . . . sunsteel and moonstone.

No.

I know this weapon.

Two memories flash. First, from the darkness, a spear in my hands, pulling me out of the void and into the light.

Second—an identical match, hanging in my father Mono's war closet. *Flame of Maripes.* The weapon forged by my grandfather, the blade that ended the war and split the Bridge of our Lord in two.

Previously lost in the Caris River following my father's death.

But here it is, waiting. Wanting me to wield it.

My weapon will reveal your path.

"I want to follow my own path." I don't know why I say the words aloud, but it's better than thinking to myself. At least it feels like I'm speaking to someone. The dead voice of my father—or grandfather? The Lord of Light? My crazy mind?

And it will help you find it.

I push up from the sand, approaching *Flame of Maripes*. Even after the ten years since my father last held the weapon, it bears no scratches. Flawless carvings engrave its shaft, depicting religious prophecies etched by my grandfather. It's at least a meter taller than me, if not more, but when I wrap my hands around it, energy flows from it into my fingers, into my arms, into my heart. It's light. It's mine.

"Ruff!"

I turn, the water-wolf sitting on its hind legs, barking. Not an angry bark, but one of joy, as if I made the right choice.

"We'll see, friend," I say. "But where do I go?"

I half expect the disembodied voice to reply. Instead, the tiny creature stares at me, wagging its tail.

"I'm leading then? All right. Well . . ." I study the river. The water's flowing south, away from Lethotar, the narrower portions of the Chasm, and my people. I've started down a path away from home, so there's no point turning back now. Spear in hand, I trudge through the sand, heading away from the river and into the forest beyond.

The water-wolf follows close behind, panting at my heels. "You'll need a name," I say. "Do you have a name? Of course. You're a wolf. You can't talk. Except I'm talking to you. What a way to start an adventure."

Naturally, the wolf doesn't respond.

"I'm going to need to call you something." I pause, listening to the sounds of the forest ahead and the water behind. "River. I'll call you river. I found you there—well, more so *you* found *me*. So you're River."

"Ruff!"

"You like the name?"

Pant-pant.

"Perfect."

Up a muddy bank we go, stepping beneath the massive juniper oaks. Leaving the sand behind, I use the spear to brush bush and fern away, forming a makeshift route through the overgrowth. Before long, we stumble upon a dried creek heading slightly uphill and away from the Caris. It becomes our path, and periodically we discover small pools teaming with algae and fish. The water's too dirty to drink, though every so often, we stumble upon a tiny waterfall, and I use it as a makeshift water fountain. It tastes despicable, but it's hydration.

For hours, I trek side-by-side with River. When I'm hungry, I find mushrooms, nuts, or berries scattered throughout the forest. Sustenance is plentiful. As the sun starts to disappear deep behind the trees and the unseen horizon, we stake a campsite beneath a rocky outcropping shadowing the creek bed. I collect dried wood and a few rocks, forming a tiny fire pit.

"Now how to ignite the wood . . ." I glance at River. He—or she, I'm not certain—tilts his head. Sparks of energy resonate in my left hand, calling me toward *Flame of Maripes.* "What the hell?"

I step toward the spear, pick it up, and approach the fire. My right hand holds the weapon, while I hold the other over the wood. "What do I do next? Father? You there? Any help?"

Silence.

"Great. So you only speak when it's convenient to you?"

Silence.

Silence and—sparks.

"Ow!" Dancing along my arm, tendrils of energy sting and stab. "I need help here; I don't even know what I'm doing!"

I drop the spear, and the glow fades. "All right. Progress. So the power is linked to the spear . . . but not entirely. Because the sparks formed before I touched it." Kneeling, I pick the spear up again, the energy flowing back into my arm.

"Now . . ." I glance toward River. "Why didn't this happen when I was walking? And just holding the spear?" The stinging continues, like my arm's asleep. I'm getting used to its annoying presence. "Maybe . . ."

I probably look absurd, but I bend my knees, point the spear at the dried wood, and shout, "Fire!"

Nothing.

"Ugh! What do you need from me?" The forest is already starting to chill after hours without the sun. In my anger, I envision the comfort a simple fire would bring. As the emotion builds, the knives in my arm dig deeper. From my hand, an arc of yellow light branches toward the wood, enveloping it in an inferno of crimson flame.

Anger shifts into surprise, and the pain in my arm fades. "Okay, okay, now we're getting somewhere. Not sure how, but it's something."

I sit down in the dust, enjoying the flames. River struts to my side and places his head in my lap. Magic. We've always had legends, stories of wizards and sorcerers capable of incredible feats. Of course, we've all heard what my father did above the Chasm. But this . . . it's something new.

I scratch River's forehead, and beneath a canopy of rock and wood, we drift to sleep.

XII

I wake. In pain. Terrible pain. My stomach, my mouth, my head, my freaking tongue. It burns. All of it.

To top it all off, it's raining.

We're beneath the outcropping, but the torrent periodically blows a wave of mist and salty water onto my face, even as I lay writhing in pain. I moan, trying to move and scoot further back and away from the storm, but I can't move. Legs lock, arms dull. I can barely open my eyes. River, for his part, curls closer to me, whimpering.

My brain, trying to break through the hammer pounding my skull, contemplates the sickness. Is it because I used my new power? Or something I ate? There's no way to know. I'm immobilized, acid welling in my throat.

The storm fades, but the eternal agony continues. I lay in my own oral excrement, hyperventilating. It's as if my skin is on fire. Fading in and out of consciousness, I vaguely recognize the shape of dead rabbit dropping into the dirt before my eyes. River curls up next to me. He hunted. I can't move to eat, but he hunted.

Light turns back to dark and dark back to light. I plead for the pain to end—anything, to save me from endless torment. When my eyes are open, they deceive me. Shapes drift amongst shadows, dancing on the mossy rocks and trees. Creatures, immeasurably large and impossibly shaped, drift, dart, and evaporate in smoke. Fear grips my soul. I just want it to end.

At some point, my fingers manage to grip the spear, as if my new power can heal me. I try to will the energy to kill whatever afflicts my body—or, in the alternative, to kill me, ending the pain—but the spear doesn't respond. It can't hear my plea.

Here in a ditch, lost in a forest, the People of Light's chosen one will die. I've failed them.

◆ ◆ ◆

I awake again. The pain is gone. I don't know how long it's been, but I'm alive.

Hungry—and thirsty, but alive.

As I sit up, River bounds into the clearing, a squirrel in its mouth. The fire from a few nights ago is an ashy soup, drenched by the rain. I can't remember if it stormed more than once. Everything blurs together. Dripping from the outcropping above, though, is crystal clean water. I stand beneath the droplets, quenching my thirst. I collect another round of wood from the brush on the other side of the creek—which now flows freely—and ignite it, just like last time.

"Here's to hoping I don't get sick a second time," I mutter to River. After skinning it with my spear, I stab the squirrel with a sharp stick and cook it over my second fire. Breakfast. Or lunch? Dinner? More like all three at once.

After finishing the meal, I strip and bathe in the creek. I'm filthy, vomit and other bodily fluids are everywhere. It's disgusting, and I wash my clothes too, both the grey tunic top and the leather, parted dress. While they dry on warm rocks, I drift lazily back and forth in the water. It's refreshing for both my skin and mind. River dives into the water too, floating about on its (his? I'm not sure) back and squirting streams of water into the air, reminding me of otters in the aqueducts of Lethotar.

Afterward, while donning the now dry garments, I wish for something other than a ceremonial outfit to wear. Picking up the spear, I kick sand about the campsite to eliminate traces of the fire. "It's time to go." I motion for River to follow, and we continue upstream.

Curving along the edge of the outcropping, a small path leads up and above the creek. Stepping over boulders and blasted tree roots, we swiftly ascend a ridge. At the top, a ghastly sight awaits.

Slumped against a tree, a dark, morphic form lies, mutilated and deformed. It's grotesque; its skin is jet-black, shades darker than my own, with white spots dotting every inch like inverse freckles. White fangs stretch over its lips.

Fortunately, it's very dead. Its throat is torn out, a bloody and mangled mess. As we approach, River growls a low, rumbling moan. I step closer to the strange creature, and River barks, roars, darts in front of me, baring its fangs and blocking my path toward the corpse.

"Okay, we can avoid it if you'd like," I say, stepping back. "But what is it?" A vengeful gleam flashes in River's eyes as I say the question. "Did you do this?" I remember the shadows from during my sickness. The creatures I'd thought were hallucinations. "Impossible."

I've never heard of any such creature. My entire life, Ero has drilled facts into my head, many of them useless about places I'll never see. I learned about the digestive tracts of the Bolog, the hunting patterns of the water-wolves, the culture of the frost giants—a creature most consider myth—the strange "cacti" of the deserts far to the south, plants capable of living without water for years on end.

And yet . . . this thing . . . it's something else.

Stepping away, we skirt around the dead, dark, demon-like corpse. "If you saved me from that, River," I say, "I owe you more than my life." As we travel further from the grisly scene, River's kind demeanor returns, his (we're going with his) tail wagging and tongue panting.

With every step, I expect my sickness to return. Yet, with every step, I feel stronger. I *am* stronger. It's as if my body was fighting its new journey, but my will to create a new path won.

Perhaps I'm just imagining the metaphor. It was almost certainly something I ate. Nevertheless . . . I like the symbolism. If I'm the subject of prophecy, might as well give substance to every moment of my life.

Like the first day—after the beach—River and I trudge through the forest, finding a new path away from the creek. We're slowly heading uphill, and if the dated and murky map in my head is accurate, I'm traversing the hills of the former Kineto clans. If I continued following the Caris River, I would have eventually reached the Emerald Falls, spilling over the cliffs for hundreds of meters before lazily entering the other valleys and the expansive plains beyond. The only real way down the immense cliff-face is the Gates of Vicor. The final battle before my father's death, where he watched many of his brothers- and sisters-in-arms fall. To properly reach Vicor and its nearby fortress, I need to veer away from the river.

I gulp. I've heard stories from the survivors of our final battle, especially those who also fought by Mono's side at the Gates. They called it the bloodiest and longest battle of the war. I dread what I will find. But, seeing as I don't know *what* I'm looking for, it's the only destination I have available. If I'm to discover my own destiny, I must go *somewhere*.

"I just hope I don't run into any more of those fiends." River growls, somehow knowing exactly what I'm thinking. "You're smarter than you let on, aren't you? Well, with you by my side, no fiend can get me. I like that name for them, too. Fiend. I think it'll stick."

◆ ◆ ◆

Three more nights pass, and other than an upset stomach following poorly cooked rabbit, I'm sure my sickness has passed. On the morning of the fourth day, I crest a ridge. To my right, a little ways away, the Caris River reaches a massive cliff face and flows over the edge. Beyond, the vast plain and rolling hills of the Three Valleys spread in their glory. Joy wells in my soul as I witness a visage I never hoped to witness.

To the left—some three or four kilometers away by my reckoning—nestled between two giant, rocky monstrosities, sits the decrepit fortress known simply as the "Gates of Vicor."

It's occupied.

By now, I'd thought the Holy Empire had simply abandoned

the Three Valleys. Since my father's death, no one has seen evidence of their activity on the other side of the Chasm. As I traveled toward the Gates, I'd seen no traces of any people—anywhere.

Faced with the truth in front of me, it all clicked into place. If the Holy Empire held the Gates of Vicor, they would indefinitely trap us beyond the Chasm, even if we managed to somehow rebuild the bridge.

So, after ten years, their troops remain, ever vigilant. The fortress itself wasn't very large; two towers buttressed the rock faces, and an immense wall spread between the two vantage points. Beneath the wall, various buildings built of the same stone spread out haphazardly in no order. Then, an empty plain and rocky bluff . . . and the actual town of Vicor, abandoned and ruined and burnt to a crisp. Flags fly from the parapets of the fortress beyond, however, signaling its occupancy.

"All right River, what's next?"

He sniffs the air, whimpers, and lies on his belly. "I agree. We wait until nightfall."

I step away from the ridge and out of sight of the towers. There's no telling whether they can see me against the trees from this distance, but there's no reason to risk detection. Once I'm a few meters into the trees, I lean against a trunk, considering my options. River follows and flops at my feet like a loose rag. He's tired.

Sighing, I lift *Flame of Maripes* into a battle stance. While I've not been training for the Legion like others my age, I've learned enough about how to use the weapon from practicing with my classmates. The reach of a spear cannot be matched, especially a spear like *Flame*. However, I'm not interested in practicing my attacks, guards, and counters. I need to see what I can do with my newfound power.

"All right, River, if I'm correct, then the energy is somehow inside me . . . but when I'm holding the spear, it like . . . channels it more powerfully? Or allows me to direct it in specific ways?"

No response from the wolf. He continues to pant, drool dripping onto the dirt next to his front paws.

"All right, well, here goes nothing."

Sparks flash between fingers. I choose a bush at random, envisioning it igniting in flame. I want the bush to burn; I *need* it to burn. My arm numbs, daggers stab my veins, but a beam of light leaves my hand, descending upon the poor plant. It burns. Way too quickly.

"Oh, shoot!"

I panic, not sure how to avoid a forest fire. Without thinking, I wish for the flames to die. In a similarly bright flash of light, it listens, energy sucking right back into my hand.

"Well . . . that could be useful."

I prance around the clearing, considering my options. What else could my power possibly allow me to do? I approach a sapling—it's not much taller than I am. I grasp *Flame of Maripes* in both hands, swing it back, and slice in an arc straight in front of the baby tree, envisioning a slice straight through the bark.

The spear doesn't touch, but a noticeable slice drives almost entirely through. So . . . not only can I blast fire from my fingers, I can enhance my weapon. Perfect.

XIII

The next few hours pass by as I practice my abilities. Day turns toward twilight, and I halt for rest and for food. As the sun sets beyond the Emerald Falls and across the valleys, I stop my practice, worried the flashes of light will alert the troops within the Gates of Vicor. Sitting on my ridge, observing the fortress, I'm unsure of my next steps. While practicing, I hadn't considered what to do once darkness arrived.

River shuffles to my side. Nibbling at my tunic, he pulls me away from the cliff's edge. I follow. We head into the trees, down a trail I'd not previously noticed. It winds down a slope, and before long, I can see my vantage point to the right and above the tree line. Minutes later, we've cleared the trees, and as the sun hides behind the mountains, we near the edge of the abandoned town of Vicor.

The Holy Empire doesn't have troops patrolling the town—surprising. I'm sneaking close to their fort at night, and given the lack of torches or light around the decaying structures, I can easily dart from shadow to shadow, remaining invisible to the towers buttressing the Gates of Vicor.

Beneath ruined windows and crumbled walls, I chart a path through former homes and shops. I imagine legionnaires probably lived in many of these buildings, prior to the city's demise. Strips of cloth indicative of Legion colors tatter about in the wind like mice. Supposedly, I lived here a lifetime ago, when Ero stayed closer to the front lines with Mono. I can't remember that far back, though.

When we near the center of town, a scraping noise scratches stone. It's like chalk on a classroom wall back in Lethotar. I stop, River at my feet. He's growling. Like when we found the fiend. Great.

I turn around—right into a trio of fiends, creeping down from the roof of a burned-out house. I'm starting to understand why the Holy Empire has no presence here. We've walked into a nest of demons.

Spear raised, I prepare for their attack. Two charge; one waits behind, pacing. Before they reach us, River leaps, tackling the left fiend. A scramble ensues, but I have no time to watch as the other one taunts me. It screams an inhuman cry—like a goat, but a higher pitch.

It strikes, its arm flinging forward and *stretching* like an elastic rope. With my father's spear, I swipe, imagining the arm tearing in half. With a sickening crunch, bones break, the arm fractures, and blood splatters the dirt. It falls to the ground, writhing in pain.

No time to watch.

River grapples with his fiend, the third still pacing some ten meters away. Holding out my hand, I imagine River's assailant bursting into flame. An energy lance leaves my palm, striking the dark creature, and it erupts, skin boiling and smoking. River rolls away, unscathed. The third fiend howls, backs away, and runs down an alley, out of sight.

"No way the towers missed that flash, better—"

Out of the alley, dozens of fiends crawl, charging River and me. They're not too fast, but they're fast enough.

I take off in a dead sprint away from them, deeper into town. Another dozen or so fly out of another alley, as if . . . herding us. Not good. "River, I'm about to do something insanely stupid, you better trust me, boy."

The larger group of fiends is behind me and a bit to the right. A small pack forms on our left—toward the Gates of Vicor. I abruptly change course, charging the group head-on. Gathering my mental strength, I envision a blast of flame throwing the pack against a nearby wall. Light lances, flames erupt, screams resound, and we're running through their smoldering remains.

I'm not unscathed. My skin feels like its boiling too, daggers continuing to stab my wrist. I look down, and it's crackling—blistering. All right, so there're limits to my power. Need to pay close attention. Spear probably helps limit damage to my body, if I channel through the weapon.

We're not out of the fire yet. With a glance over the shoulder, I see a ravenous horde of fiends charging me. Only one direction to go—toward the Gates of Vicor. Though they're aching from running, my legs carry me over crumbled walkways, dirty puddles, and patchy, overgrown grass. The closer we are to the fortress, the more I recognize its true immensity. The wall is huge, at least fifty meters tall, and it's still a good half a kilometer from me. The cries and screams of the fiends sound like they're right at my ankles, but—

The fortress screeches. No. The gate at the base of the wall—it's rising. In the dim moonlight, a party of soldiers on horseback gallops into the ruins. At this point, I don't care if they're Holy Empire. They can save us from the demons at our heels.

I barely feel the minutes pass. Feet on stone. Cool breeze through the hair. Screaming. Constant, evil screaming. Then—shouts. Men, speaking in an incomprehensible language. Rounding a corner, the cavalry are charging down a main road toward my enemy. I duck to the side of the road, pointing and screaming at the creatures behind me. Lances and swords at their sides, the soldiers converge on the fiends, slashing and swiping and carving them to pieces.

After only a minute or two of fighting, the beasts disperse, whimpering. My heart's beating like a drum in my chest, and River circles around me, wagging his tail. We're safe.

Except we're not.

The knights turn, face us, and slowly trot toward our position.

"River, you need to leave. Now. Wait for me here. I know you can survive." I scratch the wolf's head. "Do you understand? You need to go. Back to the forest."

He tilts his head quizzically.

"No, I don't know what they'll do to you. Probably view you as vermin. Go!" I point toward the trees. He's fast enough to outrun the fiends. I think.

He nuzzles my knee. It's too late. The horsemen surround us, lances pointed at my chest. The men shout words and sounds back and forth between each other, speaking their strange language. One horse trots ahead of the others. River leans against my leg.

"Accursed one," says the helmeted soldier in my language, "how did you escape the pens?"

Raising my hands above my head, the spear pointed to signal nonaggression, I say, "I did not escape. I . . ." I don't know what to say next.

"Of course you escaped. Where else would you be from? Back to the mines with you."

The mines? Oh no. "Wait! I am from Lethotar! I'm . . . an envoy come to speak with your leader!"

"Lethotar was destroyed. You lie. Drop your weapon. It's time to return you to the pens."

"I'm telling the truth!"

The soldier kicks his horse forward and whips his lance around, knocking me to the ground. "Comply. Now."

While I could fight, unleashing my power, I don't think I can take them all. I nod, wincing at the pain in my chest. I drop *Flame of Maripes* to the dirt.

With a roar, my water-wolf lunges at the horsemen who assaulted me.

"River! No!"

With a casual stab of his lance, he skewers my friend in the shoulder. River drops to the dirt, blood dripping and staining dark, matted fur. I reach for *Flame*, but I've been caught unawares. Another soldier approached from the side, and his boot now rests squarely on the spear's shaft.

"Why?" I scream. "Why kill him?" My lungs are dry and coarse with sorrow. I fall to my knees.

The soldiers give no response. They bind and gag me, push me toward the city, and leave River whimpering in the mud. I have no time to mourn the loss of my friend, my guide, my family. He'll die out here, fighting the fiends—or from blood loss—because I thought it smart to explore a city beneath the watchful gaze of the Holy Empire.

So instead, the next step of my journey will take me to the pens. And, based on the soldier's words, to the remnants of my people beyond Lethotar.

XIV

Darkness. Infinite darkness. It reminds me of the place between life and death, after I smashed into the Caris River. Except instead of water, dark walls in a space only a meter wide and two meters tall surround me. An underground coffin, with only a metal, windowless lid above my head.

I scream for hours with no response. Now, I cry.

"Father? Grandfather? Lord of Light? Where are you? Why have you forsaken me this entire time?"

Silence.

"Did you save me from the waters just to die in this hole?

Silence.

"And you let River die."

Silence.

I fall to the ground, curling in a ball. There's just enough room to lazily drift to sleep. This is the end, I know it.

Hours. Days. Weeks. I don't know. At least twenty times, they've opened the hatch above me, dropping a canteen of water, a bucket, and a wafer of bread.

Only one image repeats in my mind—the spear piercing River's shoulder, the water wolf flailing into the dirt. Why hadn't I fought? I know the answer, of course. I would have died immediately. Yet, there is honor in dying to save those you love. My father died for Lethotar. Though, his sacrifice at least had meaning. Fighting to save a water wolf and inevitably failing? Idiotic suicide. My life would result in waste for my people and the Lord of Light.

Do I care? I don't know. I want the madness to end. The Lord of Light has failed me, why shouldn't I fail him? My people wanted to use me . . . they already believe I've failed them, so why not make their belief reality?

A thought nags, gnawing at the recesses of my fluttering consciousness. I was captured. The soldiers didn't want to kill me. They'd said . . . they'd said Lethotar was destroyed. Those two facts mean something, but I'm not sure what. I need to think. It's impossible to think. How can I think in this soul-crushing darkness?

My hand sparks.

My fingers twitch.

I breathe.

My hand glows, bathing the tomb in faint, white light.

It's not a lot, but it's enough. My heart rate slows, though anger simmers. I should have created a glow days (weeks?) ago. All right. The soldiers had said "back to the mines with you." Meaning, they're using slaves to mine the mountains beneath the Gates of Vicor. And if they captured me, they have more of my people trapped nearby. I'm in a torture chamber of some sort, perhaps for punishment of disruptive slaves.

They're treating me like a slave because . . . well, the obvious. They hate the People of Light and believe we're accursed. Orcs. That's easy. However . . . they believe Lethotar has been destroyed. Why? These soldiers stand guard at the Gates to protect against a future attack from my people. Right? That's the strategic approach. Unless—

If the Holy Empire wants to subdue their captive population, they need to destroy all hope. By convincing even their own troops they won the war, there's no chance hope returns to the slaves. No one is coming to save them.

Shuffling footsteps above signal the next food cycle. Extinguishing my hand, I prepare for what's to come. I can survive the darkness. I can withstand anything. I know my purpose.

I'm going to save my people—the People of Light.

◆ ◆ ◆

I'm thrown in front of a broad-chested man, a dark beard drowning his face. His skin is a golden tan I've never seen before. It's strange. Exotic. Terrifying.

He speaks words in his foreign tongue, and a man next to him translates, saying, "We don't have a record of your existence. Who *are* you?"

I say nothing.

A firm hand strikes my cheek; I taste blood.

"You will answer," says the translator. "You are speaking to High Guardian Ricarian, Liege of High Rock and Champion of Lethotar."

My mind races at the words, considering all of the possibilities. There's too many. I've never heard of High Rock—maybe a new name for the Gates? I decide to speak.

"My name is Ermo—daughter of Mono, Warrior of Light and Vanquisher of the Holy Empire—and he was son of Maripes, who your people murdered in cold blood."

For only a moment, the eyes of the translator widen, and as he relays the words, Ricarian's similarly flare. "You lie," says Ricarian through his translator. "We defeated you, the accursed, over the Chasm, we cast down the city of Lethotar, and your people have scattered to the wind."

"Do you really believe that? Or is it . . . is it a story you've told your people, a lie to convince them you won when you actually lost?" I don't know where the words come from, but they sound . . . right.

Another smack. More blood. The translator didn't even transmit my words. I can't—

My eyes flutter open. I expect to find the walls of my prison again; instead, water splashes my face.

"Wake up."

Words. In my language.

"What? Who?"

"Get up, girl."

I push upward from the ground, eyes adjusting to dim light. Around me stand a dozen or so men and women of all shades—my people. I've found them.

My thoughts spill all at once. "You're alive! How are so many of you alive? We thought you all must be dead. It's been so long—the fact you're alive—this changes so many things. If we escape, if we return to Lethotar—"

"Lethotar was destroyed ten years ago."

I look up at the man; he's holding a pail of water. He confirms my suspicions, even through the hazy fog clouding my mind. "They've tricked you. I'm from Lethotar. My name is Ermo, daughter of Mono, the son of Maripes—"

Murmurs flurry throughout the crowd. One—or both names—are recognized. I smile.

"How?" someone says. "Why have we heard nothing from you?" He means from Lethotar.

"Uh . . ."

"So you all just abandoned us to die," says the man with the water, "to slavery, to imprisonment at the hands of the Holy Empire?"

I'm at a loss for words. My head's spinning, it's throbbing, my knees buckle. "I'm sorry, I don't know—"

"Oh Tathias, she's just a girl, let off. Let her tell the story. If she's part of Maripes's family . . ."

"Maripes?" says the man with the pail, apparently named Tathias. "Maripes failed us. He's the reason—"

"My grandfather was a great man," I shout, "he tried to save us when no one else would!"

"Your grandfather wasted his life on a cause that would never succeed. Where is he now? He retreated from the Gates before the battle was over, leaving us to die."

I fall to my knees, shaking. Tears stream down my cheeks. "But you don't understand. We won."

"No, even if Lethotar survived, we've not won," says Tathias. He looks over his shoulder at the man who supported my story. "Erin, tell her. No. Show her."

A woman approaches—Erin—grey hair stringing down past her shoulders. Her wrinkly, grassy skin reveals age, but she holds out her hand to help me stand. "Ermo, daughter of Mono and granddaughter of Maripes, we are honored by your presence. What little hope you bring, we do not deserve, for we have lost all faith in a better tomorrow."

"Erin?" I say. "You are . . . Erin? High Priest of Clan Wi?"

"I am the same. You know your history."

"I am daughter of Mono, but I am also daughter of Ero."

Erin nods. "Ero was a good student. A great student. Then—he is still alive?"

"Yes. Yes! All of Lethotar lives. I swear."

Erin grunts. "Even if Lethotar lives, we have a greater problem on our hands."

She steps back through the crowd, and I follow, the men stepping away. Beyond them, the faces of a few children peek between legs and hide in shadows, but they are few and far between. It's mostly men in this dark, damp place. My eyes having adjusted, I recognize it for a cave system, yet it also resembles a sewer system. Rocky outcroppings intermingle with flowing troughs and pipes.

"How long have you all lived down here?" I ask.

Erin leads me into a new tunnel. "Ten years. Since the fall of the Gates of Vicor, they've kept us trapped in these tunnels, every so often taking crews into the mines to drill for sunsteel and moonstone. They drop meager food to us, randomly steal a dozen or so away, and they're never seen again. On latest count, there's maybe a thousand of us down here? At one point, they trapped nearly five thousand in these sewers."

"Only five thousand? But . . ."

"Yes, at one point, the Three Valleys housed nearly a million. We don't know what happened to everyone else. There may be camps all across the region, but there's no way to know."

"They're working you to death."

"Beyond death, Ermo."

We approach a cliff, water rushing through metal grates and below, toward a small pool. Piled beneath the cascade, dozens of bodies decompose, rotting and festering beneath the mist. Surrounding the corpses, black shapes dart, crawl, and—

"Fiends," I say.

"We call them shadow wolves," Erin says. "And they form from our dead."

"What?"

"Every man and woman who has died in these tunnels has turned into a shadow wolf."

I encountered them outside—north of the Gates of Vicor, in the ruined city."

"Makes sense," Erin says. "The sewers most likely connect. A few, or more, escaping from below? Makes sense."

"They are terrible. Evil."

"That's what the Holy Empire says. That's their justification to continue calling us demons. For enslaving us. They believe shadow wolves live in our blood. That it's a curse. But you want to know a secret?" She doesn't wait for me to respond. "Look closely at the pile of dead at the bottom of the cliff."

I squint, examining the corpses. I look up, toward the waterfall, noticing the light streaming from above. Back toward the dead, I see a few dozen fair-skinned men. Soldiers of the Holy Empire. Wait—not just soldiers.

"They don't trap just our people down here," Erin says. "There's only a few, and they mostly keep to themselves, but they trap paleskins down here too. When they die—or when their soldiers die from disease, or some other cause—they turn into shadow wolves too. It is a curse upon this place, not upon any particular people."

"How do we stop it?"

Erin shifts her gaze toward me, as if she's expecting me to say more. The words don't arrive.

"Ermo," she eventually says, "I am still the High Priest of the Clan Wi. I know our scripture by heart. The moment you arrived, I knew the truth. I know who you are. Do you know?"

Swallowing, my dry throat threatens vomit. Some hours ago, I knew my role. My path. But seeing my people like this? I don't know what I can do. How can I save them? They're broken. Shattered. Defeated.

"Does the Lord of Light speak to you, daughter of Mono?"

I laugh. I fall to the dirt, holding my sides, laughing. "Speak? I thought once. You wouldn't believe me. You wouldn't believe the words, nor the path I've taken since those words. The Lord of Light doesn't speak to me. He's abandoned me, like he abandoned all of us."

Erin nods, as if it's the answer she expected. "I'd be worried if you said the Lord of Light speaks to you."

"Wait, what?"

"The Lord of Light does not speak to anyone. The Lord of Light merely moves and acts through his people, giving them power and strength to do what is right. You can only *be* a vessel of the Lord. Speak with the Lord? No. But if you are a vessel, the Lord's thoughts *are* your thoughts."

My hands. My power. I glance at my fingers, at the water, at the shadow wolves far below. Energy crackles between fingers, blades of white light skipping through the air.

Erin notices. "Ah, so you know of what I speak."

"There was a moment where I decided I would save you. I would find a way, but they . . . they give no way forward. The Holy Empire has broken me too."

"You are not broken. You're merely bent."

XV

Three days pass, and I spend them regaining my strength alongside my people. I quickly recognize the strange society built into the underground of the Gates of Vicor. The community is close-knit; everyone knows everyone, and they give to those in need . . . even the enslaved paleskins. Erin introduced me to a small group of them on the second day, hidden down a crevice in a corner of the sewers. Their eyes showed their terror, but they accepted the food we brought.

When the Holy Empire opens the gates each day to either return miners or acquire new ones, everyone prepares. They ensure those weakest are hidden away in secret places. When the slave masters arrive, I notice a group of large men block the path toward the paleskin camp; it's curious, how my people protect the weakest of the enemy.

On the fourth day, I tell Erin I'm ready. I tell her it's time for action, even if I don't know what will happen.

The soldiers of the Holy Empire open the gate at dawn, sunlight streaming through. Ten men and women are pushed through, their arms beaten and bloody. Ten of us, including me, step through the gate as the next victims of the mines.

Walking forward, we enter a courtyard surrounded by an immense stone rampart, archers standing at the ready atop the parapets. Without word, they march us straight under an iron gate, down a rocky path carved into a cliff-face, and into a dark, damp cave. Within minutes, the darkness fades, and we arrive at the brilliance of a sunsteel mine.

I recognize the golden metal, dripping from the rock surrounding us. While the art of smelting sunsteel and moonstone disappeared with my grandfather, his relics, and the artifacts of those who came before, litter the holy places of Lethotar. To see the Holy Empire desecrating our holy places? My blood boils.

The Holy Empire soldiers place picks in our hands, and for countless hours, we toil, splitting rock from steel and stone from ore. When the sun nears the end of its path across the sky, they march us out of the cave and back to the sewers.

I wait another week, resting alongside my people, conversing with Erin, and learning their stories. For many hours, I watch the shadow wolves, their haphazard movements creeping above the corpses. I see Erin's point. They're not evil. They're a mark of evil, but the creatures themselves? They are something else entirely. They're just beasts, living on instinct.

At the end of the week, I join another mining crew. We take a different path, entering a cave filled with moonstone. We drill. We mine. We carve the metal from the rocky veins on which they form.

Another week. More life among my people. More stories. A girl, only eight years old. She was born inside the sewers, it's the only life she's known. I tell her of Lethotar, but she cannot comprehend the beauty of our true home.

I continue visiting the paleskins, Tathias acting as my translator. As rude as the big man had originally been, he's kind to these poor souls trapped by their own kind. Tathias learned their language years ago, and one of the paleskins, Victor, asks questions about our religion and the Lord of Light. They all seem skeptical, but . . . I've not once heard them call us accursed. They understand the evils perpetrated by their own people.

It turns out the Inquisition sentenced them as *accursed* for acts it deemed "immoral." As Victor lists their "crimes," I further recognize the absurdity of the Holy Empire's position. Condemning someone for how they choose to love—what divine being could proclaim such a rule? Others stole to survive because they wanted food for their family. Noble in heart, even if "illegal" in the eyes of the law. Certainly not deserving of a life in bondage. The more time I spend with the paleskins, the more I recognize our similarities. They deserve a future beyond one trapped beneath the yolk of the Holy Empire, too.

Four more cycles. I pass from mine to mine, living with my people, working with them, suffering alongside them. Each evening, I slip into a distant cave . . . and I meditate, considering the possibility of another soul existing within my own, urging me to save the people around me.

Yet, what can I do? None of us are armed. I'm unsure the extent of my magic, and if I overexert myself, will I die due to my own idiocy? Still, as I talk with my new family, I learn their fears. Hopes. Dreams. They've been beaten, but they're still the People of Light at heart.

While in the mines, I sense the power encapsulating the Gates of Vicor. When I held *Flame of Maripes* weeks ago, energy channeled through the sunsteel blade and moonstone shaft. Surrounding me here, in every square meter of rock, sunsteel and moonstone binds the mountain together at its core. The power concentrated in my spear flows through everything. Yet even though they stole my spear, I can sense the power ensconcing me.

On the seventh trip to work in the mines, I halt in the middle of the courtyard, my comrades continuing past me. I sit, crossing my legs.

Shouts surround, and a soldier of the Holy Empire rushes toward me. "I wish to speak to" —I conjure the name in their tongue—"Ricarian."

It's a risk. It's a huge risk. But I know it will work.

The soldier grabs my arm and drags me away.

◆ ◆ ◆

They've thrown me to the dirt beneath a massive, wooden throne, on which sits Ricarian. It's been over a month, but I recognize his ugly beard. Strings of words pass between soldiers—taunts and jeers, most likely. Even through multiple conversations with Victor and his cohort in the sewers, I've only picked up a few dozen paleskin words.

"Girl, I remember you," he says through his translator, "you're the one we found out beyond the East Gate. Why did I know you'd be a problem? We should have just killed you. But we can *always* use more miners."

I steal a glance around the room, resisting the urge to draw forth power into my hands. As I suspected, *Flame of Maripes* hangs behind the throne on the wall. And on Ricarian's belt—

"What are you looking for?" He steps down from the throne. "Are you even listening to me, cur? You are our slave. We own you. You deserve no better in this life."

On his belt. A hammer. A massive hammer, carved from the same metal, formed with the same engravings, as *Flame of Maripes*. Impossible.

If they're mining sunsteel and moonstone, they're still trying to find a way to—

His steel boot connects with my shoulder, flipping me onto my back. Standing over me, he uncouples the hammer from his belt. The translator stops speaking, and Ricarian shouts indecipherable profanities, spit dripping from his lips.

I close my eyes. It's now or never.

Glowing energy races down my arms and along the bones of my fingers, veins pulsing with power. Surrounding us, everywhere, immeasurable tons of sunsteel and moonstone interweave through rock, lie waiting in storerooms, and . . . in both *Flame of Maripes* and the hammer in my captor's hands. Breathing in, I open my eyes.

Ricarian's swinging the hammer over his shoulder. With my right hand, I call for *Flame of Maripes*, and with impossible speed it flies through the air—and into the chest of the commander, blood spraying across my face. His fingers release Maripes's hammer. For I know that's what it is. It's infamous in our legends.

The room explodes in a frenzy.

As do I.

Red bile dripping from his lips, Ricarian falls to his knees. I fluidly roll to the side, pick up his hammer, and twist so I'm behind him. I withdraw the spear from his back, the metal sliding effortlessly from the wound. I shouldn't be able to hold both weapons, but I'm drawing energy from the mountain around us. Hammer in my left, spear in my right, pure power coursing through . . . everything. As long as using magic in this way doesn't burn me to a crisp, I'm ready to fight.

Soldiers converge, and I cycle through the forms, twisting the spear in a wide arc. The blade slices and dices, and as one or two soldiers slip through the arc, the hammer connects with skulls, shoulders, knees. Within moments, the room clears of enemies, either falling to me—or fleeing in fear.

Already, pain reaches my joints, and I remember the moment when I almost torched my arm by drawing too much power. I tighten the siphon—though I need a trickle to hold the weapons, but I'll release the floodgates when necessary. Spear in hand, I can more easily channel the power through the weapon itself, straight from the rocks into the shaft and blade. Battle fury is enveloping my mind, and a small part of me recognizes I'll probably die today.

It's worth it.

Leaving the throne room, I step into a stone hallway. It's deserted. Remembering the path from the courtyard, I slowly jog until I reach a stairway. No enemies. Ascending, I arrive on the second floor, where I assume archers wait, armed. Well, here goes nothing.

Darting onto the wall, a dozen or so archers stand ready, arrows raised. Fortunately, they're pointed down, not toward me. I ignore the first few archers, instead drawing energy from my hand to lance through their legs. It's not enough to incinerate them like the fiends, but the jolt cracks bones, and the soldiers topple, some falling into the courtyard below.

Like a bolt of lightning, I strike, impossible to hit. Arrows whistle, but before they reach me, I'm gone, slicing *Flame* through the next soldier. Once again, my enemies fall or flee. It's almost too easy—disturbingly so.

No one should hold this much power, I think, but I push the thought away. The Holy Empire, and all its followers, deserve death. For too long, they've been allowed to run amuck across our lands, enslaving and butchering the People of Light. They're—

The last soldier falls, leaving me standing in front of the path toward the mines. I rush down the pebbled path, kick an unsuspecting spearman off the cliff, and sprint into the caves. Three armed guards await, but I leap over a railing, land between them, and dispatch them with a sweep of a spear, energy lancing from the tip as it connects with their armor. Immediately, I release my flow of energy, hoping I've not already expended too much.

"What in the Three Valleys?"

I look up. Tathias is standing there, shovel in his hand.

"Hi," I say. "I'm here to rescue you all."

"We thought you were dead," he says. "Thought you'd given up, back in the courtyard."

"Nope. Come on. We've got to get everyone out of the sewers and beyond the Gates. It's time to go home."

XVI

The fortress is eerily quiet as the last of our people exit the sewers. Corpses litter the courtyard, but not a Holy Empire soldier is visible. After scouting the fortress and dispatching stragglers, Tathias and I concluded any who lived escaped westward to their camps in the valley below the ridge. It won't be long before a full force returns.

"I don't know how you did it," Tathias says, "or what you are, but you scared them. They had nearly three hundred soldiers stationed in this fortress. You only killed a few dozen, but you made them believe you were an army on your own."

Our people pass through the East Gate, heading toward the ruins. To the strongest, we hand swords and spears collected from dead soldiers or the armory. "We're not out of this yet," I say. "We still need to pass by the fiends—the shadow wolves." Looking out toward the ruined city beyond, I think of River, most likely torn to shreds by the beasts. "There are hundreds out there."

"Yet you defeated the Holy Empire single-handedly," says Erin, approaching us from the side. "You can't handle a few shadow wolves?"

"I don't know how long I can keep up what I'm doing." I eye *Flame of Maripes* and its accompanying hammer, resting against stone. Looking at my arms, I notice black strands along my veins. "It's killing me."

"You can do it," Erin says. "You know you can. You know what's happening."

"Sure, the Lord of Light is using me as a vessel. But I'm the one taking the actions, making the choices."

"Are you?" Erin's eyebrows raise. "Do any of us really have a choice in life?"

"Now's not the time for philosophy, Erin," says Tathias, "we need to keep moving." He walks along the wall, looking west over the edge. "Troops on their way up the ridge road."

"All right." I nod. "Let's go. I'd almost rather face the shadow wolves than an army."

"Well, this time you have your own army, too," Tathias says. "After today, we'll follow you anywhere."

After retrieving my weapons, we descend from the wall and pass through the East Gate behind the last of our people. We're about to close it when a crowd of forty or fifty paleskins shuffle out of the sewers. Of course—how could we forget?

"I understand if you don't wish for us to come with you," Victor says, Tathias translating. "But . . . we have no home. Your people have shown us kindness. The Holy Empire is evil, and we want to join the People of Light. We've all agreed." With his final words, everyone standing behind him nods vigorously.

I smile, glancing at both Erin and Tathias.

Erin nudges my shoulder and whispers, "Say the words. They are yours to wield."

I close my eyes for a second, calling forth the scriptures. "Tathias, please translate. Victor: You and your people are always welcome in Lethotar. 'So says our Lord of Light: to turn away the least fortunate, even your greatest enemy, is to turn away me.' Perhaps together, my friend, we can begin a new story between your people and the People of Light."

"We welcome the chance to prove ourselves."

"That's the beauty of it. You have nothing to prove. But we'll have plenty of time to talk—now, we must escape this place."

Victor and his people pass through the gate, following everyone else. The crowd of a thousand or so people gather about half a kilometer from us, and after we shut the iron exit to our former prison, Erin and Tathias lead me to the top of a boulder.

"You've rescued us," Erin says. "It's time to speak. You've already shown the grace of the Lord of Light to Victor and his people; now show his courage."

I gulp. "All right." I step forward, *Flame of Maripes* in hand. For now, Tathias holds the hammer.

"Go on," Erin adds.

I cough. Here goes nothing. "People of Light. My friends. My family. You've only known me for a few short weeks, but I thank you for welcoming me into your arms. Now, we return to Lethotar. It burns my soul that we never knew you still lived, yet I am glad I arrived to find some of you still alive."

I click the spear on the boulder. It feels right. "My father, Mono, defeated the Holy Empire above the Chasm. Many of you knew him when he fought at the Gates of Vicor, but the Holy Empire has lied to you for so many years. Lethotar lives. You live. And together, once we return to Lethotar, we will rebuild our people, strike back into the Three Valleys, and rescue all under the thumb of the Holy Empire." I glance at Victor, standing near the back with his people. "I see a future where we build a world without needless distinctions; where all come together under the banner of the Lord of Light in peace and prosperity. That world begins today."

Murmurs of fear, but also hope, echo through the crowd. Good enough.

"But first, we must pass through the shadow wolves. I will do what I can to protect us, but . . ." I don't know what else to say. I look toward my—my advisors, for that's what they are.

"But Ermo, daughter of Mono, granddaughter of Maripes, our new Lord of Light, will guide us!" Erin steps beside me, her arms raised. I see her true colors, the power of her voice once used as High Priest. "She is the Lord incarnate, come to save us from our enemies!"

Tathias roars, but it's not anger, it's joy, and the crowd replies in kind. Even the paleskins—I'll need to stop calling them that—join in. After the crescendo fades, I smile, whispering, "I can be the Lord of Light."

"You already are," Erin says.

With a loud metallic scrape, the East Gate rises behind us. Cavalry march out of the gate in formation, banners flying from lances like flags in the wind.

"Now's the time to prove it, then," I say. I hold out my hand, and Tathias places the hammer in it. Both weapons stand ready.

From above, clouds roll in from the east, as if preparing for a cataclysmic showdown. Drops of rain splatter against the boulder. Even though it's been years since any of these men or women have held a weapon, they form ranks, just as I imagined the Legion's ranks formed above the Chasm around my father. As lightning slices the sky, a new Legion stands outside the Gates of Vicor.

I leap from the boulder onto the rocky plain, my—my *soldiers* walking in formation behind me. Our position presents a slight elevation advantage over the forming cavalry, but if we push forward about twenty meters or so, we'll give them only incline to charge. Reaching our new position, I take a few additional steps forward, turning to face the line of troops. My army. Tathias and Erin are right there, a few meters away.

I turn back to face the massing force of the Holy Empire, raising my spear. "So says our Lord!" Shouts resound as I speak words they've not dared utter for ten years. "We fight for him as he fought for us. We fight for our love as he fought for us. We fight for Lethotar as he fought for us."

A louder war cry reverberates, but power courses through my veins, and I use it to embolden my words. I'm hoping even our enemy can hear them. "And when I return to your side, my sacrifice will usher in a new age. A Daughter of the Lord will rise to the throne, and *no longer will the world know us as the accursed ones. No longer will they know us as the orcs.* They will know us as the People of Light, our true form. The People of Peace. *The People of Love.*"

My soldiers have grown quiet, hearing words many have forgotten from their scriptures. I'd almost forgotten them over the past few weeks, but a chance memory—from my childhood, from the day my father Mono died—resurfaced. The words father Ero told me on that day . . . the words everyone believed were about me.

For they are. I am who they believe me to be.

I point *Flame of Maripes* at our enemy, and in response, they charge.

◆ ◆ ◆

Like an earthquake, the ground thunders, the hooves of a thousand horsemen pounding toward us. I fall back into line with Erin and Tathias, spear and hammer at the ready. We don't have many shields, but we have plenty of spears, and they all point toward the enemy cavalry.

"I'm not sure I'm ready for this," I mutter, but a comforting hand—Erin's—rests on my shoulder.

"You're writing a legend into existence, Ermo, who's ever ready for that?" she says. "You're doing things no one thought possible. No matter what happens, this day will live in infamy, either in our minds, or in the minds of the enemy."

"As for me," says Tathias, "I'd prefer to remember this day. I want to see Lethotar one more time before I die."

"I want to see the forests along the River Wi again," says Erin. "You know, I knew your grandmother, Vona. A good woman." She smirks. "Kept Maripes in check."

"Thanks for the pressure," I say. "Let's just strike down an entire army. We only see their cavalry, who knows what else they've got ready to come through the gates."

The horsemen nearing our ranks, the clatter of hooves drown out any other words we might say. Bending my knees, I prepare the first salvo. I remember my practice, both in the woods and in the caves. I envision a bolt of energy lancing through *Flame of Maripes* and striking the incoming soldiers. I release the thought, power channeling through my soul and the sunsteel at the tip of my weapon.

Light flashes. Dust erupts. Horses fall. Soldiers scream.

Then their line is upon us, reaching the crest of the hill.

Tathias and Erin step in front of me, raising spears and shields to face the onslaught of hoof and lance. A horse topples right in front of us, scarlet blood soaking the dirt. Another horseman con-verges on Tathias, and with *Flame*, I surge forward, superhuman strength striking the beast and flinging it backward. Tathias grunts in thanks, then shouts an order to the front lines. I don't know his actual background, but he quickly slipped into form as a comman-der of instinctual soldiers.

Our line's holding—we have the greatest spearmen in the world, after all—and we settle into a rhythm. The Holy Empire's troops begin to dismount, their mounted position no longer advantageous. Our lines trade blows, But for the most part, we stare each other down. When I feel I have it in me I strike with another energy blast, and slowly, it looks as if we might whittle down our enemy through attrition.

Then, half an hour into the battle, a new line of troops emerge through the East Gate. Fresh infantry, clad in steel plate. Of course—the cavalry were a delaying tactic, giving time for the heavier troops to make their way up the cliff.

At some point, Tathias, Erin, and I return to the boulder to achieve a better vantage point on the battle. Columns of infantry pass through the Gates of Vicor, then—

The columns begin to crumble. A commotion, forming from behind. The troops turn to face away from the actual battle, and dark shapes push through, gnashing and slashing at the Holy Empire.

"The dark wolves. How?"

"The people we killed inside," I say. "They've turned. Three sides to the battle now." I look over my shoulder, toward the ruined city of Vicor, standing between Lethotar and us.

The previous trickle of rain grows, turning into a downpour. It's soaking our skin, clouding our eyes, drenching our meager clothes. Both Holy Empire troops and our own soldiers slide around, a mud bowl forming. Even as infantry at the Gates tackle the dark wolves, hundreds of infantry enter the fray, converging on our line. We need a new strategy if we're to win.

"Do you both trust me?" I say. "No matter what I propose?"

Tathias looks to Erin, who nods. "You are the Lord of Light to us on this battlefield," he says. "We will follow you in life—and to our deaths."

"Well, let's hope it doesn't come to that, but here goes nothing." I leap from the boulder, bounding through our troops. "Into the ruins!" I shout, rallying them toward my voice. Slipping through crowds of wounded and elderly, I hope my face shows hope, rather than fear. "If the Holy Empire fears us as demons, if it fears the dark wolves, the idea of us as 'orcs,' then let's show them true fear."

It's a crazy enough idea to work. I know our soldiers holding the back line as we escape will suffer casualties, but someone must pay the price. We were going to face the dark wolves eventually anyway, so might as well force the Holy Empire to face them at the same time if they want to pursue us.

Reaching the back of the crowd of refugees, Tathias and Erin help me direct everyone to follow. Without question, they agree, the fear apparent in their eyes not from moving, but from the battle. Everyone can see the fresh troops approaching.

"We're going to need to run," I say. "We need to break through the dark wolves before they can converge as a horde. I saw it once, it was terrifying."

"Into darkness to find light," Tathias says. He hands me my grandfather's hammer. "I'll continue directing the rear guard. We'll retreat when we can."

He leaves, probably heading to his death. I hope that's not the case. We continue toward the structures ahead, and I recognize the street where I was first captured, secretly hoping we'll find River alive. Instead, I find what I knew I'd find. A mangled corpse, bones bloodied and crippled. He never stood a chance. My eyes water with tears, even beneath the downpour, and I stop, only for a moment. I motion for the crowd to continue past us, and I step to the side of the road with Erin.

"He saved my life," I say. "This wolf. This corpse. His name was River. He saved me more than once."

"He saved *your* life so you could save *our* lives," Erin says. "Every action has meaning, even if you can't see it at the time."

"Perhaps . . . but his death wasn't necessary. He died for no reason but a misunderstood belief that he could save me."

"Is that not what you're doing now? Could he have saved you by some miracle?"

"He was just a wolf."

"You're just a girl."

I wipe away the tears, understanding her point all too well. I jog back to the front of the column, and despite her age, Erin keeps pace. Before long, we're stepping beneath the ancient arch of a crumbling wall, entering the central portions of the city. I don't look back, trusting my people follow close behind. Despite it being mid-day, the rain darkens the ruins, similar to the night long ago when I first traversed its streets. Before long, we're walking down a main causeway, and—

From the alleys, dark shapes emerge, visages of people yet crawling on all fours like the dark, inhuman beasts they are. Except . . . they're not attacking. Our crowd walks through, and the creatures simply . . . watch.

"Why aren't they moving?" I say, asking the question we're all thinking.

The crowd murmurs behind me, and Erin's voice comes from a few steps behind. "I can't answer that question any better than you, Ermo."

We continue further, keeping our pace steady. Around every corner, dark wolves (privately, I still prefer the term fiend) stand and stare, watching us pass by. A thought begins to form in my mind, but I don't believe it. I can't believe it. Yet—

"They know. Somehow. They know."

"Know what?" says Erin.

"Who I am."

"Ah. Perhaps."

Their eyes. They contain an intelligence I'd not noticed before. They're something more than just creatures. They're shadows of those who came before. Their former selves.

"Have you ever considered why the dark wolves exist?" I ask. "What creates them here, rather than anywhere else?"

"There's a million possibilities, each as crazy as the next when you say them aloud."

"But one of them is right."

"Correct, there is a reason, even if we never know it."

I wonder if the answer is more obvious than we want to admit. It's a question to consider later, when we're through this mess. We're nearing the far side of the ruins, the Kineto Hills beyond. Those forests, where I first survived with River—weirdly, I miss them.

We round a final corner, but we immediately halt. Between a decrepit stone bridge and our position, hundreds of fiends sit on their haunches, waiting. At the front of their horde, a giant fiend, more beastly and horrific than the others, paces. Unlike its companions, it has massive, dagger-like fangs, and its eyes glow yellow. Unlike the others, it truly looks like a wolf.

River.

Of course. He died here, in this forsaken place. He, too, became a fiend, like everyone else.

I hand my hammer to Erin. Once again, her strength surprises me, and she hefts it onto her left shoulder. I hold out my free hand, pausing my people in their march toward freedom. I approach the shadowy mass. Erin cries in protest, but my palm remains outstretched. "I've got this. You said you'd trust me."

I approach River. As I approach, the beast growls, but I still my heart. I smile. The growl subsides.

He kneels.

I'm acting on instinct, so I have no other choice. I reach the shadowy creature's side; it's nearly three meters long and a meter wide, much larger than River had been in life. Just large enough for me to ride. I leap onto its shoulders, *Flame of Maripes* in hand. It rises to its full height, larger than a horse by my estimates. It howls, and behind it, the other fiends join a chorus no longer sounding of death. It's a song seeking life.

"This is my path, Erin," I say, once the cry subsides. "Now lead your people home, to Lethotar. I'll meet you at the Chasm."

"You truly are the Lord of Light," she says, and the people behind her nod in affirmation, even the paleskins mixed in with the throng, even though they barely understand our words.

"No, remember, I am simply a vessel."

"Is there a difference?"

I chuckle, knowing Erin will appreciate reuniting with Ero. Dad. They'll enjoy having a philosophical companion of similar wit with whom to spar. I hope I have the chance to see him again too. We shall see.

Without giving a response, I nudge River forward, and he marches toward the crowd, his army of fiends in tow. He's not a beast. None of them are, really. I'm thinking they may need a new name. Perhaps dark wolf *is* fitting.

The crowd continues past me, my new army filing through my people. Together, we will find vengeance against those who destroyed their souls.

XVII

We reach the center of the ruins, where a group of my soldiers, led by Tathias, sprint by us. I'm happy to see Victor fighting by their side as well, and three or four other able-bodied paleskin men and women. A massive column of Holy Empire infantry is hot in pursuit, though they're cautiously eyeing the watchful gaze of dark wolves from the alleys. When they see my contingent, they halt, forming rank.

I don't wait. I point my spear toward them, and, as if sensing my intention, River charges, her followers in tow. And from all around, masses of shadows converge from the side streets.

It's still raining, though it's beginning to fade. Even so, electricity charges through the air, bolts of lightning striking from cloud to cloud. As I aim my spear toward the column of infantry, I envision a new scene in my mind. Power surges from my spear and toward the clouds, and then—

A lightning bolt strikes from the sky, straight into the enemy formation, and then—

Another bolt. Another. Bolt after bolt connects, guided by my mind. For once, though, I don't feel tired. I feel invigorated. I see my path forward, I'm practically drawing energy from the very power of knowing what we're about to do—River and I, will make something new.

We crash into an already decimated line, troops charred and blackened from lightning. Few remain standing, and the creatures tear them to shreds. Turning around the next corner, our army finds a much larger force. We charge. This isn't a battle; it's a slaughter. The Holy Empire stands no chance. I've already won.

Stepping over a horse butchered on the battlefield, I withdraw my spear from a heavily armored soldier I've just defeated. I'd thrown *Flame of Maripes* like a javelin, stopping his charge toward me. All around, dark wolves are clobbering groups of soldiers to pieces.

Beside me, River walks, a weird, purple tongue wagging out of his mouth. I know this wolf, and his soul, even if it wears a different mask. He's my friend. My savior.

He's starting to glow.

I step in front of him, looking into his eyes. "River, you know you're the real hero of this story. I'll sing your praises for all time, to my children, their children, all future generations will know you were the thunder needed to bring an end to the misery at the Gates of Vicor."

The weird, purple tongue reached out, licking my face. It's like sandpaper, but I don't mind.

"I will miss you."

His shadow dies, brilliant specks of light exploding into a cloud and floating toward the sky. The rain having subsided, the lights merge with sunlight. Across the battlefield, other dark wolves fade into light. Like fireflies, their souls glow, having found peace at last. Perhaps it's because they received vengeance . . . but I have a feeling its more because no more will the torture they experienced be extolled upon another person. Whether it was one of the People of Light at the hands of the Holy Empire, or a soldier of the Holy Empire acting upon the orders of their horrendous regime, or the pitiful oppression placed upon unsuspecting souls by their Inquisition—no more. It all ended today.

"Goodbye, River."

FINALE

Ero stands above the Chasm, just like each day since his daughter leapt to her death. Its raging depths have claimed both his lover and their daughter. He can see how the Lord of Light would revel in such symbolism, but he thought so much more would come of her life. She was destined for greatness. To save their people. None of it made sense.

He drops a rose over the edge, watching it flutter and float along the air currents. Looking up, he stares across the kilometer-wide expanse toward the other side. It's silent, as usual, except . . . out of the trees, a crowd forms.

Impossible.

Hundreds of figures stand on the edge, looking toward him and the fractured bridge. After a moment, they part. He can't tell for certain, but it looks like one particular figure has approached the ruined, cracked, crystalline end of the old bridge, and they're holding a staff above their head.

For a moment, Ero considers whether he should sprint along the bridge to the tiny town sprung at its entrance. He takes a few steps back. Is it an enemy army? Has the Holy Empire come up with some new sorcery to cross the Chasm?

Squinting, he notices lights flickering on the far side of the Chasm, beneath the feet of the staff-wielding figure. Wait—no. The figure is walking toward him, crossing above empty space. No—that's not accurate either. The figure's forming a bridge beneath their feet, *rebuilding the path across the Chasm.*

Truly impossible. If it's the Holy Empire—

It's not the Holy Empire.

"Wha—"

My love, look more closely.

Ero whips around, searching for the source of the voice. Mono's voice. Maybe he'd finally cracked, the weight of losing his family too great to handle.

Just look.

Ero turns back toward the Chasm, the empty space rapidly closing. Behind their leader marches a throng of proud yet disheveled figures. People of Light, somehow returning home. And who is their leader?

She—they're definitely a she—uses the staff . . . no, wait, a spear . . . to paint the bridge across the sky. The woman . . .

Ero falls to his knees. Ermo. His beautiful Ermo, returning across the Chasm, performing the impossible. She's holding *Flame of Maripes*, using it to reunite the People of Light with the world.

At her hip, an object. A hammer. Maripes's hammer, perhaps? No time to contemplate the possibilities. All Ero can see is the smile on her face as she recognizes her father, waiting.

As their faces near, he recognizes not only her features but the visages of people long thought dead. Lost colleagues, former friends, and many others he can't wait to meet. More important-ly—paleskins, walking side-by-side with their green- and olive- and grey-skinned counterparts. Smiling. Laughing.

In harmony, the future begins.

"Welcome home, Daughter of Light."

ENEMIES OF LIGHT

COMMISSIONED FOR GENERAL WELLOR
The northern regions of the HOLY EMPIRE, in the years following the end of the second WAR OF THE ACCURSED.
From Esmeraldi in the south, to the northern branches of the River Wi in the north, I have endeavored to portray the Empire's domain with with accuracy.
INQUISITOR'S NOTE: We have reviewed this map for authenticity.
0   20   40   60   80   100
Kilometers
The Accursed Mountains
Eltorn
Ruins of Vi'ome
Mesin
Axal
Lacramor
Tethys
Illis
Esmeraldi
Hethen

PROLOGUE

Ero walks beneath the crumbled archway, his robes trailing. Burned and tattered longhouses spread out in front of him, and the haggard faces of more-than-starved souls stare at the ground.

"Three-hundred-forty-two survivors." A scribe approaches from the left. "What are our next steps?"

"Is Ermo still here?" Ero pauses, clasping his hands above his stomach. "Is our Daughter of Light nearby?"

"No sir, but she left you a letter." The man holds out a scroll. "Though . . . I think there's something you should see before you read it. Or, more aptly, *someone*."

"Lead the way," Ero replies, after taking the paper from the scribe. "And your name, friend?"

"Cora, Second Scribe of the Vanguard of Light." The scribe takes off at a healthy pace, leading Ero deeper into the depressing prison camp. Leaning against a mangled door, the broken and dead body of an inquisitor of the Holy Empire stares lifeless at the sky. The scene is disturbing, but it's no more sickening than the past four camps they've discovered in as many months.

If only Ermo would slow down her path of vengeance. There is so much for them to explore together. He needs her by his side, so they can unravel the truth of what the inquisitors were exploring. What power were they trying to unveil through their experiments?

Near the back of the camp, a larger stone structure rises, and Cora leads Ero through the door. Inside, a number of other investigators catalogue documents and contraptions held within the bastion's walls. Paying them no mind, the scribe walks straight down a stairwell into a rocky basement. Before long, Ero and the scribe face two cages: one, holding an inquisitor, and the other . . . containing a shadowy visage, like one of the fiends Ermo described fighting—and then fighting alongside—in front of the Gates of Vicor. Both the inquisitor and the creature appear docile, their eyes glazed in a peaceful stupor.

"You've given them poppyweed then?" Ero asks.

"Yes," says Cora. "We were surprised it worked on it."

"Of those we've found at the other camps, it's worked to varying degrees of success. What's special about this one?"

"Well . . ." Cora picked up a stick from the ground and slipped it between the cell bars—which, Ero noted, appeared to be made of moonstone. The stick neared the fiend, and—slid straight through its form.

"Curious," Ero says. "Very curious. I assume the moonstone blocks it from escaping?"

"Correct," says the scribe. "Like the others, we're unclear as to why this fiend still lives, not having disappeared with the others during the battle. We have a few theories."

"As do I," Ero mutters. "As do I. The ghost-like nature is particularly telling. And the inquisitor?"

"He won't speak. But he's the most high-ranking one we've caught. Adjutant, only two steps removed from the High Inquisitor."

"Well done. So why couldn't this wait until after I've read the letter from my daughter?"

"She wanted you to see this spectre of a fiend first. She believed it a signal of something well beyond our understanding."

"I see." Ero turns toward the scroll in his hand, unraveling it. His eyes widen at the very first few sentences.

> *Father. I believe I know the truth now. About me. About my purpose. About the Lord of Light.*
>
> *I travel southward. Our vanguard pushes toward the ancient border between the People of Light and the Holy Empire. I must converge upon an army building there, bringing about a path none expect this war to take.*

Something is coming. Something none of us could have expected. The fiends? The Lord of Light? The High Inquisitor? They're all connected in a way I don't yet understand. But I know one truth: the Lord of Light speaks to me, and you'll never believe his words.

I will always love you, Father, wherever my path takes me. When the war ends, we will be together. I promise.

Love,

Your Daughter, Ermo

Ero crumples the scroll and its terrifying words. Yet again, she dives into the unknown without consulting him or any of the other priests. And if she is right—and something even greater grows on the horizon—she will need all the help she can get. Tears well in his eyes. Too bad she's dead set on saving the people of the Holy Empire.

I

If we are to unite our peoples, we must understand their stories. Their lives. I've sat with the few paleskins now living in Lethotar. Learned their past. Their hopes and dreams. But they were hurt by the Holy Empire. I need to learn to love those who still swear allegiance to its banners. – From the Journal of the Daughter of Light

The streets of Esmeraldi chirp with life. Sand raptors dart from roof to roof, and the town criers belt the news of the day. Supposedly, the Duke of Taris is arriving, but I have no idea who he is. Around me, in the street, the boots of soldiers clatter on cobblestone. Traders and workmen rush from job to job, chittering about the blazing heat.

Me? I'm walking to market with my younger brothers, their grimy faces igniting with joy. It's a rare day mother and father let them out alone, especially with only me, their big sister, as their guide. They're surely imagining the treats, savory and sweet, waiting at the baker's stalls. They're about to be sourly disappointed.

"Come along, Nori," I say.

He's staring at the company of soldiers marching by in their crimson armor. "I'm trying to find Koric!" he shouts, but I place a hand on my hip, and he scurries toward me.

From my side, Henry snickers, and Nori lightly punches his twin. The two boys begin playfully smacking each other, and I sigh, reaching between them.

"Boys!" As I separate them, their exaggerated smacks bounce off my arms. "This is why I can't take you anywhere."

"No, Mom and Father won't let you take us anywhere because you always lose us." Henry steps away, the freckles on his face stretching as he grins. "Too absorbed in your own mind, they say."

"Absorbed," I reply.

"That's what I said."

Grabbing each of their hands, I drag them along the dusty road. "Come on, this isn't what I wanted to be doing today, and I'm sure you both would love to be playing in the mud. But it's important you learn the markets so you can start to come here, too, for the family. I won't be around forever, you know."

"We're twelve now, we know the way!" says Nori. "Straight along the—"

"But you don't know how to talk to people *in* the market. Now hush. Pay attention."

"Yes, Roan," they say simultaneously. I can't tell if they're mocking or serious. These boys will probably be the death of me.

After a few more blocks, we're entering the large central market of Esmeraldi. It's where everyone comes if they're looking to buy or sell anything.

First stop: the brewers. Of course, they don't peddle their drinks directly—sale of alcohol outdoors is strictly forbidden by the Inquisition. But scheduling shipments? That's a bit different.

"Richard, Erik," I say, approaching their little tent. "How you doing this fine day?"

"Roan, good to see you, your mother and father are well?" Erik raises a hand in greeting while Richard stares into his books. "What are we in the mood for today?"

Here's where we always need to be careful, and I pinch my brothers' shoulders to make sure they're paying attention. "The tavern's running low on our stocks of Sandman Stout and Harbinger Ale, what shipments can you set up in the next few days?"

Richard looks up. "Straight to business then. Five barrels of Sandman at the warehouse. We don't expect another shipment for a few weeks. That'll be high prices. Two hundred a barrel."

I pinch my brothers' necks again, hoping they won't start roughhousing. For now, they're dutifully staring up from beside my skirts, even if they're zoning out. "Two hundred a barrel? Certainly you can do better than that. I was talking with Theo just the other day about the prices in his warehouse, and—"

Erik leans in. "That scoundrel? His product is a rip-off, that's not real Sandman—"

"Tastes like Sandman, and he's charging seventy less a barrel than you." I let go of my brothers and cross my arms. "And I've heard whispers from a few others that you've 'only had five barrels' of Sandman for a few weeks now. Wouldn't want word to get around that you're playing people. How do we know *you're* offering genuine Sandman, anyway?"

Erik's eyes narrow. "Careful Roan, just because—"

I subtly straighten my collar, revealing the snakehead brooch beneath. "Don't forget my other associations, Erik. Don't cross me. Don't cross us."

Richard sighs. "We don't forget. We can offer one-hundred-forty a barrel. No lower."

I smile and hold out my hand. "Deal. Now don't forget to stop by soon, we've not seen you around the bar lately!"

We whirl through the market, scheduling shipments of flour, poultry, beef, and other assorted foods for the rest of the week. Not until we end with a visit to the sweets section of the market do I have an opportunity to test my brothers. I buy them each a roll before we chat on the way home.

"What did you learn?" I ask.

"Well, you really knocked some sense into that first pair," Nori says. "But I was confused by a few of the things you said."

"Though it was pretty wicked how you pulled that intimidating stunt on them," says Henry, "referencing the Serpents. Still can't believe they accepted you."

"Remember, you can't tell Mom. Or Koric. Only Father knows." They both vigorously nod, certainly happy to be in on my secret. "But you're right, intimidation is key. But I think you're missing another key detail I included in that exchange. What did I lead with?"

"Uh . . ." Henry stutters over his words, still chewing way too much of his sweet roll. "What's it called?"

"Undercutting!" Nori shouted, a bit too loudly. "You pulled out a counter-offer without calling it a counter-offer because you implied you had another source."

"And what do you know about Theo?"

"Theo is hated by almost all the other distributors," says Henry. "No one wants to lose business to him."

"Correct, so by—" A hiss releases from a nearby alley. We're just a few blocks from home, and this is *our* territory, so I know the signal. "Boys, wait here for a second."

Without waiting for their response, I slip into the shadows. Leaning against a sandstone wall, I hiss and await a response.

"Little snake, your presence is needed tonight," says a disembodied voice. "At the Red Raven. After sundown."

"Do I need to bring anything?"

"Absolutely nothing. We will have everything you need."

I nod and hiss, acknowledging I can attend. I receive a returning hiss before I head back into the streets. My brothers are both cocking their heads.

"Serpent business," I say.

"Oooooh," murmurs Nori. "A secret mission? A heist? An assassination? What is it?"

"Boys, enough. That's not what we do. You know that. Now let's run along. It's time we were home."

* * *

I catch my father on a break from tending the bar just as the afternoon transforms into evening. I pull the list of confirmed shipments out of my pocket. "Here's what we've got. Ten barrels—five Sandman, five Harbinger—ten pounds of flour, a dozen chickens, a hundred eggs—"

"Thank you Roan," says Father, "I can read the rest of the list. You did well. How'd the boys do?"

"I *think* they were paying close attention. It's never easy to tell with those two."

"I know what you mean."

I step into the kitchen and away from our bar, hoping he follows. He does. "I've got other news, wanting to make sure you're aware."

He nods. "Go ahead."

"Cover for Mom for me tonight."

"Of course." Father was once a Captain of the Serpents. Mom hates it. Hates if any of us associate with them. But Father gets it. Knows why I joined.

"I'm headed to the Red Raven for a mission," I say. "Got the missive on the way here."

"The old alley hissing technique, I assume." He scratches his beard. "Interesting."

"What do you mean?"

"Well, Roan, you know I'm supportive of your choice to join the Serpents, but you still need to be on your guard. I'm surprised they're looping you into a Red Raven mission so quickly."

"Should I be worried?"

"No, no, you're in good hands with Aarin. He knows he'd answer to me if anything happened to you."

I chuckle. "I thought that life was past, Father."

"It never really leaves you, even when you seek blessings of the Creator every week and swear by the Inquisitor each day."

"Don't be that hard on Mom's beliefs."

He sighs. "You know I love her, but she's obsessed. What has the Inquisition and the Church ever done for us? Hm?"

I eye the open door. "Careful, Father." I don't believe all his heretical thoughts, but I understand his concern. It's not like what the Serpents do is in line with the Inquisition's teachings, after all. Quite the contrary. Still, openly speaking his thoughts . . . you never know who's listening.

"Sorry, you know I'm just sick of the nonsense they're spewing into Koric's brain," Father adds. "Holy War, future of the nation, all that. The war ended years ago, what are they still spending so much money on?"

"I don't know." Whoops, looks like I've sent him on a rant.

"I swear, if you would have seen the city under Emelia's rule, you'd get what I'm saying. Now she was a ruler. The High Inquisitor's a piece of work, I tell you. Still don't think his story about her death adds up, you know—"

"Yes, Father, I know, you tell us every other week." I smile. "All right, thanks for covering for me."

"If you're launching a mission from the Red Raven," he says, "I won't expect you home until the morning."

I gulp. That big of a mission. "I'll let you know how it goes in the morning, then."

"I'm proud of you. You're perfect for the Serpents"—he peeks out the door—"even if your mother doesn't get it. She'll understand, some day, when we've not had a fight in the tavern in over three years, we're the busiest bar in the district, and our shipments flow freely through the streets."

"Just like you, I'd do anything for this family," I say.

II

Officially, Lethotar is at war. But every acre we reclaim past the Gates of Vicor feels hollow. They've burned the entire valley. The only hope we find is in the rescued faces of our people. A hundred thousand saved since Liberation Day. A small victory, in light of the desolation brought upon us by the Holy Empire. – From the Journal of the Daughter of Light

Mother's busy manning the tables, and I help her most of the evening. But as night falls, Father gives me a nod. I feign a cough and head upstairs. After gathering a dark cloak, a set of lock picks, and a small dagger, I'm ready. The moon is high above as I sneak out our third-story window.

It's an easy climb down the gutters to the alley below. Rats scurry, diving into the sewers. It's not a long walk through the streets to reach the Red Raven, and I arrive as the final hint of sunlight disappears over the horizon. My destination sits on the side of a hill facing west, the outskirt slums of Esmeraldi spreading out on the other side of the river. We aren't living in the best district, but I can't imagine living out there, amidst the smog and smoke of the Empire's factories. After watching the fading purple twilight, I push through the entrance of the Red Raven and into a dimly lit bar. It's practically empty, save for a few soldiers throwing dice back and forth across a table.

I approach the bartender, but without a word, he points at a door near the back. I nod. It opens to reveal a set of stairs heading into rock, and I follow them downward. Based on my estimate, I'm now *inside* the hill. At the base of the stairs, I find another door, but it's locked. I knock.

A few seconds later, a voice says, "Who is it?"

"Roan."

"Roan?"

"Roan, second Snake of the Serpents, daughter of Tork." I roll my eyes, thankful they can't see my annoyance. "Here on behalf of a missive received this afternoon."

Silence, then the door opens. A diminutive man in a leather coat greets me with a short bow. "Mistress Roan, welcome."

"Thank you." I dutifully curtsy.

"To the corner," he says, pointing with a rough jab of a thumb. "Aarin's waiting."

I nod and slip past the doorman, spying Aarin quickly in the dim lamplight. He's a handsome fellow, though even if I had an interest in him, I know Father would slit his throat if he touched me. With brown, slick hair and green eyes, he's one of those people who you listen to when he walks into the room. It's a sort of gravitas, even when we all know his words are falsehoods. But more importantly, he's a true leader within the Serpents. Everyone knows, even under his façade of half-truths, that Aarin has the best interests at heart for every person he trusts.

And somehow, I've earned his trust.

I slide into the booth. Next to Aarin lounges his sister, Yarika, and I'm sitting next to Carter. A few seconds later, Jacob arrives, pulling up a wooden chair. Interesting choice of crew.

Aarin rests his hands on the table. "Thank you, all of you, for coming on such short notice." He grins. "We've got a once-in-a-lifetime opportunity before us. This isn't my idea though. I want to turn the table over to Yarika. This is all her."

Interesting. I try to remember what I know of her, but my mind turns up blank.

Yarika whistles between her teeth and downs a shot of a dark whiskey. "Boys—and girl, sorry Roan—you're going to love this. So you all know how I work as a cleaner in the palace, yes?"

I hadn't known, but her comment triggers a cascade of potential missions at her mention of the palace. Anything to do with the royal family or the Inquisition is going to be big. I can barely believe Aarin thought of me for this mission.

Yarik continues, oblivious to my inner contemplations. ". . . so last night, I was cleaning the hallways down near the vaults, when High Inquisitor Trallius walks by with an entourage of three attendants. They're all carrying various objects wrapped in crimson cloth, and I act ignorant, continuing to sweep the floor. I heard them clearly say, 'straight from the Mountains, these came. We needed to get them out of the way of the front.' Now I don't know what they're going on about, clearly something valuable. I watched them set the artifacts in a preparation room for processing and paperwork . . . but not yet in the vault. And when I cleaned the hall again today, they were still there! Not secured yet!"

Aarin nods. "So you see why we called you all here on short notice. We've got an opportunity. Sneak into the palace, grab the artifacts before they're placed in the vault, and sneak back out with our prizes." He looks around the table, as if expecting responses from us all. I follow his gaze, noting Carter and Jacob look just as stunned as I feel. Aarin adds, "Well, don't all voice your excitement at once!"

I try to bite my tongue, but the words slip out. "So we're going to infiltrate the most heavily guarded building in the entire city for a few artifacts? What's the catch? What's the market we're tapping? What's the valuation on these?"

Aarin taps his fingers on the table. "Good questions, Roan. All good questions. Your answers: yes. No catch. I've got buyers lined up. And invaluable. We're talking sunsteel and moonstone artifacts. From before foundation of the Empire, if how Yarika's describing them is accurate."

"I pulled up their coverings today and checked them," she says. "They're definitely sunsteel. The Church might really want these, but we've got some collectors out west who will want them even more."

Jacob furrows his brow. "Aarin, you are a crazy person, you know that?"

"Yes, I'm quite aware," responds the Captain. "What of it?"

"I think I'm going to need to turn in a favor from when I saved you from being stabbed and sit this one out."

Aarin nods. "Fair enough, I'll be seeing you." He waits for the man to leave before adding, "I expected he'd pass. So I figured this would be a great way to cash in his favor."

The table erupts in tense laughter, though it's definitely a clever move. It makes me wonder, though. Jacob's a legendary thief among the Serpents. If he's spooked by this heist, should I be as well? But Aarin's all in. He's not done anyone wrong, and I've been given an opportunity to prove myself. Like I told Father earlier in the evening—I'll do anything for our family.

"Well I'm in," I say. "What's the plan?"

Aarin looks to Carter, who simply nods in acquiescence. "Well, my young friend, the first part involves the little squad of soldiers upstairs. They just so happen to be part of a contingent set to attend a royal banquet tonight. And it just so happens that they should already be asleep due to the powerful depressants my friend upstairs slipped into their drinks. We've got our way inside." Aarin places his right hand on the table; his left hand grasps the snakehead broach beneath his pressed collar. "For the Serpents."

I place my hand on his, caressing my own broach. Carter and Yarika both follow suit. In unison, we say, "For the Serpents!"

And with that, I've joined a suicide mission.

III

I wish I could know what my grandfather knew. He walked the hallways of the Holy Empire's palace—supposedly. What did he learn? Did he have a chance to barter, or did they strike him down on the spot? Did we ever have a fighting chance for peace? – From the Journal of the Daughter of Light

I scratch the leather caressing my skin. The soldier closest to my size is actually considerably smaller than me, so everything is snug. Too snug. I'm going to be sore all over. But we robbed the soldiers blind, leaving them naked in the alley outside the Red Raven. All for the Serpents. According to Aarin, the cocktail they were fed will leave them knowing not a thing by the morning.

And so here I am, scratching at too-tight leather and disguised as a man. The red, fiery sword of the Inquisition adorns my chest. There's a spear roped over my shoulder, though I'm much more comfortable with the dagger secured at my hip. An iron helmet covers my face, though we cut my hair to ear-length and rubbed dirt on my cheeks to better mask the fact I'm a woman.

I'm astounded by their faith in me. It's illegal for women to fight in the army, and any caught are immediately executed. Aarin must have a particular reason for bringing me on this mission if he thinks it's worth risking a woman going undercover as a soldier. I, for one, revel in the thrill of potential exposure. If they discover me, I'll run. They won't recognize me by the time I'm home and out of the armor, anyway. They won't ever catch me.

Though, I'm not sure whether I should take the whole affair as a compliment or not. People have always said I look similar to Koric. He might be my older brother, but I'm still a woman. Then again, when we were kids, I always managed to disguise myself as a boy when his band of miscreants ran about town. I have particularly boyish features—why not use them?

"So," says Carter, "we've got their armor. We're on the way to the palace. What's the plan once inside?"

We're walking along Tower Boulevard. According to the information Yarika coaxed out of the soldiers prior to their . . . incapacitation, we're masquerading as three soldiers in the Third Battalion of the Skirmisher Horde. Those units are so large, it should be incredibly easy for us to blend in. When you've got a thousand comrades, it's easy for someone to believe they've simply never met you before, but yet you still belong.

Aarin pauses for a moment, pulling Carter and me into a nearby doorway of a closed shop. "It's simple. We join the pronouncement in the Grand Hall with our fellow soldiers." He grins, excited. "Then, during the ensuing feast, we sneak into the servants' corridors, Yarika meets us, we head to the vault, we steal the prize, and we slip out into the night."

"Sounds easy enough," I say, hoping my words illustrate a confidence lacking within my mind. I don't doubt we can survive, but the plan sounds pretty absurd.

"See Carter?" Aarin says. "Roan's onboard. She doesn't even know what her role is yet, and she's onboard!"

"Sir, what is my role?"

Carter laughs. "Oh, what's different about you compared to us?"

"I'm a woman? What, are you going to do, reveal me as a woman to cause a distraction during the feast?"

Aarin laughs, not answering at first. He motions for us to continue walking toward the palace. It's igniting in light, ready for the revelry and festivities. "Roan," Aarin finally says, "we would never betray you! Though I admire your ingenuity. That *would* be an effective way to create a distraction, given how . . . starved a skirmisher unit can be. Anyway. No, it's not because you're a woman. It's because you're small."

Of course! I can fit into places they cannot. They're going to use me to break into the vault if the artifacts aren't in the preparation room. The thought terrifies me, but also . . . I can't believe I get to pull off a heist. Father will be so proud. "Sounds like fun." I hope my grin's hidden under the helmet's shadow. "Can't wait to see what I'm sneaking through."

"Well, I don't even know," Aarin says. "Yarika's planned most of this mission, I'm just along to make sure it happens."

"I'll need to thank Yarika then."

"You'll have your chance in a bit."

Our conversation quiets as we near the gates. When the guards see us, they motion us right through, recognizing our uniforms. Way too easy. Once we're walking up the steps toward the palace's main entrance, I notice the dozens of other soldiers on their way inside, too. The excitement in their eyes—it's the look my brother has when he talks about serving in the military. Hopefully, Koric isn't here. He'll see straight through my disguise.

Passing beneath the massive marble pillars, we enter the luminous main hall. The constant throngs of soldiers heading deeper into the palace guide our path, and before long, we've traveled through another set of double-doors into the—

I've never seen anything like it. I've lived in Esmeraldi all twenty years of my life, and I've never stepped foot in the palace. I guess I didn't know what to expect.

For at least a hundred meters, a massive cavern of a room extends, filled with swarm upon swarm of soldiers. Servants mill about, serving the troops drinks and hors d'oeuvres on crystal platters. The royal family—and the Inquisition—they've outdone themselves. They're spoiling our troops. I can see why my brother loves life in the army if this is his usual going-away party.

"Stay close," Aarin whispers as he strides between us. "No rousing of suspicion. We listen to the Inquisitor's speech, we find my sister, and we get out of here as quickly as possible."

"Understood, Captain," Carter mutters. "All of this is just so shiny, though . . ."

Aarin knocks the man lightly on the back of the head with a

backhand. "Just remember the greater prize."

"Yeah, yeah." Carter's gaze drifts about the room, but he stays close.

Aarin leads us toward the wall on the left, where black columns display the red and purple flags of the Inquisition. Far in the distance, a dais and podium hold a table filled with regally dressed dignitaries. While we wait and observe, a servant—not Yarika, unfortunately—offers us a drink. We each decline, though I can tell Carter's hungry for champagne worth more than a month's wage in the tannery where he works. A few minutes later, a man in a dark robe, trimmed with red velvet, approaches the podium. The ruckus sounding throughout the Grand Hall dissipates as attention turns toward him. High Inquisitor Trallius, in the flesh.

I've never seen him either. Koric has spoken about him a few times around the dinner table, having heard his inspirational speeches to the troops. He sounds like just another old man to me, but even Father respects him, regardless of piety.

"My friends!" Somehow, the old man's voice reaches us in the back of the Grand Hall. "My friends, I am so glad you are all here to celebrate before your departure. You are our vanguard; the men who prove every day that the Holy Empire—that Esmeraldi—is the greatest nation in the world."

Applause ripples throughout the crowd. Once it fades, Trallius says, "It's been countless decades since the assassination of my dear sister, Empress Esmeraldi. It's been thirteen years since the tragic martyrdom of your High Prince in his great victory over the Accursed. I have tried to rule faithfully in their stead, and I hope you have found my reign faithful to their memories. As I attempt to honor them every day, you now have the opportunity to honor them in kind."

"Intriguing," whispers Aarin. "I'm curious as to where this is going. Trallius has never led us astray."

I roll my eyes, though I know he's right. He might zealously push religion down our throats, but it's not like the city's in bad shape or anything. The gangs still have quite a bit of freedom, and from what Father's said, Empress Emelia was taking efforts to root out the gangs. She may have been more tolerant of religious differences, but she wasn't perfect. Still, she was loved by the people, according to Father.

And Trallius? Trallius is just a creep.

"We'll see," I eventually mutter. Everyone ignores me, so I return my attention to the podium.

"I have consulted with General Wellor," proclaims Trallius. "They've discovered a pocket of holdout Accursed deep in the mountains, and we've selected your battalion to root them out! It's a great honor, and you will bring glory to your families and your villages."

Whispers flirt with the air and cascade into a roar of cheers. We join them, though I'm unsure why we're so excited. I thought the Accursed were defeated years ago? The High Prince died for us on some bridge or something, striking down the enemy with one single blow. We all heard it from the mouths of soldiers who'd been there at the battle.

"So tonight, you celebrate," continues Trallius, distantly oblivious to my misgivings. "Then, you journey together to bring glory to the Holy Empire, to Esmeraldi, and the Church of Light!"

Whoops and hollers rebound, and as Trallius steps down from his dais, Aarin tugs my elbow. "It's time."

I nod, and I follow him, Carter not too far behind us. We slip to the side of the immense ballroom, hustling into an alcove cleverly hiding a servant's door. There Yarika waits, ushering us into the hallway.

"I'm about to begin my round cleaning the area around the vault," she says. "No time to lose. Everything should be ready."

"Wonderful," Aarin says. "Do I tell you enough how you're a genius?"

"No brother, you could tell me a lot more. I'd appreciate it."

"I'll try to do so."

The group follows Yarika down a long spiral stairwell. Based on my bearings, I'm pretty sure we're now *under* the ballroom. A long corridor spreads in front of us, and Aarin's sister leads the way, ardently ignoring any potential risk of hidden guards. She knows this place, though. If she thinks it's safe, it's probably safe.

At the end of the long, dimly lit corridor, we round a corner and come face-to-face with a massive steel door. Off to the side, a smaller wooden door rests.

"In here, in here," she says, pointing to the smaller entrance. "This is the preparation room."

If Yarika is right, the artifacts will just be sitting on the table, ready for us to steal. We enter, and—

They're nowhere to be found. It's an empty room with a few shelves, a wooden table, and a small grate in the wall.

"All right," says Aarin, "You're up, Roan."

"I thought we'd have artifacts to steal right from here," I say. "I mean—"

"We had hoped, maybe, but the plan was always to sneak you directly into the vault. I told you, because you're small. We can't pass up this opportunity now, can we?"

I swallow. "No. All right." No time for hesitation, what would Father think? "Let's get to it."

Yarika and Aarin both smile. Aarin says, "Good girl. Carter, help me with this table."

Together, the two men lift the table and slide it over to the wall. Aarin hops onto it, removes the grate, and holds out his hand.

"You might want to remove your armor," notes Yarika.

"Right, can't be getting stuck in a vent," I reply.

I pull off the chest plate and armbands, leaving me in merely a white tunic and black pants. I hand the armor to Yarika before I place my hands on the lip of the tiny tunnel. I pull upward, getting my elbows and chin over the edge. Aarin roughly grabs my thighs and pushes, and before long, I'm inside a tunnel little larger than a laundry chute.

"All good?" Aarin's voice.

"All good," I say, unsure whether the sound will properly

rebound. "I'll see you on the other side."

Carefully, I pull myself forward, no light to guide my path. I hear a skittering—most likely a rat—but I ignore the sound. I can't imagine the droppings or other disgusting refuse through which I'm probably dragging myself. Reaching a fork in the tiny tunnel, I turn left—the direction toward the vault. Just a few meters later, I discover a drop-off.

Great.

I'm stuck face first with less than half a meter in any direction. The tunnel's ended, I'm staring down a vertical shaft probably two meters or more, and I can't—

Wait, yes I can. What am I saying?

I double back to the fork, scooting past the original turn down the path I didn't take. Then, I start crawling back toward the preparation room, but only for a moment. The quick detour allows me to reposition so my feet head toward the drop-off. Moments later, my feet hit air, and I rotate so my eyes face the vent's ceiling. My legs lock with the ledge, and I slip down to the bottom of the shaft.

Easy.

I crouch and push open the grate blocking my way into the vault. Slipping into the room, I discover my prizes.

It's more than I could have imagined.

Hundreds of artifacts line the walls in glass cases, from swords clad in innumerable jewels to armor coated in a subtle gold. There's more wealth in the room than the rest of the city combined.

Not only riches fill the space. Adorning the walls—and the ceiling—magnificent paintings display ancient battles and scenes from untold legends. I recognize a few, like the original war against the Accursed. Others are more difficult to decipher, like a strange landscape filled with shadowy ghosts. I've never even heard of such creatures.

On another wall, a painting shows two parties facing one another, a table between them. From what I can tell, one side is filled with people from the Empire, others of distant sand nomads. A long-forgotten treaty, perhaps? I don't—

Blast it, there's not enough time to observe all the artwork. Gingerly, I tiptoe toward the front door.

And stop.

This is *my moment.*

If I grab something now—something small—they'll never know. They won't expect me to share it with them and include it in their spoils. I can take it home, keep it for my family, find my own seller. I'd set my parents up for life.

Quickly, I search for something easy to steal among all the larger artifacts. Easier said than done. Everything is big, or bulky, or awkward. Even the jewelry looks like it would stand out like a sore thumb. Until . . . there. A tiny blue orb with two rings—one silver, one gold—surrounding it. Perfect.

It's hanging from two metal hooks, dangling in the dim light. Lifting it from its home, I loop its metal chain over my neck and slip the orb down my shirt. I carefully hide the necklace beneath the cloth of my tunic. Satisfied, I turn toward the door to let my team inside.

Wait, what?

Standing in the room, conversing with one another: High Inquisitor Trallius in his dark robe and a man in a full suit of plate armor. They've not seen me. How? I'm right in their line of vision. More importantly, how have I not seen them before now? Or heard them?

I crouch, sneaking toward their position and listening.

"High Inquisitor," says the larger man, "we can't keep sending massive bands of skirmishers. We need new tactics."

"Oh? Is that so?" Trallius's voice drips with contempt. "It's how we won the war the first time. We overwhelmed them with brute force."

"I'm telling you, something's changed. The reports I'm reading from my captains in the valleys . . . they have a new weapon. Our men are calling her a demon, capable of striking down armies with a single—"

A sharp crack resounds through the vault. Skin-on-skin. I chance a glance quickly enough to see the inquisitor's hand sliding away from the face of the other man—who I'm guessing is General Wellor. Must be, based on Koric's description of him. I squeak in surprise, their eyes shift toward me, and then . . . they disappear, their forms shimmering and fading like mist in the early morning.

My eyes widen. What? What did I just see? A vision of some sort? I rack my brain for answers, considering all the options, but it doesn't take me long to figure out the most likely explanation.

There's an artifact touching my skin. We'd always heard such things held power, but . . . I look down at my chest, and against my skin, inside my shirt, the small orb dimly glows.

I shake my head in disbelief, but I don't have time to consider the implications. After approaching the door to the vault, I place my ear against its cold steel, listening for any sounds. Frankly, I'm surprised I've not heard Aarin and the others yelling for me to open up.

I find only silence.

Strange.

Perhaps they're just being quiet in an effort to limit noise echoing upstairs to the ears of others in the palace. Whatever the reason, I need to let them in. I can't carry very many artifacts on my own. And we can't leave here with only the orb. With my ear still pressed against the door, I prepare to rap knuckles on the cold steel.

Then, I hear it. The faint sound of whimpering, somehow slipping through the sealed vault. Yarika, perhaps? Why would she be—

With a groan, the door begins to creak. A million gears shift and spin under the weight of the entire palace.

I stumble away from the door. Given its size, it will take some time to open, but that doesn't give me much hope. I need to move quickly. My friends have been captured, presumably, and I'll be next. What faces us? Death, most likely. Sneaking into a secret vault of the palace while impersonating soldiers had to constitute treason—or worse.

I sweep my eyes around the room, looking for a place to hide. Except that's impossible. Every cabinet, filled with golden armor and shiny weapons, is locked tight. And there's no hole in which I could slide out of sight. What am I thinking? I need to leave right now, right through the vent I crawled through.

Careful not to bump into anything, I dart toward the grate still resting against the wall. Without pausing, I crawl through and stand in the vertical portion of the shaft. Turning around so I'm facing the vault, I crouch, reach outside, and pull the grate into place. It fits snugly; I can only hope it doesn't appear disturbed.

Turning back around, I grope for the ledge above. My fingertips barely reach it, and with a soft grunt, I lift myself upward. Fortunately, I can use my feet to lodge myself against the shaft wall, and without much effort, I'm soon sliding down the tunnel back toward the preparation room. When I reach the fork in the vents, a problem arises.

If Aarin and the others have been captured, I'm trapped. What am I going to do, slide into the preparation room right into the arms of their captors? My weapons and disguise are both out there. Now, if I grab the outfit when no one is looking and pull it into the vent with me, I can wait until all the commotion clears and sneak out. Or, I could try the other fork of the vent.

My heart races, the overwhelming danger sliding into focus. I'm going to die. There's absolutely no way out. I've failed the Serpents, I've failed my family, I've failed Father. I'll be branded a traitor, and by proxy, they'll target him too.

And my brother, serving in the military.

Koric!

If I find him, perhaps he could help me escape. No, wait, who am I kidding? He'll probably turn me in. I can't trust him. Back to square one, trapped inside a vent with a few dozen rats probably ready to feast on me when I die of starvation.

Jokes on the rats, I probably taste terrible.

Only one viable option. I need to find my disguise and pull it in here with me if they've not already noticed it.

Slowly, slowly I slither toward the preparation room's grate, its light dim. And—something's blocking my vision. A bundle.

I reach it, my hands grasping blindly. It's my armor, tucked inside the vent by a Serpent. I can't believe it. One of those three decided to hide my presence. Probably Yarikia—I can't imagine Carter or Aarin having the foresight to tuck my things out of the way. Getting caught about to steal from the vault is a hundred times better than actually having someone *inside* the vault.

So what next?

I can't make out words, but the shouts of guardsmen from beyond the preparation room and outside the vault indicate I'll have no luck escaping through the way we came anytime soon.

But if I go back down the vent and through the unexplored fork, who *knows* where I'll turn up. Might discover an inquisitor's bedchamber.

Shivering at the thought, my limbs relax. At least for now, there's no way for the palace guards to know I'm in here.

Until one of my co-conspirators talks.

IV

I want to know about the people of Esmeraldi. Who are they? What are their hopes and dreams? Why do they fight so fervently for an order of zealots blinded by bigotry and power? Do the people believe we're evil, or only think as such because they've heard nothing else every day of their lives? – From the Journal of the Daughter of Light

Hours pass. At least, it feels like hours. My eyes struggle and droop. It's certainly the middle of the night now, the party most likely over. For some time, I've not heard a peep from outside. If I'm going to escape, there's no better time. So . . . here goes nothing.

I slide forward, reaching the grate. No noise. I push it open, careful not to drop it to the ground below. I pull it horizontally into the vent and place the bundle of armor on my back. Pulling my body over the grate and to the edge, I peer into the empty space.

It doesn't even look like anyone was ever there. No sign of a scuffle. No sign of my crew. I'm all alone.

Carefully, I pull the bundle of armor from my back and dangle it in the open air. With a light toss, I drop it onto the table. I come next, carefully scooting outward, headfirst. I roll over so my joints are parallel with the corner of the vent, hanging toward a floor less than a meter away. I'm not sure how I'm going to pull this off without making noise.

Breathing, I stretch out my arms and remember my days doing handstands with Koric in the stable. Laughing. Crying. Our heads bruised. All I need to do is fall and catch myself. Easy, right?

Right.

I fall, bracing for impact. The space separating me from the floor instantly disappears, and my hands land squarely on the ground, the descent aching to pull all of my body down on my head. Bending my elbows with the fall, I push in return, attempting to spring back and cushion my fall.

It . . . somewhat works.

Before I know what's happening, I've crumpled on the ground, but at least I crumpled gently. I stand and shake my head, just hoping no one heard a thing.

Okay. First step, out of the way. My bigger problem? The grate. If I leave the vent uncovered and someone returns to the preparation room, they'll know it was touched. So, gingerly, I pull the table back against the wall. Fortunately, it's not too heavy and doesn't scrape against the stone floor. Once in place, I stand, reach for the grate, and move it back into place.

All right, step two complete.

I push the table back into place, and while preparing to head into the hallway, I recognize a problem.

I have no weapon. Aarin and the others hadn't taken time to hide my spear. If I'm going to flee through the palace disguised as a guard, I need to look the part. Lacking a spear? It's a serious flaw.

Well, pouting isn't going to change my circumstances. I quickly dress myself in the skirmisher's uniform, taking care to put every piece of armor in place so I fit the part. When tightening the leather chest plate into place, the strange ringed orb presses against my skin. It's strangely warm to touch. At least if I escape, I'll have something to sell.

"Aarin, someone's coming."

Yarika's voice. What the hell?

I don the helmet—the last piece of the uniform—and rush into the hallway. Yarika, a panicked grimace forecasting her fear, scurries beneath pillars and torches. She charges right toward me, and I hold up my hands to stop her.

She runs right through me.

For a moment, I recall the moment inside the vault when I witnessed the conversation between the High Inquisitor and his general. A strange magic is afoot, and I do not like being wrapped inside it.

I turn around, following Yarika back into the preparation room. There, life-like images of Aarin and Carter wait. Yarika says, "We're trapped. There's nowhere to run. Aarin, I'm so sorry. I thought it would work."

Carter's eyes widen with fear, and he paces, his arms resting behind his neck.

"It's all right," says Aarin. "We'll find a way out. We always do. First things first, we need to get Roan out of—"

"No time," replies his sister. "Hmm. Here. Hide her armor in the vent."

"Good thinking."

"If we're going down, why not have her go down with us?" mutters Carter. "Maybe revealing she's in there will help them let us off easy, you know? Tit for tat?"

"If you think we're going to sell one of us out, Carter, then I should probably kill you right now." Aarin steps toward the man, his dagger half-unsheathed. "We protect our own."

Even as Aarin says the words, Yarika's bundling up my armor and shoving it into the vent. And there, resting against the wall, is my spear.

Clearly, I'm watching some sort of flashback, but why wasn't it there when I escaped the vents? If the guards who captured my crew noticed three spears for only two people disguised as guards, they would have searched for me. Right?

I approach the spear. As I near it, it shimmers, almost as if snapping into focus and refracting the light of its past away from it. Outstretching my arm, I attempt to grasp its shaft.

With a slight jolt, almost like a bee-sting, my fingers snap to the spear. I grasp it in my hands, bringing the spear into my moment in time. Moments later, the visages vanish, just as a guard with a sword drawn rushes into the room. He disappears too.

A few seconds pass before I hear my own breathing, labored and wheezy like I've just run laps around the city walls. I'm holding a spear, a piece of wood pulled from the past into the present. It's impossible.

But it happened.

I pull the necklace out so its tiny orb is resting against the chest guard rather than my skin. Two visions, both after I started wearing this artifact. Whatever it is, it's powerful. It may have just saved my life. Now I'm not so sure I *want* to sell it.

After staring at the orb with lingering lust for longer than I should have allowed, I push it back beneath my armor, careful to tuck it in a space between cloth and leather so it's not touching my skin. I have no idea how it works, but in my mind, it makes sense for touch to trigger it. Right? Once I'm satisfied it's safely hidden again, I rush out of the preparation room and into the vault's long hallway.

It's empty. Thankfully. I slightly jog toward the stairwell tucked into the wall about halfway down the hall. Up, up, up its spiral I climb, and before long, I'm sneaking back into the massive ballroom where the festivities occurred hours before. It's empty.

I just might escape this nightmare.

Mere moments later, I pass into the palace's outer hall. It's empty too. I think. The doors to the stairs leading outside and into the city near. I've almost escaped; I'm almost safe. The only thought on my mind is returning to my family.

As casually as possible, I walk toward the exit—and run right into a massive crowd of soldiers all facing the palace gates. They're silent, staring at a small wooden stage haphazardly constructed in the plaza. Torches surround it, lighting up the scene and darkening my position at the back of the crowd. No one notices me creep up behind them, and for now, I'm blending in with the other soldiers.

All is quiet.

"Esteemed warriors of the Third Battalion, horde of the northern marches and harbinger of the doom of the Accursed . . . you have traitors among you."

The speaker is at the base of the stairs standing on the stage. I squint, trying to identify him. I think it's the High Inquisitor. Does the man ever sleep?

"Standing behind me"—he motions with his arm, revealing three figures kneeling with hoods over their heads—"are vagabonds who attempted to break into the Royal Vault of her Highness Emelia II, may she live in our hearts forever. They attempted to supersede and undermine us even as we fight to protect them from evil. Can you believe it? Can you believe treachery has found its way to Esmeraldi? Well it stops today. Their lives end."

I hold my breath, entranced by the scene. Every soldier watches, waiting, anticipating the blood about to spill. My crew, Serpents, about to die. I should be up there with them. But I'm not. And if I'm to survive, I can't react. I can't cringe. I can't cry.

A large man in a dark coat drags an axe onto the stage. He approaches the first of the incapacitated figures and removes the hood, revealing Aarin, gagged and bloodied.

Trallius approaches, and, with a scepter slipped out of his robe, he pulls away the cloth binding Aarin's mouth. "Any last words, traitor?"

"Oh go to hell," Aarin says.

With inhuman speed, the axe zings through the air and slices his head cleanly from his shoulders. His body crumples, slumps, dies.

Yarika's next. She doesn't say a word, and she dies more gracefully than her brother. The poor girl. Braver than us all, risking her job for a brilliant con.

They reveal Carter last, and the moment his gag falls, he blubbers nonsensically, tears evident even from my distant vantage.

"Speak up boy, I can't hear you," says Trallius.

"There was a fourth!" cries Carter. "If I tell you where she is, will you spare me?"

"Of course you can have a moment of redemption."

Carter's body trembles, shoulders slumping. "She's hiding in the vents." That bastard. "She was inside the vents when the guards found us. She's just a scared kid, she's probably still hiding there."

"Ah, thank you child," says the High Inquisitor. "But to reveal truth only in the face of death? You are still a traitor." He flicks his wrist.

The executioner's blade swings, a sickening crunch signaling the end of Carter. Though he betrayed me in the end, he didn't deserve his fate. He was only trying to live. I probably would have attempted something similarly, with a blade above my neck.

The courtyard silences. Soldiers stare at the bloody mess before them, and I tense, not knowing what comes next. My mind's racing; I need to find a way to sneak out of the battalion and into the alleys of Esmeraldi. Once I'm away from the pack, I can easily find my way home.

Trallius whispers something to a set of royal guardsmen—I'm guessing he's sending them to "find" me at the vault. As the two men in shining plate rush away, Trallius raises his hands. "Third Battalion, it is time for you to begin your march. The Accursed Mountains await you. Glory awaits you. Bring death to your enemies, and bring honor to your families."

A cheer rises from the soldiers, their spears rising. I quickly join them in an attempt to blend in, and seconds later, the horde begins to move through the gate. I have no choice but to follow.

The column moves down the steps and onto the broad avenue leading through the center of the city. We're headed toward the North Wall. My best chance will to stay near the back, slow down, and slip into an alley—

Another column fills in behind us.

I'm no longer near the back. I'm in the middle of this damned battalion.

I'm a woman, trapped in the middle of a horde alongside a thousand sweaty soldiers leaving Esmeraldi. We're marching

toward a war hundreds of kilometers away.
    I'm doomed.

V

The Council still treats me like I'm some sort of tool, designed to execute their will. They're convinced if we stay put beyond the bridge I built, we'll be safe. Well I'll have none of it, and neither will my legions. We're going to save our people. And we're going to save the people of the Holy Empire. – From the Journal of the Daughter of Light

Shit. Shit. Shit. I'm so screwed.

We've been marching for hours, straight through the night. As dawn arrives, we enter a war camp filled to the brim with soldiers from all corners of the Empire. And I'm the only woman. Years ago, I would have ached at the opportunity to join the military. But it's illegal. My father made it painfully clear what would happen if I joined. Public humiliation—for me and my family. To join the army, as a woman, was a slight on the honor of your family, both informally and in the eyes of the Inquisition. A woman joining the army? It's as if the woman said the men in her family were incapable of fighting themselves.

So of course, the Inquisition used it as an excuse to brand heretics and ship them off to who knows where. Or kill them. So I'm definitely doomed.

Focus.

Koric. I need to find Koric.

We reach the center of the immense compound, and from my position in the crowd I can see a sergeant—I think he's a sergeant, based on the yellow plume sticking from his helmet—hand a scroll to a man sitting in front of a wooden table. For a moment, the man reads its contents before rising. He steps onto his chair.

"Third Battalion, welcome to the Army of Wellor! We are honored that you have joined us today."

A guttural "hurrah" rises from us.

"Yes, yes, you're excited to make it to the battlefield. Aren't we all? The fourth sector of the camp is ready for you, with all the supplies you'll need, tents and all. Claim your tents, see the quartermasters for supplies, and rest up. We march northward in the morn."

Before I can even catch my breath, we're moving again. After a short jaunt through the camp, we reach a massive field filled with single tents no larger than my bed, tiny cots rolled underneath them. Near the back, a long ditch spreads, and I can practically smell its stink from here. Unfortunately, it reminds me of a truth I've been holding for hours.

I really need to piss.

It's the first test. If I'm to somehow disguise myself in this camp long enough to find Koric, I'll need to blend in completely. I can't *not* relieve myself.

Wow, this really wasn't how I expected my first major mission with the Serpents to go. I've been thrown into hell with absolutely no way to escape.

Tent assignment is a free-for-all, so I grab one quickly far from the latrines and near the edge of the sea of canvas. Without fail, I follow the massive throng of men heading toward the ditch.

As we near it, I see a long line of latrine huts.

Oh, by the Empress. Thank the Inquisition for its harsh imposition of sanitary rules on the war camps of our Empire.

* * *

And now, I'm back in the camp hiding beneath my tent.

Yawning, my eyes droop. It's been a long night; I'm amazed I didn't fall asleep or fall over due to exhaustion on the walk here. I'll need to rest, but I should probably figure out my next move.

If I can find Koric, he'll have ideas. But I don't even know for certain if he's in this army. I search my memory for answers, trying to recall what unit he serves with. He's a Captain—I know that much—of an elite unit of swordsmen. I think. The Company of Blades? Is that what it's called?

I'm . . .

I'm—

* * *

I jolt awake, my head twisting frantically.

Right. I'm in an army a province away from home, disguised as a man in a skirmisher battalion. The sun's still fairly high in the sky, so it's most likely mid-afternoon. My back's sore from sleeping on the ground, but at least I found sleep.

My mind settles into place, considering my circumstance. Based on the surrounding snores, most of the men in the Third Battalion of who-knows-where are still asleep. That means I have a moment to think. Like I planned before slipping into unconsciousness.

My thoughts drift, remembering everything that's happened over the past day. The Serpents called on me to join a mission. With Aarin and Carter, we snuck into a celebration honoring troops of the Empire, using it as cover to infiltrate a vault beneath the palace. I crawled through vents, found a magic orb—I can feel it pushing through the cloth beneath my chest plate—and had visions of the past. Very strange.

Then, the other Serpents were executed. All dead. Except for me.

The weight of it all hits me like a wall of bricks. All dead. Aarin, the first Serpent to believe in me, dead. He protected me even to his last breath. And Carter—screw Carter. Yarika though, she didn't deserve her fate. Her plan had been flawless. We were simply unlucky.

So now, I'm stuck in a war camp. If I run, I'm a deserter. They'll chase me as I sneak out, kill me in the forest, and I'll never see my family again.

If I turn myself in, the same thing happens.

So I have one path forward.

I conceal myself. I am a member of the Army of Wellor, a soldier fighting for the honor and glory of the Holy Empire. I must wear a mask, survive the war, and find my way back to my family. There is no other path forward.

And Koric's going to help me—if I can find him.

Even as I resolve the problem, tears well in my eyes. Yesterday, I took my baby brothers to the market to teach them how to barter. I waited tables in my family's tavern. Now this?

Why me? Why am I set on this path?

For a second, I consider what Mom would say. Not Father—I have no idea how he would survive as a woman in a war camp. But Mom? She always taught us to believe the basic tenets of the Church. The Lord God, the Almighty, rules over all, the final arbiter of our fates. The Church and its Inquisition enacts his will upon the world, ensuring the Law is followed. And when you are at your worst, the Lord God reaches you in darkness and lifts you into light. The Lord God lifted the Holy Empire out of darkness, wielding its sword against the demons of the world. We are God's blade. We are God's shield.

I shake my head. How's any of that supposed to help me? I don't see the Lord God reaching for me. My predicament is of my own making. In fact, the Inquisition would say I'm violating the Law. The Lord God would wish me punished for my crime. I'm dishonoring the Empire, the Church, and my family.

Yet . . . if I serve in the army—the Lord God's blade and shield—wouldn't that mean I'm enacting the Lord God's will? We're headed north to fight the Accursed. If I kill Accursed, I'm cleansing the world of their evil. They're the ones who killed Empress Emelia, after all.

I ponder the question. If I'm to take the Church's teachings at face value, it says the Lord God works through people in moments not known until the events have passed. I can have faith in this moment. The Lord God is working through me—setting me on this path. He's the final arbiter of fate, after all.

Right?

Doesn't matter. I must adopt such a view. When someone asks me why I fight, I must speak with truth and conviction. They cannot know who I am. They cannot see through my shadow. They cannot learn of my deception.

I wipe away tears, drying my hands on the tent flaps. All right. Time to find my brother. I sit up and straighten my armor. No one's really seen me in light as a soldier yet; would my current appearance deceive everyone into believing I'm a man?

I lift my helmet for a moment, checking the length of my hair. We'd cut it short prior to infiltrating the palace; I muss it again to ensure it looks dirty and rough, unlike the more common, straightened hair women wore. For once, my fairly flat chest would come in handy, though I'll need to keep my wits about me regardless. Keep my armor on. Stay quiet. Speak only when necessary.

All right. No use waiting any longer. I crawl out of the tent, tighten the spear into its harness on my back, and head into the camp.

Koric, wherever you are, I can't wait to see the look on your face when I find you.

VI

Thirteen battles in as many months. I don't find joy in striking down the soldiers of the Holy Empire. I wish we didn't need to fight. I wish there was another way. But how else are we supposed to save our own people? We can't just sit on our hands. We must show them truth. – From the Journal of the Daughter of Light

For an hour, I wander the war camp, intensely aware of my surroundings. I try to soak it all in, make sure I know where everything is. Number one lesson Father taught us: always know where things are. If I'm ever in a situation where I need to flee through this camp, even if we're about to abandon it tomorrow . . . I need to be ready.

So there's six major battalions, each with their own staging field. If my estimate is right, then, this army has at least six thousand soldiers—a sizable force. General Wellor is in charge—he's the man I witnessed the High Inquisitor slap in a vision. Interesting. I vaguely recall them saying something about the enemy having a secret demonic weapon?

Anyway, stationed between the six "sectors" of the camp are barracks for specialized units. If my brother's company is here, he's most likely in one of those larger tents. They're private, though. It's a perk of serving as a career soldier. No way in unless you're invited.

Situated on a bluff above the hill is a larger pavilion. I'm guessing it houses the general. Near the center of camp, an immense stockpile of barrels, boxes, and wagons forms the "warehouse," run by the quartermaster mentioned when I arrived with the rest of the skirmishers.

Wow. I'm already starting to think of myself as one of them.

I consider my options. I've explored camp. I *think* I know where Koric might be. But how to figure out if he's actually here?

I approach the warehouse. I expect to find one man. In reality, it's actually a dozen or so running the whole show, dishing out supplies left and right. I suppose I'll need gear. Right now, all I have is a spear. Was I supposed to bring anything else with me as a soldier?

Fortunately, there's a line. I watch what everyone else requests. Canteens—good, because I'm parched. Daily rations. Great, also starving. Cloak and boots—could be useful, especially at night.

I furtively wait, watching the queue dwindle. I try to ignore the aching fear biting my bones. At any moment, anyone could accuse me of being a woman. They have no reason to suspect—but the fear remains. I clench my hands, trying release tension. The more I act afraid, the more likely someone will be suspicious of me.

It's my turn, and upon reaching the table, one of the warehouse workers asks, "Battalion?"

"Third Battalion," I reply.

He scribbles a few notes in a book, barely looking at me. "Standard set or specialized?"

I furrow my brow, not knowing what he means. "Uh . . . standard." I hope that's the right answer.

"All right." He raises his left hand, and a young boy approaches with a stack of supplies. Everything I hoped for, including a full canteen and a few days of food. All of it is looped in a bundled bag which would slip over my back during long marches.

"Thank you," I say, taking care to keep my voice level. I loop it all over my shoulder. "One more thing. I have a friend in the Company of Blades. Where are they?"

The man looks up, clearly confused. "Company of Blades?"

Shit. Is that wrong?

"I think that's what he called it."

He shakes his head. "Oh, you probably mean the Company of Slaying Swords."

"Oh. Sure. Yeah, that sounds right."

He shakes his head again. "Third barracks on the left."

"Thank you."

"Move along now, there's a line, can't you see?"

"Right, sorry sir."

I scurry away, heading back toward my tent. Fortunately, the sectors are numbered and organized with lettered signposts along the rows of tents, so it's easy to find mine. 6-1B. I drop the supplies, nibble on a piece of stale bread, and down a swig of water. All right. I know where my brother is.

Now what the hell do I say when I find him?

* * *

I approach the green canvas. A soldier stands absentmindedly against a flagpole. From its heights, the standard of the Company of Slaying Swords waves; I recognize it from my brother's armor. Now that I see it, I feel incredibly foolish for failing to look for it. I would have recognized it immediately upon walking through this part of camp.

No matter. I step up to the guard and clear my throat. "Excuse me, sir," I say, "but I'm here to meet with Captain Koric."

"Koric?" He looks me up and down, a puzzled look on his face. "What would Koric need from a skirmisher-rat like you?"

Oh, so people look down on my battalion. Good to know. "We're friends. Trained together in Esmeraldi. Thought I'd tell him I made it to the army. Finally."

The man squints.

He's probably not buying my story. I need to think of something else to say, and fast. My tongue's going numb, though. What if he suspects my—

"He's not 'ere at the tent," says the soldier. "Captain Koric's at the training grounds. Where else would you expect him to be?"

"That sounds like Koric," I mutter, trying not to speak too loudly. "Thanks . . ."

"Char. Name's Char."

"Thanks, Char. See you around."

His eyebrows rise, as if slightly amused. I step away, shuffling toward the training grounds noticed during my earlier exploration of the camp. They're around a hill near the center of the tent city. It doesn't take me long to reach the wooden barricade surrounding the cleared sparring space. If I hadn't seen them earlier, the sounds of constantly clinking and clashing metal would have led me in the right direction.

I slide inside and take a seat on one of the surrounding wooden bleachers. The training grounds are little more than an underfunded arena, with a fenced pitch and various practice equipment strewn about. Dozens of men, many of them shirtless, tackle and wrestle with one another. The whole scene is incredibly strange. The grunts and slaps and smacks are positively amusing.

Near the center of the ring, four men in blackened leather armor prance around one another, their longswords held in careful guard. Their helmets and shields rest against a fence-post a few meters away. It doesn't take me long to recognize the matted brown hair of my brother, his pale, freckled skin shining brightly. The red emblem of his "Slaying Swords" is visible, even from my distant seat.

I watch—mostly in awe. It's been years since I've seen my brother fight. He's brilliant. It doesn't take long to recognize Koric's fighting the other three on his own. Two of his partners attack simultaneously, forcing Koric to dip out of the way of one attack while countering another. Like a dancer, he steps over swings and leaps below thrusts, all the while placing his blade in deadly positions.

Before today, I never realized the skill he possessed.

"Hello there, young one."

I jump at the sound of the voice, looking around for the source. Seated a few rows behind me, an old man with a starkly white beard and barely-peppered hair sits, hands intertwined above his knees. He's not wearing a helmet, but his tunic bears the insignia of the Slaying Swords.

"He-hello," I stammer, nearly forgetting to deepen my voice.

"Admiring the work of the Swords, I see. And yes, it's that obvious. What's your name? Where are you from?"

I don't know how to react. So far, no one's actually asked my name—merely my battalion. Frankly, I'd been starting to think soldiers don't care what my name is, especially because I serve in one of the skirmisher hordes. I think fast, considering a name capable of triggering significance in Koric's mind.

"Nori," I say. "From the south side of Esmeraldi. Near the Red Raven, if you know it?" Another signal for my brother, hopefully, if he remembers any of Father's tales. "I'm a friend of Koric's."

"Didn't know Koric had any friends from the south side of Esmeraldi—or who were skirmishers in the Third Battalion—but I suppose I can learn something new today. Name's Yarwin, Keeper of the Slaying Swords." He holds out his hand.

I tense, only for a moment, then reach out and shake the older man's hand. "Pleasure to meet you, Keeper Yarwin."

"So polite," he says. "Someone taught you well."

"My parents made sure I knew protocol."

He nods and stares into the distance, as if considering an idle thought of more importance. "So why are you here looking for Koric?"

"I didn't say I was looking for him."

He shakes his head. "You said you were friends with Koric without me prompting you."

"Fair," I say, internally cringing. I *really* am terrible at hiding my intentions.

"And, you stopped by the tent just a few minutes ago asking for him." He grins, as if mocking me.

"How—"

"Never mind how, I think it's time Koric reunited with his old friend, don't you think?"

I sincerely hope my face doesn't immediately redden, because I feel terrified. I open my mouth, but Yarwin stands, shouting, "Slaying Swords, stand down from Drill Seven! Koric, report. Slaying Swords, commence Drill Nine!"

I have no idea what any of the words mean, but mere seconds pass before Koric jogs toward us.

I gulp.

He arrives.

"Captain, you have a friend here to say hello. He was staring you and your squad down with quite a bit of fervor."

Fervor? Did he really have to describe it like I was drooling over them?

My brother briefly salutes the older man before turning toward me. With the helmet partially concealing my face, it doesn't seem like he recognizes me. His sister.

I smile, hoping to shed the initial weirdness of the interaction. "Captain Koric, Nori of Esmeraldi at your service. I'm serving in the Third Battalion, a recent recruit. We met a few months ago at the Red Raven, don't you recall?"

His eyes don't reveal a single sliver of recognition as I drop my keywords. Instead, his eyes drift toward Yarwin. "So Nori here just plopped down and started chatting to you?"

"Quite the contrary, Koric, I plopped down and started chatting with him."

"And your thoughts?"

"I think Nori here is someone you should hear out, whether you actually know him or not."

Koric shrugs. "I think I agree." He steps forward suddenly, wrapping me in a massive hug before I can move. "Nori, it's great to see you!"

Surprised by the sudden change in mood, I return the hug while still sitting on the bleacher. Once my brother steps back, I smile and stand. "I told you I'd make it into the army! It took months, but I made the cut for the skirmisher horde right before they set out for this here camp."

Koric shakes his head. "It'll be good to catch up with you, I'd say. Yarwin, with your leave, I'd like to end my training early today."

Yarwin chuckles. "You're the captain, not me." He waves his hand dismissively in the air. "I'll see you at dinner. And I like this one." A finger wags at me.

I'm not sure if Yarwin liking me is a good or a bad thing, but I'll take it. I give him a curt nod, and before I know what's happening, Koric's striding out of the training grounds; I'm trailing close behind.

For a few minutes, we walk in silence toward the edge of camp, only pausing momentarily as Koric chats with a guard near one of the barricade gates. After clearing Koric and I—apparently captains can come and go from camp as they please—the guard ushers us out, and we're suddenly striding through forested woodland.

We continue our wordless hike until we've reached a large outcropping overlooking arboreal hills far into the distance. I can just barely identify the winding Queret River arcing toward the invisible capital further beyond the horizon. As we near the edge, Koric turns around, draws his blade, and . . . targets me.

I stop, holding up my hands in supplication. "Koric, what are you doing?" I drop all pretext, letting my voice reveal its normal tones.

"What am I doing?" His voice cracks. "What am I doing? Roan, what the hell are you doing here? You're going to get yourself killed, not to mention ruin our family in the process!"

I take a step away, trying to drown out his anger with distance. "I understand this doesn't look good, but I have a perfectly reasonable explanation—"

"It's you, isn't it?" Though he still sounds angered, he lowers the blade. "You're who they're looking for."

I shake my head. "What do you mean?"

"We received a missive this morning, from the Inquisition. They suspect a member of the Third Battalion may be a fugitive on the run. For breaking into one of the royal vaults. Was that you?

Please tell me it wasn't you."

Tears well in my eyes as I involuntarily shake. "Koric, I'm so sorry to put you in this situation, I know what your career means to you, I screwed up huge. I had an opportunity to hit it big and I bit off more than I could chew. Mom has no idea. The whole family has no idea where I am. Father may suspect what happened, but he probably already thinks I'm dead. I have no idea what to do."

Amidst my blubbering, I barely notice my brother drop his weapon completely and rush forward to wrap me in his arms. "Roan, Roan, it's all right," he says. "We're going to figure this out, together. It'll—it'll be just like when we'd play War with the boys down the street. You remember?"

Wiping away the tears, I laugh. "You're kidding, right? You're going to help me?"

"You're my sister, what do you expect me to do? Turn you in and let them string you up as a 'harlot' or something even more ridiculous?"

I take a step back, scratching my forehead. "This is all so overwhelming, Kor. Sorry, Captain Koric—I'll need to make sure I don't slip into familiars."

"We're alone, it's fine."

"You know what I mean."

He smiles that half-crooked grin I know too well. "Yeah, I do."

"In the past day," I say, returning to my rant, "I joined a heist, snuck into a vault, watched my crew executed, and marched who-knows-how-long to the middle of nowhere. And now, if I flee away from camp, I'll be branded a traitor and deserter. Then they'll discover I'm a woman and do unhuman things to me as a villain in the eyes of the Church and Inquisition."

Koric nods. "So what's your point?"

"How do I get through this?"

"Do you trust me?" he says. "Do you believe I can get you through this?"

"I do."

"Then you're no longer a member of that dreadful skirmisher horde. You're joining the Slaying Swords, and you'll always be by my side."

"No," I say, stepping away from him. "No, this is too risky for you. At least if I'm in the Third Battalion there won't be a target on your back too if I'm caught."

"Roan . . ." He rolls his eyes. "Would you rather take your chances with a thousand idiots, or just a few dozen?"

"On second thought?" I say. "Deal."

VII

As we've retaken more and more ground, I'm uncovering more and more caches of our sacred texts. There's so much I was never told. I don't think Father Ermo's even read these books. I'm beginning to construct a theory . . . and it's more heretical than anything I've said yet. – From the Journal of the Daughter of Light

I'm standing next to Koric, dressed in new leathers matching everyone inside the tent. We stashed my spear in the forest—fortunately, the specialized companies have their own quartermaster, so no questions were asked as we acquired new gear for me. Our hope: someone finds the spear in the forest, discovers the abandoned tent in the Third Battalion, and believes the "fugitive" has attempted to flee the camp.

"Company of Slaying Swords!"

The commanding force behind my brother's words illustrate his authority inside the tent. Everyone stands from their comfortable positions, whether lounging on their beds or playing a game of cards on a table in one of the room's corners. In seconds, the whole unit faces their Captain. Koric. My brother.

"We've been waiting for this day for a long time, my friends!" He spreads his arms wide in a welcoming embrace. "Tomorrow, we march for the Accursed Mountains, where we *finally* take the fight to the enemy. Our predecessors bearing the sigil of the Slaying Sword fought at the battle before the Gates of Vicor, and it's about time we returned to repay the favor and bring glory to our name once again."

A chorus of huzzahs echo around the tent, a strangely crazed gleam twinkling in the eyes of many of the men. I notice Keeper

Yarwin leaning back in a chair off to the side, looking slightly bemused.

"Before we leave, I have an announcement," Koric says. "As is my right as Captain of you fine men, I have taken on a ward. Company of Slaying Swords, meet Nori, a son of Esmeraldi like many of us. He will study under us, instead of wasting away in the Third Battalion alongside skirmisher scum."

A wave of chuckles crinkle the room, but Koric holds up a hand to quiet the men. "Treat Nori as one of us, for he will *become* one of us before long. He's got a lot to learn, but we've got a long journey ahead of us as well. We'll do introductions in a bit, but for now, back to your lounging. Tomorrow's going to be quite the day."

With a flick of his chin, the men drop out of attention and return to their leisure. It's all quite jaw-dropping; I never could have imagined my brother holding such authority over dozens of men. But here he is, conducting them like a band on a Friday night in our parents' tavern. He's a natural leader. He deserves his role.

And he's putting all of it on the line for me.

"Nori." His words knock me out of my internal contemplation. "Follow me to the back."

Without waiting for a reply, Koric strides down the narrow space between the beds of soldiers, and I follow close behind. I probably look like a puppy; most of these men are at least thirty, if not older. Many of them look older than my brother by at least five or six years. His position as Captain, at his age, says a lot about their respect for him. If only they knew his treachery . . .

Stop it. I really need to stop it. I can't keep undermining our plan by feeling sorry for myself or believing I deserve to be turned over to the Inquisition. I don't, and if Koric believes I deserve a path forward, I need to trust him.

We reach the back of the tent, where a single bed stands off from the rest of the group. From beneath it, Koric pulls a cot and a pillow. Convenient. I hesitate to ask what happened to the last Captain's ward. Hopefully he didn't die. Maybe he's now a member of the Company.

I set down the few supplies we gathered from the quartermaster and rest my new weapon on the ground—a sword, safely in its scabbard. I plop onto the cot. It feels more homey and comfortable than the lumpy ground I slept on earlier. Too bad we'll be moving in the morning. I sincerely hope these cozy accommodations move with us.

Already, I'm feeling ready to handle everything coming my way. I go over the plan in my head again. I am Koric's ward, conscripted out of the Third Battalion. Since, technically, no one ever knew who I was or knew me as part of the Third Battalion, it's practically like I was never there. And, for the next few weeks as we travel northward, I will train under my brother and the rest of the Company of Slaying Swords.

Father taught me to use a dagger growing up. I know the basics of the blade. I'll need to strengthen my muscles to handle the heavier weapon and acclimate to the longer reach of the sword, but Koric assures me I can do it. He knows my strengths.

With the Company of Slaying Swords, I'll stay relatively out of the eyesight of most soldiers. It'll decrease, according to Koric, the number of people scrutinizing my form. On our way back to camp, he commented on my disguise's effectiveness. He said my build helped—I sent him a scowl for those words—but the hair and dirt were a great touch. I looked like a young man, freshly recruited at the age of nineteen or eighteen. Given I'm only a year or two older, I can fit the role easily.

As for relieving myself, changing, and all the other awkward moments easily capable of throwing off our game? We just need to be very, very, careful. But Koric, again, assured me everything would work out just fine.

He said I could trust him—and trust the Company. We aren't telling them, of course, that I'm a woman, but Koric also said they wouldn't bat an eye at weird interactions between the two of us. An unspoken rule within the Company, Koric said, was not to question the behaviors of any soldier on the road. The Inquisition asked a lot of questions, judged many behaviors, but amongst the Company, trust, respect, and brotherhood were honored above all else.

If two soldiers wished time alone together none would judge, lest they be removed from the Company.

When Koric explained this all to me, I rose an eyebrow at the implications, but I didn't push the subject. If we needed to sneak away for a bit without anyone batting an eye, all the better. Apparently the disregard for such sojourns was so ingrained in the Company, Koric's men most likely wouldn't even notice we're gone.

"Nori?" came Koric's voice. "Ready?"

Pushed out of my silent, centering meditation, I nod and rise to my feet. "I'm at your disposal, Captain Koric."

"Then it's time you met the rest of the Slaying Swords."

* * *

There are forty members of the Slaying Swords in total, making me the forty-first. Koric introduces them in squads of four—each with their own specialty. I note their skills don't all pertain to combat. For instance, Yarwin leads the clerical staff of the Company. All four of them can fight, of course, but the Slaying Swords also need a bookkeeper, cook, and supply officer.

I can't remember all their names, but in addition to Yarwin, Koric's own crew—the soldiers who were training with him earlier in the day—stand out in my mind. Jamus, Marik, and Weston. Oh, and there's Char, the awkward doorman. I remember his name.

Koric's crew? They're the most intimidating men I've ever seen, their very eyes like daggers into my own soul. If anyone in this war camp could uncover my secret, it's those three, based on how they scrutinized every *centimeter* of my body.

The three—plus Koric and I—are sitting in a circle at the back of the tent. Their eyes linger, studying and prying apart my soul. I ache to yell at my brother for placing me in front of them, but I can't give away our relationship. I am his student, nothing more.

"So Nori," says Jamus, his dark eyes meeting mine, "You've somehow convinced Koric to take you under his wing."

I nod, reticent to speak. Even my slight fidget sends shadows splaying throughout the room. The sun now hiding behind forested hills, we're resting in the barracks by candlelight.

"Why do you wish to be a member of the Slaying Swords?" says Marik. His blond hair stands out among the mostly dark-haired Esmeraldians in the Company—I'm guessing he's from the north, somewhere along the coast.

"I joined the Third Battalion to bring glory to the Holy Empire," I say, recalling and mimicking words from the Inquisitor's speech the previous night. The subtle, deepened tone I've added to my voice is slowly becoming more natural. "We must strike down the foes of the Empire and bring glory to the Church—and the Inquisition."

Silence, for a moment, then everyone, including my brother, burst into laughter. They slap their knees and each other's shoulders, grins sprouting across their faces.

"What's so funny?" I mutter.

"Nothing," says Koric. He raises his eyebrows. "Do any of us in this room look like holy men?"

I furrow my brow, remembering the religious rhetoric spouted by my brother at the dinner table every time he returned home after a campaign. "Do we not fight for the Empire?"

"Of course we do," says Jamus. "But above all else? Every man in this room, including you, fights for one another. We fight for each other, not for the Inquisition. This is the first and final rule of the Slaying Swords. We receive our orders from the General, we follow them, and we *protect our own.*"

I'm already beginning to see why my brother joined them in the first place—and why he rejected moving up the ranks in one of the larger units. In some ways, the Slaying Swords were just like the Serpents on the streets of Esmeraldi.

"So the Company . . ." I stumble over the words, not sure how to ask the question. "The Company is not officially part of General

Wellor's chain of command? Technically, you're a mercenary troop?"

Marik glances at Koric. "He catches on fast." He runs his fingers through his blond hair. "Yarwin!"

Seconds later, Yarwin appears, a notebook in hand. "I was just about to begin writing my notes for the day. Is this urgent?"

"We're just educating good ol' Nori here about the Slaying Swords and its role in General Wellor's army."

Yarwin wrinkles his nose. "Of course. Surprised Koric didn't inform him up front."

Koric gives a sheepish grin but says nothing.

"Anyway," continues the old man, "the Slaying Swords are an officially chartered Company under the Enforcer Act issued by the Emperor's Court prior to the Border Wars almost half a century ago. We pay and train our troops outside the command of the Inquisition's overseen military, but can receive contracts from those same armies. We can also take jobs as guards for caravans, towns, and the like, or go root out bandits in the countryside. But we are not mercenaries; if we take up arms against the Empire, we lose our charter and our lives are forfeit. If we sign a contract for a campaign, we must see it through; otherwise, we likewise lose our charter."

"I think I understand," I say. "So what's the contract for the Slaying Swords say regarding this campaign?"

Yarwin glances at Koric as if asking for approval. I note the exchange, beginning to comprehend the power dynamics of the Company. Koric barely twitches, but the subtle shift in his eyes and lips signal affirmation.

"Once we reach the Three Valleys," says the old clerk, "and once the battle lines are drawn, we're to infiltrate the enemy lines, seek out their leaders, find their secret weapon, and assassinate them."

VIII

We've always believed the War for Heaven—when the Lord of Light first struck down his enemies—was against the predecessors of the Holy Empire. But the enemy described in the texts? They're not human. We call them demons, or fire-spawn, or reapers, or leviathans, or any other manner of foul names. I can't accept a world where we distorted our view of a people not much different from us so drastically—especially when they lived just across the mountains. What's more—their description is eerily similar to that of the fiends. Curious. – From the Journal of the Daughter of Light

With brutal efficiency, the war camp disbands the next morning, deconstructing into a thousand wagons and thousands of soldiers all marching along the high roads headed north. The Slaying Swords, in particular, somehow manage to fit all their supplies into two wagons drawn by four horses—an impressive feat given the size of the tent, to say the least.

I'm walking alongside Koric. Our company trails one of the larger battalions with the Third Battalion following behind us. The dust of the road coats my mouth. The sun's barely reached its zenith; we still have dozens of kilometers to go before nightfall. I try not to think about how distant home is becoming.

"So how long is the march all the way to the Three Valleys?" I ask. "I've never seen a map of the region."

"Neither have we," Koric says. "Our contract, however, predicts a term of six months. Depending on how prolonged of a campaign the general expects, I'd say probably a month to reach the front lines, give or take a week."

"Do we have troops already at the front lines?"

Koric didn't respond to my question right away. He scratched his ear in stride. Eventually, he says, "To be honest, I don't know. I heard about the bluster spewed by the Inquisitor to the Third Battalion before it left Esmeraldi. We've . . . been hearing different reports. It may not be merely a rogue band of Accursed appearing out of the mountains. A rogue band couldn't break any of the fortresses established throughout the region."

"Have you been to the Three Valleys before?"

"No. But Yarwin has. When you get a chance, ask him. He has an interesting view on the place."

We continue in silence. Having my brother beside me keeps me grounded. I can't cry—I can't grieve—but my heart still aches following the events beneath the palace. Aarin and the others, executed for a crime they failed to commit. I actually succeeded—and I'm alive. But our parents don't know where I am. They don't know I'm with Koric. And he can't risk telling them via letter. Who knows what the Inquisition reads these days.

Overall, the march northward is fairly quiet, the chatter between soldiers stifling my memories of home. We eat and drink on the road, only stopping when nightfall arrives on the outskirts of a small farming village.

Since we're only staying for a night, we don't set up the full barracks, opting for squad-sized tents. So as the stars brighten the sky, and blisters burn my feet, I find myself huddled beneath canvas with Koric, Jamus, Marik, and Weston. It's a tight squeeze, but we all fit.

"So . . ." I say, eyes darting between the four men. "I know we're on the road, but at some point, I'm going to need to learn the tactics and techniques of the Slaying Swords, yeah?"

"Oh, he's eager to learn," says Marik. "One day on the road, not even used to the traveling life, and he wants to start training?"

I flinch at the quick rebuke. "Well, I suppose we can wait, but I've got a lot to—"

"Nope, you asked for it," says my brother. "Tomorrow morning. Two hours before dawn. We begin your training."

"Two hours before dawn? Wait, no—"

"It's decided then," says Jamus. "I'll make sure Yarwin knows." He begins to crawl out of the tent. "Boy, you don't know what you've just asked for."

I shoot Koric a glare, but he shrugs. What *nonchalance*. His baby sister, going through an unexpected regimen of physical torture before the sun even hits the sky, and he doesn't care. I shouldn't have expected anything less from him, I suppose. I did ask for training.

* * *

"Stand up."

I roll onto my back, calves aching, dreading the next smack of the quarterstaff.

"Stand up."

I push myself upward, rising onto the balls of my feet. Standing a few feet away, Yarwin wields the long wooden staff in both hands. Leaning against trees nearby, Koric and the rest of his squad watch silently.

"You act too swiftly," says Yarwin.

"Too swiftly?" I brush the dirt off my arms. "You're asking me to dodge smacks of a quarterstaff, do you expect me to move slowly?"

"Yes, I do."

The wood flies through the air. I try to slide to the right, but it smacks my shoulder with a soft crack. I stumble backward, instinctively rubbing the bruise certainly forming.

"I thought you were a part of the Third Battalion," Yarwin says. "Did they not teach you how to stay on your feet? To stay focused? To be aware? To slow down?"

"To be honest," I say, "they didn't really teach me anything." It's not a lie, technically.

"Figures," mutters the old man. "The hordes aren't good for anything but getting their men killed. Again."

I step forward, bending my knees and facing him down. "I don't see how I'm ever going to escape your attacks without a weapon to block."

"You will *only* escape my attacks when you have no weapon. If you can't fight with only your body, then you're not worthy of being a Slaying Sword." The wood flies toward my forehead.

* * *

Three days of marching. Three nights of sleeping. Three mornings of training. Now, the fourth morning.

I'm tired. Dreadfully tired. Bone-breakingly tired. Yet here I am, facing Yarwin and his damned staff once again.

He stares me down, hands in the center of the weapon. I watch, bouncing lightly on the soles of my feet. His hands shift, and . . . it clicks. I slow down, considering the movement of his hands in concordance with the path of the quarterstaff. He's swinging the wood above and to the left, but its arc, based on the positioning of his hands, will bring it down to my right. I wait.

The wood reaches the top of the arc. His hands don't shift their path.

I wait.

It's dropping, heading toward me.

I slide to the left, watching the wood fly by my eyes with only a few centimeters to spare. The quarterstaff slams into the ground.

"Well done," Yarwin says. "Again."

"Again?" I sigh, exasperated.

"You think succeeding once means you've passed the first test? No, young one, you must excel." He whips the staff upward, clipping me in the chin.

Crimson spots. All across my vision.

* * *

Six days of marching. Six nights of sleeping. Six mornings of training. Now, the seventh morning.

Without waiting for me to enter my stance, Yarwin whips the quarterstaff into a series of arcs and jabs. I step through and around them like a dance, watching his hands guide the wood—and guide me to know where *not* to be. For twenty steps, our dance continues until he nods, drops the staff, and bows.

"Well done, Nori, son of Esmeraldi. You have passed the first test."

I smile, though my body still screams for attention. But I must ignore the blisters. I must ignore the bruises. Koric and his squad are all smiling, proud of me, but I can't let their hope crack my veneer. I'm headed to war, as a woman, and I must survive.

"What's the second test?" I ask.

Yarwin steps away, and Weston approaches. He holds no weapon. In the week I've been a part of the Slaying Swords, I've heard the man say maybe two words. And as always, he continues his wordless ways, kicking Yarwin's dropped quarterstaff up from the ground. Toward me.

I catch it out of the air.

"Strike him," Yarwin says.

Holding the quarterstaff in both hands, the process of the Slaying Swords formulates in my mind. I attempt to strike, knowing I'll inevitably fail.

* * *

The seventh evening. The Slaying Swords huddle around a fire, roasting a deer caught by one of our men. We're camped somewhere north of one of the lake towns. By now, I've stopped trying to figure out where we are within the Empire's borders.

I'm sitting on a stump beside Yarwin. Koric sprawls on the ground nearby.

"Yarwin?" I say.

"Hrmm?" He strokes his beard, barely looking up from the book he's reading.

"I hear you've been to the Three Valleys before. I was told you can tell me about where we're going."

Yarwin's eyes mist, matching the smoke drifting over our heads. He glances at Koric. "You put the boy up to this, didn't you?"

My brother—I mean, the Captain, I *seriously* need to stop thinking of him as my brother—shrugs. "He asked about our destination. I told him you'd been there. I wasn't lying."

"I suppose everyone else in the Company has heard the tale. You should too."

"Oh, it's a tale?" I say, taking a sip of the mug of rum in my hands. "We hearing a story?"

Others in the company perk up. Over the past week, I've noticed people listen when Yarwin speaks. After training with him, I understand why they all respect him. He commands their respect, even when he's not Captain. Though, I suspect he was their leader not too long ago, based on how he treats Koric.

"Yes, a tale. Let us begin."

INTERJECTION

Imagine the beginning of the invasion—what, something like, thirty years ago now? They all run together at this point. I was a new recruit in the Company of Slaying Swords, just like you, young Nori. Along with the Vanguard of the Sun, we entered the valleys a few months after the initial sacking of Ut'ome.

After we passed the wreckage of that border town, we passed more burned villages and towns. Everything—burned. Not a soul in sight, until we reached the war camps at the confluence of the River Wi and its southernmost tributary.

Have you ever seen death? Tasted it in your mouth? Witnessed its tangible mark on the universe?

To reach the war camps established by the Army of Our Empress, we were forced to walk through a riverfront city formerly occupied by the Accursed. Siege weapons had decimated the homes of these people, blasting apart wood and stone. By all accounts, the battle ended at least a week before we arrived, but fires still burned, smoldering the soil and salting the gardens with ash.

And scattered about, on every street corner, every square, every alley? Bonfires upon bonfires of corpses. Charred to the bone. We hadn't defeated the Accursed who lived in that town. We massacred them.

In those days, the Company of Slaying Swords had twenty-eight members. I don't know a man who didn't cry himself to sleep that night. I can still recall the memory of approaching a skeleton and realizing it was the bones of a child.

Do you know what death smells like? What it sounds like? What it does to your mind when you numb yourself to its touch?

We trudged through that town and entered the war camp of the Army of Our Empress and found the men celebrating, drinking away their fears as they prepared for the next campaign. Less than a kilometer away, an entire town wasted into ash, and they sang songs. Hymns. The Inquisition pontificated about the glory and peace they were bringing to the Three Valleys.

You might think we've reached the end of the story—we've not. The Company received its first contract of the campaign the next day. A simple one—escort a dozen wagons of supplies to a second camp a few dozen kilometers to the east. Easy.

We reached the camp by the afternoon of our second day of traveling. We were met with massive wooden palisades protecting black longhouses. A prison camp. Or so we thought.

They didn't let us inside. The gates swung open, and a dozen inquisitors adorned in white robes walked out to greet us. They thanked us for the shipment and sent us on our way . . . but not before we heard a shriek come from inside one of the darkened buildings. The inquisitors eyed us with sneers so poignant in their message we didn't need to ask. If we said anything to anyone, we would suffer the same fate as the foes kept inside.

As we trudged back up the road, the screams we heard echoed through the wilderness and in our minds for the rest of our trip back to the war camp.

For the rest of the campaign—and we fought in the Three Valleys for many more years—we witnessed hundreds of atrocities. We committed some of them ourselves. All in the name of the Inquisition, justified because we were killing the *Accursed.* And through it all, we watched thousands of our enemy burn—and thousands more sent to secret camps hidden from the eyes of anyone except the Inquisition.

It was after those first days on the front lines that the Company of Slaying Swords adopted its one and only rule. We receive our orders from the Generals, we follow them, and we *protect our own.*

We protect our own, because if we do not, we will suffer the same fate as the Accursed. It's the only way we can find honor. Our souls died the moment we recognized the truth.

IX

What's most surprising to me, as we continue gain-ing ground throughout the Valleys? The number of their own people imprisoned behind Inquisition walls. – From the Journal of the Daughter of Light

After the twenty-second march—the twenty-third night.

"Wake up."

My mind wanders through shadows, seeing the ashy, black-ened remains of a child's skull. It's been two weeks, and I still can't get the images out of my mind. I see them every night. Instead of dreading training, I look forward to it, because it means I can wake from nightmares of imagined death and destruction.

"Nori, wake up." A sharp kick to my calf.

"Huh, what?"

Koric's face, looming over me. "You need to come with me, right now."

"Training?" I ask.

"You could say that."

I quickly slip into my armor, and I'm about to don my helmet when Koric brushes it aside. "Don't wear it. You'll stand out *if* you're wearing a helmet."

I nod, uncertain at his words. The Company has seen me plenty of times without the helmet on and no one's batted an eye, but I have no idea where we're going. Yet . . . it's Koric. I need to trust him.

I follow him out of our tent and into the crisp night air. Torches light the paths between camp sectors, and we head straight toward the heart of the mobile complex. Toward the Gen-eral's compound.

"Koric!" I hiss. "What are we doing?"

"Remember," he whispers, "you're my ward. I'm your Captain. Remember the honorifics."

"Sorry."

"Too many people know I took a ward. You must be with me at this meeting."

"Right."

We finish the trot in silence and slip into the green tent. Inside, a dozen or so men stand around a table lit by oil lamplight. Standing near the edges, in the shadows, half a dozen younger soldiers yawn. The wards of other commanders, I presume. Koric gestures for me to join them, and I dutifully stand near a table cluttered with envelopes, papers, and books. Thousands of numbers and calculations—I can't make sense of any of it.

"Ah, Captain Koric of the Slaying Swords, glad you finally joined us," says a deep voice from the far side of the table. I fidget, trying to find a gap through which I can see a face. After sliding a little to the left, I spot the speaker.

General Wellor. As I suspected—the man inside the vault when I had the vision. I hold back the urge to grab the orb around my neck. Thank the Empress I've not had another one. Skin-to-skin contact is definitely necessary for the thing to do its magic.

"Apologies, General," says Koric.

"It's no matter, we've not started. And you're not last."

As if orchestrated for dramatic effect, a man with bronze skin and two short spears tied to his back enters the room. "Apologies," he says without prompting, "but this is what happens when I'm assigned the sector furthest from the center."

"Maybe we'd give you a better spot, Haris," mutters a man standing beside Wellor, "if you'd keep the Third Battalion in line."

"Oh, are we starting this now?" The man—Haris—looks ready to pull his spears.

"*Boys.*" Wellor's voice booms. "We're three days from the front lines, and this is how you act?"

The room goes silent.

No one speaks.

Until—"three days, sir?"

I don't know who said it.

"Three days," repeats the General. "I've been waiting as long as possible to ensure no deserters"—he sharply glances at Haris, who's apparently my former commander—"can take the news back home."

I consider the implications. We passed by the ruins of Ut'ome, according to Yarwin, a week ago. Based on what everyone's said, the Gates of Vicor are at least a three-week-march inside the Three Valleys. If we're almost to the front lines . . . this is an actual war. Not an incursion by some little band of hidden Accursed. They're back in full force, stronger than when we fought them last. How? It's impossible. The Inquisition assured us they were dead . . .

I consider everything I've known of the Accursed, though. Always taught by the Church and its Inquisition, it's simply truth that the Accursed are demons who perform all manner of sins and corruptions, destroying the land and defiling each other with impurities. We were told they eat our people and worship a demon masquerading as an angel in white.

But the Inquisition never told us of their torture camps. It never told us of the villages and towns and *children* burned to the bone. Even if the Accursed are our enemy, they *aren't* what the Inquisition has taught us to believe them to be. So why couldn't the war be different than what we believe it to be? The Inquisition lies.

And so we *protect our own.*

". . . we'll be reinforcing the First and Second Battalions along both the east and west banks of the river," says General Wellor.

While I've been lost in thought, he's continued sketching the battle plans for his captains and commanders. I shake my head, refocusing on his words.

"We believe the bulk of their forces are coming down the High Road," says Wellor, "but we suspect their phalanx units will attempt to strike the eastern front. We'll be sending the Slaying Swords, along with my personal units of the Army of Wellor, to reinforce the First Battalion. The Third Battalion will also join us, while all other units reinforce the Second Battalion on the western bank."

The words confuse me. Phalanxes. Units. It's all logistics, but the other wards next to me nod along like they understand the language, so I follow suit.

"What's the composition of their forces?" Koric's voice, I think.

"From what we can tell, they've rebuilt a number of their phalanx units—what they call legions. We estimate their strength at four thousand soldiers, mostly mixed between spears and bows. They have a few swordsmen, but not nearly at the numbers prior to the Battle above the Chasm."

It amazes me none of these men are questioning the Inquisition's lies. Unless they knew? Have they always known? Or just recently? Koric mentioned the "secret weapon"—perhaps their new leader, the target of the Slaying Swords.

"And their armies are pushing in formation?" Koric's voice again.

"Yes, a double-pronged front on both sides of the river. They were able to split our forces at the last bridge twenty kilometers north of our currently entrenched position."

"Wait—the First and Second Battalions retreated?" Haris chuckles. "Oh, this is rich, I can't wait—"

"*Commander* Haris, enough of your foolishness." Wellor slams a hand on the table. "I have a final detail you must all understand."

They all freeze, awaiting the words of their general.

"The enemy? They're supported by at least a thousand of our own people."

Whispers. Murmurs. The tension in the room bubbles, captains and commanders glancing about in palpable fear. Stepping out of the shadows behind the general, a man in a white robe takes an open spot at the table. An inquisitor.

"Good evening, gentlemen," he says. "Above all else, this reality must not reach the Empire before the Inquisition prepares the people for the news. We believe they have bewitched our people, tricking their minds to believe lies and deceptions. Devilry. It's evil, all of it, and now your men will be forced to kill their own brothers."

"How is this possible?" asks a man whose voice I don't recognize.

"Rest assured, my friends, we are putting our best minds to the task of determining what power has caused our men to work with the Accursed. More importantly, we're crafting a . . . weapon to counteract their witchcraft. Rest assured. The Inquisition is hard at work to protect your souls on the battlefield."

"And until then," says a captain standing next to Koric, "We're meaty shields?"

The inquisitor's eyes flare, and in a flash, he whips his hand out from under his flowing robes. There's red everywhere, a spark, a blinding white—and the man falls to his knees, hands grasping his neck. Blood pours from a gash in his throat.

I expect an uproar; I expect someone to confront the inquisitor. Instead—nothing. His body drops, the commanders acting as if nothing happened.

Until now, I'd never questioned how the Inquisition held sway over the Holy Empire. Everyone *knows* Trallius runs it with an iron grip—he ran it even when the prince was his ward, before the man met his death at the end of the war. But I'd never witnessed the true breadth of their authority. Soldiers—the greatest warriors and strategists in our military—don't bat an eye when one of their own is murdered in cold blood by some unknown sorcery.

We protect our own. But they didn't protect this man. My eyes can't stop staring at the now lifeless corpse.

"Shall we continue?" says General Wellor. "I have a few more logistical matters to discuss."

"Of course, my lord," says the Inquisitor, and he slides back into the shadows.

"When we combine with the First and Second Battalions and their support units, we'll form a combined army of close to ten thousand troops. However, the river will divide us, so we'll utilize flag bearers along the shores to transmit signals . . ."

* * *

I don't know how long the strategy session lasted, but I'm pretty sure I fell asleep while standing for a few seconds at least once or twice. In any case, I snap to attention when General Wellor smacks the table and the men surrounding it shout an inarticulate chant. They disperse, wards heading in all directions to follow their masters.

"Captain Koric Torkson," says General Wellor. "A moment of your time."

"Sir?" responds Koric.

He motions for me to join his side in front of the table, giving me a chance to see the tactical map displayed across its surface. I don't understand any of it other than recognizing the rivers and mountains.

"Ah, so this is your ward?" says the general. "What's your name, boy?"

I swallow. "Nori, sir."

"Nori? Where are you from? I feel like I've seen you before."

"South side of Esmeraldi," I say simply. In the vault—the vision. The moment when he and the Inquisitor looked my way. Had I *appeared* to them as they appeared to me?

He nods, eyes shifting. "Same as Koric here, as I understand. I see the typical features in your chin. Your eyes."

"He's the younger brother of a dear friend of mine back in the city," interjects Koric.

"Indeed," says Wellor, though for some reason, I sense he doesn't believe my brother's words. Or doesn't trust them, at least.

"I thought you should know some news of your family," continues the older man. His hand rests on the pommel of the sword belted at his waist. "Have you heard from your sister, Roan, recently?"

He's speaking to my brother, but he's looking at me. He knows. Somehow, he knows. By the Empress, I've killed us both.

"No sir," says Koric. "Last time we spoke was when I visited my family some three months ago. What's the matter? Did something happen to her?"

The general's gaze shifts to my brother. "I'm surprised you've not heard. No letters from home?"

"None. My father . . . he doesn't look fondly on my choice to join the military."

"Ah yes, the Great Serpent."

Koric stares at the table. "That was his name once, you are correct. He put that life behind him."

"Pardoned by the High Inquisitor himself."

His gaze slides to me again, as if he expects a reaction. I bite my tongue, even if my mind screams. I'm going to die in this tent. I can barely make out the robed figure still standing in the shadows behind the general. Waiting. Watching. They're baiting us. *They know.* And as for Father's pardon—I've never heard of it before. Did Koric know? What is Wellor talking about?

"He earned that pardon," says Koric. So he *does* know. "He risked his life for the Empire, earned his freedom."

"And you exemplify the best qualities of your father," says the general. "The same cannot be said for your sister. We've received a formal warrant for her arrest. Signed by the High Inquisitor himself. Your whole family's been questioned, though everyone says the same thing—she disappeared one night, never to be seen again."

I can't see Koric's eyes. I want to know what he's thinking. I'm certain he won't turn me in—at this point, he's harbored me for far too long for either of us to escape if they know. What options do we have? If the inquisitor were to step in, could we even escape? I'm sure Koric has witnessed their sorcery before, but I doubt he knows how to fight it.

My brother leans into his fingers, slightly crinkling the paper map beneath them. "My loyalties are to the Empire, General

Wellor. If my sister were a threat to the state, if she were an enemy to us all, and I knew where she was? I'd kill her myself. She thought she could follow Father's old ways, clearly, and it got her killed. If they've not found her, she's probably dead in a ditch or sold to Taris. Or far worse."

"I'm sure you would kill her," says the General. "I've heard the stories of your rage amidst battle. So you've not heard anything about her? No sign, no letter, nothing?"

"Nothing."

General Wellor nods. "Well, if you do hear anything, I'm sure you'll resolve everything quickly and efficiently so it doesn't disrupt the campaign. We can't be running formal executions and interrogations in the middle of a war. And if you *have* heard something, and you're lying . . . you know what that would mean for you. And the Slaying Swords."

"I'm well aware, sir. You have my word."

"See that I do." The general turns to face me. "Your Captain is a good man, young Nori. Follow him closely. Learn from him. Protect him with your life."

"Thank you, sir." It takes everything in me not to shake. "Yes, he is a good man. I'll do as you say. Sir."

"You're both dismissed. May favor find you on the battlefield."

"You as well, General Wellor," replies Koric.

X

My conversations with Erin—and with Victor—indicate a reality we cannot ignore. It may be the key to defeating our enemy. The people of the Holy Empire? They are good at their core. Even many of its leaders. Victor says many people even suspect High Inquisitor Trallius lies about the circumstances of Empress Emelia's death. If we are to win, we must win the people. For there are many simply waiting to strangle the Inquisition and destroy its hold on the country, if given the chance. – From the Journal of the Daughter of Light

We return to the tent in silence. There's no way for us to discuss what happened with the general. We can't risk anyone overhearing us, and it's too late in the night to escape into the forest for a private conversation. I drop onto my cot beside my brother, but sleep eludes me. Based on his tossing and turning, it eludes him as well.

The general knows. He must know, the way his words bit into both of us. His eyes . . . he recognized my face. My hand plays with the tiny orb still resting around my neck.

A few weeks ago, I created a cotton pouch in which it rests above my breastbone. What power am I carrying with me? The ability to steal glances of the past. To take from the past, drawing physical objects into the future. All of it impossible. But it happened to me.

Why have I held onto the damn thing for so long? The moment it's discovered, I'm doomed. Certainly the Inquisition knows what they're looking for, too. The inquisitor was hiding in the shadows, watching us the whole time Wellor stared us down.

Then why didn't the general accuse us?

Koric doesn't gather us for morning training. Before the sun rises, I notice my brother slip out of the tent into the misty morning air, and before long, I hear his hushed whispers with another member of the Company—probably Yarwin. As sunrise hits, my brother rouses the Company and pulls them together into a tight circle. Our grouping of tents partially shields us from the prying eyes of other units.

"Good morning, my friends." Koric stands in the middle, Yarwin at his side. "I have important news to share with you all." He pauses as if expecting a response, but Yarwin nudges him in the side. "Right. So first things first. We're almost to the front lines. Only three days. We'll be crossing the river today to the east side with the General Wellor's army." Murmurs, but no one addresses their captain directly. "More importantly—and I know not every commander is telling their men this truth—the enemy has former citizens of the Holy Empire fighting by their side."

"Impossible," says Jamus from beside me. "Fighting alongside the Accursed?"

"You've all heard the stories," says Yarwin. "Not only were the Accursed taken to the camps. If you were forced to experience the same violence as an Accursed, would you not join them?"

"Yarwin may speak truth, but do not let it leave this circle," says Koric. "Remember, protect our own. We're about to enter hell, from the sound of it. We have one mission—eliminate their leader—and their secret weapon. Whatever it is. Whatever it takes. But will you be ready to strike our own former brothers?" Koric swivels in place in attempt to meet the eyes of each man under his command. "Are you ready to face the sins of our Empire?"

We pound our chests in unison. I'm in harmony with them; by now, I've learned Slaying Sword tendencies when Koric addresses everyone at once. No one ever backs down. No one ever hesitates. We protect our own.

"Good," says Koric. "As I thought. Prepare your minds for the coming battle. Prepare for the onslaught. Hopefully many of us will live to see the other side."

* * *

One day from the front line. Morning. My final training.

We're beneath massive trees, their trunks easily ten meters wide. Their branches and leaves are far above, a tangled weave designed to catch the sky. Morning birds caw and cry, eager for their breakfast.

I walk through Yarwin's attacks with ease. I strike Weston in each limb with the staff in under a minute. I dodge Jamus's fists and kicks for the designated time. Marik only blocks my own jabs for thirty seconds. I know they're not using all their skills—it's simply a test, after all. But they still feel like wins.

And now—the final test, the test I've not yet won.

My brother. Koric. My captain. He stands before me and tosses me the practice sword. He holds a second in his right hand.

"Engage," he says.

I step forward, swinging the wooden weapon with both hands. He parries easily, sending my weapon sliding to the left. Before he can slice toward my chest with his counter attack, I dance away, bringing my weapon into a guarded position. His overhead swing crosses toward my nose, and I raise my weapon to block.

He bounces off my defense, bringing the practice sword around my flank in a wide sweep. I crouch under the attack, slicing my weapon toward his shoulder. He side-steps out of harm's way, twirling with his weapon to catch me unawares.

I lean into my attack, however, twirling in a dance matching my brother's footwork. I slip into a one-handed grip on my practice sword, extending the reach of my weapon. I just need to touch him to—

His forearm sweeps around, cracking into my wrist. I drop the practice sword to the mossy ground. The full force of the blow causes me to stumble, and I slip on a rock, falling to the forest floor.

"Get up!" says Koric. The force in his words sting. "Get up and win. The war begins tomorrow, and you can't even make it through the damn motions of a scripted encounter."

I attempt to rise, but a sudden kick from his boot sweeps into my feet. I sprawl, tasting mud. Spitting, I roll onto my back in time to see a wooden sword swinging from above. I brace for impact, but a quarterstaff intercepts the practice weapon.

"Enough," says Yarwin. "Jamus, Marik, Weston, leave me alone with Koric and his ward."

Silently, the three men march out of the clearing. I push up from the ground, scooting from under the two crossed wooden weapons. Koric glares at the older man, but a look of pained sympathy dominates Yarwin's face.

"Koric," says Yarwin. "Three and a half weeks of training, you can't expect more than this."

"We are going behind enemy lines tomorrow, and you believe this to be enough to survive a fight?" Koric throws the wooden practice sword into the bushes in disgust. "Look. Fear, all in the eyes. Didn't join the war for the right reasons, and this is what happens. When you use war to run away from your problems, you will die."

With a sharp crack, the quarterstaff smacks Koric against the ear.

"Ow." My brother takes a step back. "Yarwin, what—"

"Look at her," Yarwin says. "Your sister. You're her last hope, and she's done everything to make it easier on you."

Your sister. He knows. Yarwin knows. Yarwin knows?

They both see my looks of confusion as I scoot against the bark of one of the massive trees. "Sorry, Roan, I had to tell him." His demeanor shifts slightly, though crimson fury still hides behind his eyes. "He knew almost instantly."

"Does . . . does anyone else know?" I ask.

Yarwin shakes his head. "Only me. Not even Jamus or the others in your brother's squad."

"Why? Why did you let him help me?"

"You know the answer," says the old man.

We protect our own.

"The entire Company of Slaying Swords could be eliminated by the Inquisition for what the two of you have done," I say.

"That possibility became clear the moment Koric decided to protect you," Yarwin replies. "He risked the lives of thirty-nine men for you."

"I didn't ask him to!" I say. "I was going to hide in the Third Battalion, I was going to—"

Yarwin laughs. "I know, I know, child. You think you're the first fugitive to try to hide in the army? You think you're the first person taken under the wing of a company like the Slaying Swords?"

"Yarwin, don't you dare." Koric paces back and forth, fists clenched. "It's not your story to tell."

"You're right," says the man, a glint in his eyes. "It's your story. Now tell it."

"No."

"Boy, do it."

INTERJECTION

Roan, do you remember when I came home, telling Mother and Father I decided to join the military? The looks on their faces? The look on your face?

I remember your eyes, seeing your older brother leaving. You probably felt I'd abandoned you. I can't imagine what the twins thought of me. Joining the army? Fighting in wars hundreds of leagues away from our home?

I betrayed everything our family stood for. But I had no choice.

Earlier that day, I'd made my way through the market, locking in shipments for Father. You know, the usual. Completing them early, I decided to go visit Tylor. You should remember him. We had talked about visiting the baths.

I headed to his apartment. But when I arrived, I found slimy bastard inside—an inquisitor—pushing Tylor against the couch. My friend was drugged and unconscious. I shouted for help, screamed for it, but I was the only person nearby. Rushing into the room, I threw the man off Tylor, grabbed a pot from the wall, and bashed the man's head in. It all happened so fast . . .

I leaned against the couch, tending to my friend's wounds. It only took a few moments for his groggy mind to awaken, but he couldn't remember what led to the assault. We sat there in tears, recognizing a terrifying reality—our lives were most likely ruined. I killed an inquisitor. We were under no illusions. The Church would not believe we were innocent.

And then the soldiers arrived. But not the royal guard—Yarwin, and the Slaying Swords. They witnessed the scene. They recognized the consequences. And they believed us. They gave us each a choice—flee from our lives and find a new life elsewhere, or join their ranks. They could hide us. We both joined the Slaying Swords on the spot. Hiding the evidence—eliminating all traces of the inquisitor from Tylor's house? Impossible.

Yet for at least a year, Tylor and I trained with the Slaying Swords without worry. Then, the Inquisition arrived. But not for me—for Tylor. They'd found evidence of the murder of an Adjutant Inquisitor in his house. Without question, they went to arrest him, but Tylor killed himself on the spot.

Do you know why? It should be obvious. Rather than let himself be captured, tortured, and reveal the truth of who killed the inquisitor, he took his own life. He saved me. He sacrificed himself.

Together, we fled into the arms of the Slaying Swords, and they have protected me as their own. And now you've forced me to protect you, risking all of them in the process. The least you can do is learn to protect yourself.

XI

You know what still stumps me? Where did the dark wolves—the fiends—come from? What magic caused their creation beneath the Gates of Vicor? They weren't evil; when we restored them, we revealed a deeper truth about their nature. But what magic caused them? Was it a natural law of the universe, or did something else cause their formation? – From the Journal of the Daughter of Light

I stare at my brother, seeing the pain in his eyes. I remember Tylor. His best friend—and he was who Father blamed for convincing Koric to go "gallivanting off into the wilderness on foolish adventures." We never imagined the horror described.

"I'm so sorry," I say. I step forward, embracing him. For a moment, he stands completely still. Then, his arms wrap around me. I can't hold back the tears.

"I can't lose you too," he says. "I can't lose you too."

"You won't," I say. "I may have stumbled my way into war, but I'm by your side to the end. I may not be as good a fighter as any of your men, but I'll be watching your back regardless."

"You might die tomorrow."

"By all accounts, I should have died three weeks ago when I attempted to steal from the palace vault."

He laughs, and despite my tears, I laugh too. A third chuckle joins us, and as we break our embrace, we glance at Yarwin slapping his knees.

"She's right," he says. "Your sister is living on borrowed time. I may not follow all the Church's teachings, but I'm a spiritual man. Destiny brought your sister to us—maybe there's a reason she's by your side. Don't flaunt the power of fate!"

"You're a crazy old man, you know that?" I say.

"I'm quite aware."

We all share another chuckle before Koric begins walking out of the clearing. "It's time we head back to the Company," he says. "This was good. Important. Good for you to know, before tomorrow, that Yarwin knows. In case, well, you know."

"Neither of us is going to die," I say. "Or we'll die together."

"That's what worries me the most," he says. "I can't solely protect you. I have my mission—and the lives of the rest of the Company—to protect too."

"When it comes down to it," I say, wiping the tears from my cheeks, "forget about your duty to me. Sacrifice me, if you must."

He strides out of the clearing; Yarwin and I follow close behind. "You know I won't ever do that," he says. "I won't lose you like I lost Tylor."

* * *

Halfway through the day, the sun high in the sky, we crest a hill. Spread to our left is the River Wi, its slow, meandering flow contrasting against the mountains rising in the distance in nearly every direction. Across the river, the formations of the Second Battalion occupy entrenched positions along ridges and culverts.

Directly to our north, the First Battalion awaits us, hundreds of spearmen occupying similar fortifications. In addition to the hundreds of skirmisher units, archers support the First Battalion, occupying a ridge above the lower trenches. We've also set up a few catapults, apparently, though they don't look like they'd be particularly effective in a pitched fight.

I don't know much about battlefield tactics, but the position looks strong. We're out of the forest now, facing a cleared plain along the riverbank. Any enemy approach must charge across nearly a kilometer of cleared ground. Though . . .

"Koric," I say. He's walking next to me. "Our positions. Why won't the enemy just . . . flank us? To the east or west, through the foothills?"

"Starting to attempt to think like a tactician," he replies. "I like it. I confess, I don't know enough about large army tactics to answer your question. I assume the battalions have scouted the hills and determined them impossible to traverse with the size of the enemy force. Either that, or we have units stationed out there—maybe recon units that can manage hit and run tactics—and they're forcing them to meet our fortified positions. It's dreadfully difficult to move an army on anything other than a road."

"Oh." A bit more in-depth of an answer than I expected. "Makes sense. So what's our role in all of this?"

He slaps my shoulder. "You really didn't pay attention much during the briefing, did you?"

"Hey, to be fair, it occurred in the middle of the night. Do you expect me to understand things on two hours of sleep?"

"I'm very well aware you've done quite a few things on fewer hours of sleep." He glances toward me. "Like choosing to join the Slaying Swords."

"Precisely, without sleep, I can't think straight."

Waving a hand, he brushes away the jokes. "So that's what we're going to figure out. But General Wellor's personal guard? Best heavily armored troops in the entire Empire. They'll be serving as the primary vanguard on this front. In theory, we should be able to avoid the bulk of the fighting. We're not a front-line unit, after all. We're more like a recon unit. Hit and run tactics."

"Or assassins." I hope he can see my smirk.

"In this instance, yes."

I look at my brother—I've given up thinking of him as my captain—and I notice his eyes darting back and forth across the battlefield. What's he thinking? Where is his mind going, in this moment? Trapped between fulfilling their contract and receiving payment . . . and ensuring the Company survives. Ensuring I survive.

"Is Yarwin joining us on the battlefield?" I ask.

"Every one of us must go. You as well, though I'm sure you already know that. A ward stays by the side of their commander through it all. To the end." He glances over his shoulder. "Jamus?"

A few moments pass before the man trots up to walk beside us. "Sir?"

"In the morning, Wellor plans to move the army forward to smoke out the enemy. Based on the last reports, they're encamped just a few kilometers up-river. So tell me, what are your thoughts on us moving ahead tonight? Camping in the hills to the northeast?"

"It would be risky . . ." while we walk, Jamus runs a hand through his hair. "Yet, if we find a hidden position, we could drop ourselves behind enemy lines with a vantage point on the battle tomorrow. We identify our target, flank in from the side, and get out behind Wellor."

I can't help myself. "That sounds like suicide. Planting ourselves far from support? If the battle goes south during the day, and we're trapped, what happens then? We'll certainly be captured, killed, or worse."

"Presumably their commander will be stationed at the rear of their force," Koric retorts. "If we're to complete our mission, our only chance is to drop behind the enemy."

"It'll be just like the battle on the Colored Plateau," mutters Jamus. "Just like it."

"The Colored—"

"Brutal battle, Nori." Jamus looks away. "Brutal battle."

"How—"

"He's somewhat messing with you," says Koric, "but he's not wrong. We lost ten good men that day. Desert frontier bandits are brutal fellows."

"Do I even want to know?"

"Probably not."

I sigh, still uncertain of what's about to happen. I think back on the past month. Everything started the moment I climbed into the vent inside the vault's preparation room. If I'd not hidden, my blood would have seeped into the stones in front of the palace alongside Aarin and the other Serpents. Now, when I consider it all, I'm weirdly happy I'm here, beside my brother, facing the Accursed.

Sure, I never wanted to join the army. What woman does? Yet here, beside Koric, Yarwin, and the others . . . at least I have a place. People who wish to see me succeed. The Serpents used me for their secret missions. They didn't *really* care about me.

Though, I miss my parents. I can't imagine what they're thinking. Or, for that matter, Henry and Nori—the *actual* Nori. Do they understand what's happened to their big sister? Do they know she attempted a capital crime to impress a few street thugs? Do they know Father approved of her going with them?

Now I'm on an adventure, and what Yarwin said yesterday makes sense. I've never been one to think about destiny or fate. And I certainly never imagined a crazy adventure with my brother, of all people, to the furthest reaches of the Empire. Facing down Accursed together. It all must mean something, right?

It's one way to think about the battle before us. A tiny part of my brain whispers a more likely truth; tomorrow, we'll die, and we'll rot in unmarked graves beside the River Wi.

I shudder. I prefer the hopeful thoughts quite a bit more.

* * *

We move forward with Jamus and Koric's proposed plan. A few hours later, the forty-one soldiers of the Company of Slaying Swords discover a cleverly hidden cave in the foothills of the mountains spreading eastward. From our vantage point, we see our army entrenched. To the north, we see nothing; no phalanxes or legions, no secret weapons, no minions of witches or demons or whatever else supposedly fights beside the Accursed.

Instead, dressed in our dark leather armor, the Slaying Swords blend into the trees and caves. We cook ourselves a final meal. As night falls, we bundle deep in our secret cave, darkness enveloping us all. No fire at night, lest we signal our position to any enemy scouts.

Instead, bundled in blankets, swords in our hands, we listen to Yarwin. Old Yarwin. We can't see him.

But he speaks, nevertheless.

"All forty of you," he says, "are men I would die for. I know your stories, at least the parts that matter. I've seen your eyes. I know the truth in your soul. And so tonight, dream dreams of home. Of hope. Of love. Who we face tomorrow? An enemy unlike anything you've ever witnessed. The Accursed—that's what we call them."

Silence, except for the constant drip-drip of water deeper in the cave.

"The Accursed are the greatest warriors you will ever face. Swift with the spear. Deadly with the blade. Strength unmatched. We all know what the Church teaches. What the Inquisition preaches. The Accursed are people of darkness, destined to be a blight upon this planet, a blight upon our people. I don't know the truth, but I know they have threatened our Empire before, and will do so again. So we fight them."

The old man coughs. "Just know—when your blade strikes them, you're not striking simply an Accursed. They have families, and lovers, and homes, just like us. Whether we want to admit it or not. They are a people. Do not lose yourself in the thrill of battle. Remember they fight for something they love too, and will fight fiercely. Do not underestimate their passion, or their resolve. For if you do, you will fall."

"Yarwin," says a voice from somewhere in the cave. "Do you believe the Almighty has forsaken us? Is that why, after we won the war, the Accursed have returned? Are we being punished? Did the Empire fall in the eyes of the Holy?"

"We are certainly being tested. Whether we are the ones in the wrong—do you feel like you're fighting on the wrong side?"

"We protect our own," whispers a number of voices.

"We protect our own," repeats Yarwin. "This Company is your

family. We fight together. That's the only side that matters."

XII

I've not heard the Lord of Light's voice for years now. Not since my tribulation before the Gates of Vicor. Erin said no one hears the voice of the Lord, but I know what I heard. Maybe I was a vessel, maybe my mind was just making sense of some higher power. I may never know. But someone spoke to me. And the voice was more than Father Mono or Maripes, even if it channeled their spirits in the process.

And today, before we face the next legion of our enemy, he spoke again: "You've found them. Beyond all odds, you've found them. Prepare for the end, my Daughter." – From the Journal of the Daughter of Light

"Slaying Swords, to arms!"

Koric's voice breaks through sleep like a trumpet. I sit right up, throwing the blanket to the side. Rising to my feet, I quickly belt the sword to my back and strap the accompanying dagger to my belt. Throughout the cave, the forty other Slaying Swords ready themselves. There's just enough light to see the fear—and anticipation—in everyone's eyes.

Koric stands at the mouth of the cave, blade in hand. Behind him, morning gloom blooms. And beyond, subtle sounds of stampedes and screams resound. The battle—it must have started in the middle of the night.

"Slaying Swords," Koric says, pointing outside. "The Accursed have taken the cover of darkness to advance. They're already assaulting the First Battalion; Wellor is moving into fill the gaps. Not ideal, but *this* is our chance."

He walks out of the cave, and within moments we all follow. We find him crouching along the rocky outcropping. Giving us a view of the battle below, all forty men crouch along the ridge, observing the distant fight.

As my brother said, a legion of Accursed have charged our lines. Hundreds of shielded spearmen face down our trenches, and hundreds more archers bombard Wellor's soldiers as they enter the fray. More importantly, stationed near the back of the enemy formation—near their archers—a dozen or so soldiers in white and gold armor. And—

A flash of light lances outward from the center of the armored unit and collides with one of our raised parapets filled with archers. Smoke settles; dust clears. The parapet, constructed of wood, ignites in flames.

"What in the bloody damnation was that?" says Jamus, on Koric's left.

"It's their secret weapon," says my brother. "Our target."

* * *

It's painful to watch the slaughter, but we have no choice. The open battlefield doesn't present us with a clear opportunity—yet—to approach covertly. Within an hour, Wellor's units takes a more strategic position on the sides of the fortifications, forcing the phalanx to reposition and face attacks from three sides. Whatever power their weapon possesses, though, it strikes with methodical precision. It fires infrequently, but when it does . . . hellfire and ashes.

By the second hour of battle, the men around me grow impatient. I feel their pain. We're watching our countrymen die to unknown sorcery. What does Koric expect us to do?

I'm almost ready to smack some sense into him myself when from the mountains, a fog rolls westward. Before long, we're surrounded by mist. We couldn't have asked for anything better.

Koric smiles from beside me. "Fortune sees us today and has

given us her favor," he whispers just loud enough for us all to hear. "Into the battle we shall go. On me!"

He leaps from the ridge, dropping the two meters to the gentle slope below. Silently, we all follow my brother over the edge and into an abyss of murky-white.

The fog, though eerie, is more than we could have ever hoped for. Visibility drops to only a few dozen meters within moments. We can't see the battle, but I know Koric has a map of the field in his mind. He knows where we're going. Around boulders and ridges, we traverse kilometers of ground at a decent jog.

The fog thickens; even as we near the fighting, it somehow muffles the sounds of clinking steel. We crest another ridge—the sounds of sword and spear ring clear. Moments later, the shining gold and white plates of our target's entourage appear, practically blending with the fog. They're all facing south, toward the rest of the Empire's forces.

Koric turns to face us, his eyes welling with a sadness I recognize immediately. It's the look from the other day, when Yarwin revealed his knowledge of my truth. Koric knows he'll see his brothers fall today. He'll probably see me fall today.

"Into the battle we go," I whisper, before he says a word.

He nods. "Brothers, let us end this." Holding his sword in both hands, he turns, bends his knees, and charges.

For a second, it's as if time stands still, my brother facing down a faceless enemy. Then, my knees move without any orders from my mind. I'm following Koric, and beside me, the other thirty-nine soldiers of the Slaying Swords follow their captain into the gauntlet.

It takes less than ten steps for a roar to echo through the legion, and they turn to face us. From the ridge, we couldn't see their weapons. In their hands, the shiny soldiers wield long spears; on their backs, hammers protrude, strapped ready for use if necessary.

They're terrible. Frighteningly terrible. All twelve of these soldiers turn to face us, revealing the thirteenth of their number. In the center, clad in pure white armor, a woman wields a glowing spear, a hammer strapped to her back. Both weapons emit white light—the same white light we've witnessed strike our armies a dozen times.

Her dark grey skin contrasts against her armor, and—is that red hair beneath her cowl? In any case, the twelve soldiers, plus their commander, face our forty-one. We're just a dozen meters from them, and Koric hasn't stopped our charge. He's insane. We don't stand a chance—

The woman—their secret weapon—she leaps forward, swinging her spear high overhead. When the blade strikes the ground, a shock wave billows through the soil. It hits my brother's feet, and he flies backward. A second later, the light hits me, and though it looks weaker than what hit my brother, I stumble, as do Jamus and the others. Vision spins, spots blurring and blending with the ever-present mist. Those of us in the front who falter—we're the first to die, certainly. They'll be upon us in little time.

I'm wrong, of course. What do I know of battles? A dozen Slaying Swords fly forward, their weapons ready. I struggle to my hands and knees, Koric a few meters away. Even more of our men surge forward. Jamus stands beside me, and I think I spot Marik's blond locks just beyond. Weston? Where's Weston—

All thought is lost as I witness the Accursed strike down our men. Their spears seem weightless in their hands, slicing through limbs like butter knives. We're all struggling to join the fight, and it looks as if at least one of these demon-spears falls to the combined attack of three of our men, but . . . I count at least ten Slaying Swords already laying wounded in the mud.

"Koric!" I cry. "This is madness!" I find his eyes.

"Nori, Jamus, Weston, Marik, on me!" he says. His eyes meet mine. The message is clear. *Roan, you chose this. Face the end.*

Jamus and I reach our feet, and before we know it, we're by Koric's side. Weston is nowhere to be found—I fear the worst—but Marik is with us. We turn to face the line of enemy spears, including the lightning witch leading them. Our men have retreated too, forming a line on our flanks. There's already so few of us. And I count . . . no. Thirteen still. We didn't manage to fell any of them.

"Drop your weapons!" shouts the woman—in our language. "You are not our enemy. Our quarrel is with the Inquisition, not you."

Koric takes a single step forward, his blade in hand. The fog swirls around us like rippling waves. "You just killed a dozen of my brothers, and you expect me to believe we're not your enemy?"

She takes a step forward, spear tip pointed toward the grass. "Men, reveal yourselves!"

In unison, her spearmen take off their helmets.

Every face—not that of the Accursed. Skin as pale as the stars, their brown and blue eyes reveal the truth. They are of the Holy Empire, their fierce scowls revealing how they detest us. Despise. Revile us—pity us.

"You've bewitched them!" Koric says. "You've turned them against us."

"No, my friend," says a man from the direct left of their leader. "No magic. Just truth. We fight for her because she fought for us."

Koric looks back at the Company. None of us know what to do. But we have our mission. We have our contract.

"Are you with me to the end?" says my brother.

"Always," I say, in unison with Jamus and Marik.

"Then this is the end."

We charge, our blades in hand. The spearmen don their helmets and ready their weapons. The two lines converge; death awaits us.

* * *

The clash of steel above me signals I'm still alive. My eyes flutter open. I'm face first in the grass, though my head's tilted enough so I can see the scene: Yarwin and Koric, back-to-back, standing a few meters from me. Three spearmen surround, including the lightning witch.

"Finish it," Koric says. Blood drips from his cheeks. I can see a wound in his side, though it looks like a light grazing. My eyes quickly dart around the field of vision available—I see at least three fallen foes. At least we took down a few of them. I don't see any other standing members of our Company, though a few could be incapacitated like me.

I don't remember how I fell. It was soon after the battle began. A hammer blow to the helmet, maybe. I'm not sure. Doesn't matter. Here I am, alive, watching my brother's execution.

But we protect our own, right?

I crawl toward the leg of the closest spearman. I reach his feet; he doesn't notice me. I grope for my dagger and without thinking, pull it and swipe for the man's heel.

In pain, he falls to his knees, screaming. Chaos ensues, and before I know what's happening Yarwin and Koric attack their now one-on-one opponents. Blades clash, but within seconds, their swords fly from their hands. Spear tips reach their necks.

"No!" I cry, crawling to my knees. "No, no, don't kill them!"

"Roan, no!" Koric says, all pretext of subterfuge lost. Here, at the end.

The mist continues to swirl around us. The lightning witch steps away from Koric, and before I know what's happening, I'm *rising* to my feet by a power beyond my own volition. Somehow, she's lifting me with her mind.

"Who are you?" she says. "You have a gift. You have—you have an artifact."

"Don't hurt her!" Koric says. "Kill us, I don't care, but she doesn't deserve this fate."

"She?" The woman . . . she laughs. She laughs at us. As I land on my feet, she's laughing at us! She takes a step back, her spear pointing between us. "Oh, I see the resemblance. Brother and sister? This is ridiculous. Here on the battlefield, an old man and two siblings. This is so rich."

As she walks back and forth, other spearmen approach. I count at least seven total. "Just kill us and be done with it," I say.

"We're not going to kill you," she says, "we're going to—"
In a single thunderclap, the mist disappears.

XIII

I suspect our histories are entirely wrong. Everything points to it. There's a power out there, beyond all our understanding; it's the true enemy of light. To defeat it, we must change everything. But how can we when, for the past half-century, both our nations have known nothing but war? – From the Journal of the Daughter of Light

In an instant, darkness envelops the battlefield. Strange; it's still midday by my accounting. Regardless, it's dark. And the mist? Gone. Then—figures form. Dark forms, yet radiant, surrounded by a glowing shadow. Hollowed eyes, like the blue flames in a fire. Their mouths—impossibly wide. Before now, I would have thought the Accursed the most evil creature possible.

But these—they are evil incarnate.

"To the Daughter of Light!" shouts someone from within the darkness. I don't know who says it. Dozens—no—hundreds of these figures float through the dark, their motions haphazard and coordinated like a ritualistic dance.

I stumble forward, reaching Koric and Yarwin's side.

"Our swords!" he shouts. "Do you see our swords?"

"No!" I'm not sure why we're shouting, but it's like a constant, raging wind billows all around. It's impossible to hear.

"I've got them," Yarwin says, and somehow I catch my blade as it flies to me through the air.

Suddenly, in my face—the eyes of the witch. "You!" she says. "Reveal it. Reveal your artifact. Now!"

"What?"

"Just trust me if you want to live!"

I reach beneath my armor and pull forth the orb from its

pouch, removing it from its chain. "This is it," I say.

"Step away from her," Koric says, though his heart doesn't seem behind the words. "Step—"

"It's over." Yarwin's words. "Koric, can't you see it's over? We have a bigger fight!"

The spearmen surround us, their spears attempting to fend off the strange spectral creatures. They don't attack yet. But dozens of them float—and gloat—their eyes gazing toward the witch. And me. And Koric and Yarwin.

"We had a mission," Koric says. "We had a *mission*."

"And so do I," says the witch. "I'm Ermo, Daughter of Light, and you, girl, do you trust me?"

"No!" I say. "Why the hell would I trust you?"

"Doesn't matter. Take off your glove. Hold that orb. And take my hand!"

I look to Koric. His eyes are vacant. He's staring at the ground. "What about them?" I glance at Yarwin, who nods.

"Just trust me!" shouts this Ermo.

Quickly, I pull my fingers out of the glove and drop the orb into my palm. I close my hand, feeling a strange power surge through my bones. As the artifact touches my skin, the creatures surrounding us shriek. It takes everything in me not to drop the artifact and cover my ears. The shadows charge, the evil anger evident in their dead eyes.

The woman rips off my other glove. "Now take my hand!"

I do as she says.

Nothing, then . . . everything. An energy surges through me, impossibly vast and incredibly strong, but—it's also simple. It feels right. Natural. And it arcs between me and this woman, then outward, around us. Around Yarwin and Koric. And—

* * *

Silence. Between light and stars and life and death.

* * *

Sand. Lots of sand. The sun—high above. Nothing but sand all around. I twirl, looking for the demons, but they're gone. As are the witch's guards. It's just her, Yarwin, Koric, and me, in the middle of a scorching desert.

To our left, a tower rises out of the sand, its grey stone contrasting against the browns all around.

"Well, Ermo," says Yarwin, his arms wide. "Where the hell are we?"

* * *

VANGUARDS OF LIGHT

A Sketch
of the
Desolate Plain
These lifeless lands contain only death. We know of only one location of interest. The Pillar of Power.

INTERJECTION

It is my duty to explain to you who I am. Let us start from the beginning.

My name is Kyri. I was a child of the shadowlands. The Triumvirate ruled me. I now rule the Triumvirate. And today, upon a surface-dwelling battlefield facing innumerable enemies, we initiated the first step toward reclaiming our rightful place in the world. No longer will we hide in darkness, kept apart from those who have forgotten our existence.

They banished us millennia ago for false crimes.

But I digress.

I am Kyri, and I was a child of the shadowlands. I hid among rocks, searching for food on my own. My parents died when I was six shardcycles old, murdered by the Triumvirate's scions for having a second child.

For having me.

My sister and I escaped. We lived in the Caves of Akonar, scavenging for stone-lichen. And when she died of iron-rot a few cycles later, I returned to Shade. I lived on the streets. I watched others like me die on the streets. I tried to be better.

Let me tell you how everything changed. The moment I recognized the way the world worked. When I realized I wouldn't survive if I merely *tried* to be better.

I must simply be.

I wandered through the streets of Shade, exploring the alleys of the burrow tucked beneath the Glowshard and searching for my next meal. Rats were the food of choice in those years, when I had lived twelve shardcycles. Cook them over a geyser and you were set. Delicious.

I found a whole nest of them. The problem? They lived in the basement of a gem smelter. The smithies were simply too strict. They wouldn't let anyone inside during forge-hours. Regardless, I couldn't pass up the opportunity to nab a couple dozen meals.

I made a key mistake, though.

I enlisted help.

A young shadow-thief named Eryk—he was about the same age as me—followed me around in those days. I didn't mind him. He was nice. I wanted to help him. He was stuck in the same rut I was, and we could assist one another when necessary. Together, we staked the gem-smelter.

It all was going smoothly.

As we approached the forge, I motioned for Eryk to follow. We snuck behind a particularly massive obsidian pillar and reached the back curtain.

"All right," I whispered. "Check the corners, check the stairs, then we dark downward."

He nodded, and I gently parted the fabric covering the doorway. Eryk slipped in, and I mirrored his footsteps pattering on the stone floor. As our night-eyes shifted to match the forge's dimly glowing magma, I recognized the truth immediately. We made a terrible mistake.

Inside the forge-smelter stood a smithy introducing three soldiers to newly minted blades. The moment we turned the corner, they saw us.

Their eyes met ours.

Eryk yelped. "Hello, we . . . we didn't mean . . ." His words blubbered and blustered and deformed into nonsense.

"Stop talking," I muttered. But it was too late.

They stepped forward, picking up their blades, igniting them in an inferno of smoke and flame.

I froze. Eryk froze. We stared at our deaths.

In those precious seconds, I recognized an emblem of one of the men. His misty figure, adorned with an ashen cloak, bore the sigil of the Vanguard. The explorers of the deep. And this one was a Scion.

For years, I knew I held a power craved by those above me. I turned toward Eryk. I knew both of us would die if I did not act.

I reached out, grasped for darkness, and destroyed my friend. He evaporated into dust.

Without hesitation, the Scion of the Vanguard stepped forward, sheathed his blade, and motioned for me to join them.

I

ROAN

There is too much sand. Way too much sand. And there's nothing we can do about it.

In my hand, I hold the tiny, two-ringed orb. Somehow, it transported us across the continent to who knows where. In doing so, it fractured. The cracks run along both rings, revealing maroon scars.

Whatever power brought us here, it can't take us home. Though for now, my fears should focus on a different threat—the Accursed woman who supposedly saved us.

"I'll say it again," Yarwin says. "So, Ermo, what do we do now?"

Our enemy takes two steps away before turning to face us. Koric crouches to my left, Yarwin stands ready to my right. Her eyes, like fire, examine us with an intensity I've never seen before.

Raising her hand to shield the bright sun from her eyes, she says, "I can't explain it. Not yet. I don't know what we do now. I act on instinct. Did you not see what was coming for us?"

Koric groans, rolling his shoulders. I can't imagine the thoughts—

He pulls a dagger from his hip and charges the Accursed.

"Koric," The word sounds frustrated breathed through my teeth. "Stop!"

He doesn't listen, and his blade comes within centimeters of the large woman before she deflects the attack with an armored gauntlet. My brother stumbles into the sand, eyes growing wide as he sprawls.

"Now is not the time for fighting," Ermo says, taking a step backward. Her palms rise in supplication, though fierce determination and readiness bleed from her powerful stance. I hadn't noticed my hand sliding to my own dagger.

Yarwin spreads his arms wide. "I see no harm in us calling a truce. Koric, stop your silliness."

"She killed everyone." He flips to his knees and spits at Ermo's feet. "All of us. We're just going to act like that never happened?"

"I told you not to attack," she replies, tilting her head. "I warned you. You couldn't win."

"We had a job to do. We still have a job to do."

"Koric," Yarwin says, stepping between the three of us. "Something greater is happening. Did you not see the shadows? The darkness surrounding? The power enveloping us? We've stepped into something we can't understand."

"I don't care," he says. "I failed them. All of them."

I can't take it. The bickering. I look to the horizon, where a massive grey pillar rises out of the sand. I noticed it when we first arrived a few minutes ago, but I'd forgotten about it until now. Ignoring the others, I start walking.

"Roan, where the hell do you think you're—"

"I'm finding shade," I say, "because it's way too hot." I turn to face my fellow stranded souls. "If we're going to fight, let's at least do it in comfort."

Yarwin smiles and nods, striking a path across the sand in pursuit. Ermo smirks—strangely, it excites me—and she follows, too. Koric continues wailing in the sand.

"I'm sure you'll catch up eventually," I shout, knowing he'll hear.

"How can you both be so crass?" Koric screams. "She just slaughtered our friends."

My mind pains with the memory of the dead around us. I understand his fear. His anger. I do. They were his brothers. And I'm terrified of the woman walking behind us. But . . .

"Do we have a choice, Koric?"

"We do not," Yarwin interjects.

Following a huff, I hear my brother's feet shuffle through the sand.

* * *

When we originally arrived in the desert, I was certain the tower stood a few hundred meters away. As we trek across the sand, it quickly becomes apparent it stands kilometers in the distance. Moreover, it's incomprehensibly tall. Its summit stands above anything I've ever seen before, including the Grand Cathedral in Esmeraldi.

If only the twins could see it. They would love it.

Ermo strides a few dozen meters ahead of us, leading the charge to the tower. I know I'm supposed to despise her—and I do—but the confidence she exudes intrigues me. She seems . . . certain, as if the world around her *is* the way she *believes* it to be. No one can tell her otherwise. Given what I've learned over the past few weeks about the Inquisition, her aura only further cracks my loyalty to the dogma of the Holy Empire.

She killed our comrades in self-defense. At her core, though, she doesn't seem dangerous. If she's an "Accursed," they're much more civilized than we were ever taught.

"We can't trust her," Koric says from a few paces behind me.

I glance over my shoulder, raising an arm to shield my eyes from the blistering sun. "Of course we can't. She killed hundreds of Empire soldiers. But we're in over our heads, dealing with a power we don't understand. But she *does* understand, Koric. We need to use her." I'm not certain whether I believe the words, but I *think* they'll convince my brother.

Before Koric responds, Yarwin says, "Your sister speaks a truth we can't ignore. We have no idea where we are. And I don't think she knows either." The older man wipes glistening sweat from his brow. "And in this heat, we'll die in days. No food. No water. Only that tower."

"Do you not believe we can fend for ourselves?" Koric sighs.

"No, I get it. We need to be smart. She might be our enemy, but this desert is a greater one."

I nod, glad he sees the truth of the matter. "So we don't try to kill her?"

"For now."

"Hey . . . Ermo!" I shout. "We won't kill you. Or try to, at least. Care to come walk with us instead of sulking alone?"

She pauses in stride, hands on her hips. "Sure, if you keep the wolf on his leash."

Koric audibly grumbles. "Hey—"

"He's agreed to stay his blade," Yarwin says. "So, as we walk, I'd love to hear about how in the holy light of the world we got here in the—"

Ermo's eyes widen. She's looking beyond us, not paying attention to Yarwin's words.

I follow her gaze.

A dust cloud clutters a nearby dune. It's rushing toward us, slithering and sliding along the sand. Serpentine bodies slip beneath the surface.

Snakes. It's snakes. Several thousand of them.

"Run!"

I'm not positive who said the word. Maybe we all simultaneously shouted it. But at the sight of the sand serpents, we all spring into a sprint. More like a shuffle—it's difficult to run atop shifting sand dunes.

Down one dune, up another. I don't think I've ever run so hard in my life. My muscles scream, still aching from a battle ended only a few minutes prior. Adrenaline rushes through my veins, driving my body toward the sole refuge in sight: the tower.

Ermo rapidly breaks away from us, reaching the top of the next dune. Spear in her hand, she turns, aiming it over our heads. "Duck," she says, less of a command and more of statement of fact. For if we don't duck, we'll die.

We lower our heads. A beam of light lances from her weapon. There isn't time for us to assess whether her attack harmed the swarm. We keep running, running, running.

The dunes level into packed earth. Ragged shrubbery dots the dusty plain beneath our potential refuge. The flat surface allows us to break into a full-on sprint; seconds later, a blast of granulated dirt shatters through the sound of our panted breath.

Ermo shuffles backward, somehow keeping pace with us. "They're further away than they look," she says. "Don't worry. You're fine. The entrance is right ahead."

Right. The pillar. I've been too focused on my feet. Now, the massive pinnacle rises hundreds of meters above us, windowless and pristine. Sun glances off its white surface. At its base, a tiny archway, adorned by two rows of smaller silver pillars, greets us like a hungry child.

"Roan, Roan, we're going to make it." Koric's words arrive from over my shoulder.

"I know." I slip the thought through baited inhales. "I know."

"Yarwin, how you holding up?"

"Don't you worry about me," says the older man. "I'm only a few steps behind."

We're passing by the columns, ancient and ruined. Ermo stands beside one, spear ready, ushering us toward the door. I don't ask why she paused. Whatever power she holds, it's more useful against the serpents than any weapon the three of us possess.

The last column. The archway. We're through, into darkness. Ermo steps in after us.

Her spear flashes. Light blinds, striking the archway. A thunderclap pierces the dry air. My ears ring, any words spoken by my companions lost in an ever-present buzz.

And the arch collapses in sandy smoke, enveloping us in complete and utter black.

II

ERMO

I reach deep within my soul, finding light. It glows, dimly illuminating our dusty, shadowy space. Before me, the eyes of my forced party look frantic and afraid. "Now will you trust me?" Their language is rough in my mouth. The years of learning it from my human warriors did not prepare me to perpetually speak it. "I just saved our lives from those things. We're now stuck inside a giant stone pillar. We need each other."

The three humans stare back, winded and exhausted. The obstinate one—Koric is the name I heard, I think—doubles over, his hands on his knees. The older man, breathes heavily. I'm impressed he kept up with us. And the girl . . . she seems reasonable. Well, her and the old man together. Mostly, Koric sounds like he'll be a problem.

"Let's restart all of this," I say. "I'm Ermo. I am the Daughter and Vanguard of the People of the Light and Protector of our lands. My goal was not to destroy your people, but to break the hold of the Inquisition upon them. To reunite our peoples as one, rather than fractured into two parts, held at odds . . ."

I'm glad you've arrived, Ermo.

The voice interrupts my monologue. Its words are clear, stronger than when I first heard them standing on the bridge above the Chasm all those years ago. For now, I need to ignore it. The present scene takes precedence.

". . . with one another," I finish my thought from a moment prior. Their language is rolling off my tongue more naturally as I get into the flow of its cadence. Victor taught me well.

With the thought of his name, my heart falls. I hope, following whatever happened at the end of the battle, he survived. He and the rest of the guard.

I shake my head, returning my focus to the three. "We're here now, we're in this unknown place for a reason I don't fully understand. It has something to do with a power you"—I point at the girl—"probably didn't know you possessed. That artifact you had, I mean." I pause, resting *Flame of Maripes* against a pillar and placing a hand on a hip.

"You've got quite the nerve, Accur—"

"Koric, hold." The old man raises his hand. "Ermo, Daughter of the People of Light." He bows. "I thank you for saving us. My name is Yarwin. I once was the captain of the Slaying Swords, but that role now rests in the hands of Captain Koric. The three of us here—including young Roan—represent the final three survivors of the Slaying Swords, the battalion your guards so effectively defeated. I understand you have an agenda on your mind—and you're capable of pushing the death and destruction out of your heart quite quickly—but we need time to grieve, woman. Our family died less than an hour ago. Less than an hour ago, we were prepared to die under your spear!"

I take a step back, seeing the simultaneous anger, pity, and understanding in the old man's eyes. The girl—Roan, based on what he said—is helping Koric tend to cuts and gashes still fresh from the battle. All their eyes fill with dread and boil with rage. I've been ignoring their pain.

You'll all go through hell before this adventure ends.

The voice, clear as day again. Now is not the time for the Lord of Light to inject his diatribes into my thoughts.

Right now is absolutely the time. You're much closer to the truth than I ever thought possible. I wasn't sure when this day would arrive, but I'm glad it has reached us.

I shake my head in disbelief, rubbing my temples. Two conversations at once. I can't afford to have an argument with my new companions or the mystical Lord of Light, especially not at the same time. One of them needs to leave me alone.

We don't have time for that, Ermo.

"Well? Are you going to answer?" Yarwin steps forward, fire in his eyes. "Or are you just going to stand there, muttering to yourself?"

"I lost a lot of people today too, you know," I say. "You are angry because I killed your family. Yet were you not the aggressor?"

Koric spits. "You're Accursed, we have a duty—"

"Silence, boy," Yarwin says. "If you've not already realized we're in the middle of something inexplicable, you need to fix that head on your shoulders right now. We need to grieve our brothers. We *must* grieve them. But we also have something more pressing before us. I'll ask you the same question I asked you outside. Did you not see the shadows that assaulted us from the mists?"

Koric grimaces, either in response to Roan tightening a bandage or Yarwin's words. "Yeah. I saw them. Probably witchcraft. Accursed magic from her."

I throw my hands in the air. "You're kidding, right? Those things were attacking my men too. I saved us. I helped bring us here. I don't know what those things were—"

"Why should we believe you?" says Roan, speaking for the first time since we entered the tower. She holds in her hand a cracked, two-ringed orb—sunsteel and moonstone, I suspect. "This thing brought us here, not you. Not you. Some power, through this artifact . . ."

Yarwin glances at Roan. "That's what you stole, then."

The girl nods.

I tilt my head, intrigued. "Stole? And let me be clear, the very power lighting this room right now—from me—is the same power that brought us here. *From me.*" I wave my hand all around, indicating the glow emanating in the air. With the snap of my fingers, the light extinguishes. A second later, I bring it back again. "I have a power unseen for generations. I didn't ask for it, but I have it. Through that artifact, we traveled here. Using my power. And we need to learn why."

"No." Koric rises to his feet. Yarwin raises a hand to stop him, but Koric brushes it away. "If you have power to bring us here, take us back. Take us back to the army, to the lands of our people. This is ridiculous. We aren't your friends. We aren't your allies. We aren't going to help you with whatever Accursed goal you have here."

They have no choice. The artifact is broken. It will not work again.

Well, at least the voice is being helpful this time. I gesture toward Roan. "That orb, in your hands. Do you think it still works?"

Roan looks from her brother to Yarwin, then to me. "No. It doesn't. In the past, when I've made contact with it, skin-to-steel, I've always seen things. Visions. Now . . . nothing. I feel nothing. It's scarred, it's burned, it's broken."

Koric runs a hand through his hair, clearly exasperated. "But you said . . ." He wags a finger at me. "You *said* it was your power that brought us here."

Before I can reply, Yarwin shakes his head. "You aren't understanding, my boy. She's something we don't understand. I don't think she understands herself. Her power may have brought us here, but it worked through that artifact in your sister's hands. So if that thing is broken, we can't use it to return home."

"Wait!" Roan steps in front of her brother. "What if . . . what if we can fix it here? What is this place anyway?"

"A place of ancient power," Yarwin mutters. "I'm more interested in *where* we are, personally."

"I have my theories," Koric says, resting a hand on Yarwin's shoulder. He has apparently forgotten his conflict with me. "We're in a desert, that's—"

You must join me at the top of the tower. All of you. The world depends on it.

The Lord of Light again, pushing and pushing and pushing. I turn away from the three as they discuss, trying to listen to the words in my mind.

Now. Death. Shadows. Increasing in speed, the Lord of Light's ramblings become nonsensical, bordering on madness. *War. War. War. War. My mistake. Now that you're here, you'll learn my mistake. But the world depends on it. Everything you've done—that we've done together—it's all been building toward your arrival here. Here. The Pillar. Power. Here find power—new power. In unexpected places.*

I shake my head, fighting against the urge to scream. Picking up a rock, I imbue it with light and toss it at their feet. "I'm forging ahead. Scouting our immediate surroundings, at least. Make up your minds together. Or separately. You can sulk in this tomb, but it won't change things. When you're ready to discover why we came here, I'll be waiting."

Welcome to my home, Ermo. All of this will be explained, soon. And it will all be over soon, too.

III

ROAN

As Ermo walks away, I slump against a stone pillar, exhausted. The glowing rock she left for us illuminates the room with a dim, white light, barely enough to reveal the ornate carvings engraved into the walls. Though white sand covers the ground in little dunes, the metallic sheen of the structure is unaltered by the desert elements. What is this place?

"We should go after her," Yarwin says. I look up, watching him stride away.

My brother shakes his head. "Let her go. Stay with us. We may need to follow her eventually, but hell, just slow down for a moment, old man. We need to chat, the three of us, and figure out our plan moving forward."

Yarwin pauses, looks back at us, and nods. "Fine. Koric, you're still the captain here. I'll acquiesce."

"Thank you."

I observe my brother and his mentor, noting their determination. They're scared. I am too. That much is apparent. The gears in their minds turn like clockwork as they ascertain our path. I'm attempting to answer the same question, but I can't even comprehend our options.

"All right." Koric inspects the bandages I've placed over his wounds and, with a curt grimace, closes his eyes. "Roan, you did a great job patching me up, but this is going to be rough now that the battle fever is leaving our blood. We can't trust her—Yarwin, don't give me that look, we can't—but that doesn't mean we shouldn't use her. Thoughts? What do we do? Where are we?"

Yarwin places a hand on one of the pillars and stares at the sand, clearly contemplating.

I grunt. "Koric . . . we're in over our heads. I don't know if there is a way to make a plan that isn't just guesswork." I slide up the edge of the pillar and to my feet. "I suppose . . . we could attempt to break apart those boulders. But presumably, those snakes are still out there. What were those, anyway? If we don't go outside, our only option is to explore this tower." I swallow, considering my next words closely. I don't want to upset my brother. "While I'm not saying we should trust her, she is correct. We were pulled here. I felt the power surging between us. I can't explain it. Something pulled us here, and shouldn't we wonder what that means?"

Koric shakes his head. "Don't start spouting nonsense about fate and life and God's plan for us, Roan."

"That's not what I was talking about at all."

"We protect our *own*," Koric says. "And right now, it's just you and Yarwin and me. We need to figure out how to protect ourselves from—"

With a loud smack, Yarwin's hand connected with Koric's cheek. "Don't call her Accursed again."

"What—"

"Have you forgotten any of the stories I've told you over the years? Even in the past few days?"

I nod. "I remember. What you and the company found during the first invasion. Those camps. The Inquisition's camps."

"Precisely." Yarwin walks toward one of the walls, pivots, and faces us. "Our nation has been torturing their people for a generation. The hatred runs even deeper. For too long, we've believed they were Accursed. Koric, you know better than most the evil of the Inquisition. Is it too difficult to believe we're wrong about them?"

"It's not just the Inquisition that has taught us of their devilry, though," Koric replies. "Yes, the Inquisition is evil. Her people are still *our* enemy, though. She could be deceiving us."

I frown, not sure who I agree with. I see both their points.

Though, I'm not certain how either approach applies to Ermo specifically. Her people might be evil, but . . . "How did she convince our own citizens to fight by her side? Did they look twisted? They looked happy. Happy! And they pitied us as they defeated us in battle. You don't inspire that sort of devotion through fear and cruelty."

"I don't think I understand," Koric replies.

"You took me with you to a meeting with General Wellor, remember. I saw what that Inquisitor could do. Nobody batted an eye as a fellow Captain was murdered."

Yarwin shakes his head. "Koric, you must see what she's saying."

Koric steps toward the older man. "No, I can't believe it. I won't believe it. The Inquisition may have its talons in all the wrong places, but we do not fight for them. We fight for each other. For our families in Esmeraldi. In all the cities of the Empire. We fight for them."

"Do we?" Yarwin sighs. "What good has war brought our people?"

"We've protected them against threats unknown! The giants in the Far North? You don't think that fight was worth it? Or the Sea Peoples? They raid our shores all the time. We protect our people."

"And yet we also attack, just like we are attacked. We attack and invade and attempt to crush the Accursed."

It's my turn to shake my head. Our arguments run in circles. They're in each other's faces, yelling and spitting. It's going nowhere. Slowly, I slide away from them and toward the hallway. Koric and Yarwin's voices echo within the confines of the small foyer, but with each step, they sound a little quieter. They don't notice me sneaking away.

They can continue to bicker. I'm going to follow Ermo. The path she is taking we will need to traverse eventually. Might as well start now. We may not be able to trust her, but I can learn from her without Koric poisoning the air in the room. His anger worries me, but he is grieving. We're all grieving.

I think Ermo is grieving.

I'm almost in complete darkness, the shadows overtaking, when I turn a corner and discover a waiting, glowing rock. Ermo left us a trail of breadcrumbs. I pick up the stone to use as a light and continue down the corridor. Like the entrance foyer to the tower, its walls are made of a shiny metal. Sunsteel, most likely, based on its slight golden glow.

The tunnel slopes upward a few meters later, in a subtle leftward curve. The ramp follows the outer wall of the tower, by my reckoning, and after a good minute of an upward trek, I reach a level platform. To my left, a door opens into what I imagine is the second floor. If I follow the outer wall, the ramp continues spiraling.

"Simple enough design," I mutter. I shuffle down the hallway of the second floor, and it opens into a larger room—an amphitheater of some sort. In its center, Ermo sits, cross-legged.

"Where are the other two?" she says, not looking toward me.

"Thanks for leaving a light." I ignore her question and stride down the stone steps. Trotting onto the stage, I plop and sit across from her. "They're still arguing downstairs. So. Who are you really?"

Ermo tilts her chin toward me. For the first time, I get a good look at the grey- and green-skinned woman. Her hair is cut short—artificially colored, based on its sheen. A shade of red, I think. I remember first seeing it on the battlefield. Scars line her cheeks, and her hands—they appear perpetually burned. Almost blistered, the skin an ugly pink. But it doesn't look painful. Her loose armor fits her form, though I think it's strong enough to survive a direct blow from an overhead strike. Resting on the ground next to her is a spear—that powerful spear from which incredible destruction emanates. The large hammer strapped to her back looks deadlier, but I know better from seeing her in action.

After we continue staring at each other for quite some time, she sighs. "Who am I really?" Her eyes flit away, and she almost looks like as if she's hearing the voice of another. After a quick nod, she refocuses on me. "I am Ermo, daughter of Mono and Ero, granddaughter of Maripes, Daughter of Light and Herald of the People of Light. And a dozen other names they've attached to me. Do any of them define me? I don't know. Maybe. Maybe not. None of it matters. Who I am to me matters, and I am the person who will break down the walls between our people. Between the People of Light and the Holy Empire."

I blink after realizing how I've widened my eyes. Her words aren't what I expected. Once again, she proves how she is certain of herself—and she also knows exactly who people believe her to be. "Why?" I say. "Why do you believe you will destroy a thousand years of history on your own?"

"Not alone." She glances to the side. "At least, I wasn't alone. Not until those things attacked us. I had my battalions. I had my guards. Both human and . . ." she struggled to find the right words in my language. "What do you call us other than Accursed?"

I cringe. "I'm not aware of another term."

Ermo nods. "My guards quickly adopted the term 'People of Light,' and learned our language quickly, as I learned yours. A few terms still escape me though, and there are a few frustrations, like that one. Our language had an alternative term for our people, taken from our scriptures. Orc. It's the term in our language supposedly derived from your word 'Accursed,' but I think it's been lost in translation over the years."

I nod, not sure why she's spilling so many thoughts at once. I don't mind it, though. At first, I was terrified of her. Now, I'm breaking through the facade built in my mind. Ideas swirl. Considering everything I've experienced over the past few months, could she be right?

"Tell me." I swallow. "Why are you the one to save everyone? To bring our people together? To end the wars between our people?"

"Three reasons," she says. "First. You've seen what I can do. Have you ever met another person who can shoot light with their mind?"

"Actually," I reply, "I've seen it just once. An inquisitor struck down one of the captains in the army with a strange power. Red light."

Ermo squints. "Ah, yes, their strange sorcery. I've still not determined the source of that particular power."

"These powers," I say, "where do they come from?"

"It's complicated." She places a hand on her spear. "At first, I believed it came from the sunsteel and moonstone found in my weapons. This spear." She rests her other hand on the tool hanging from her back. "And this hammer. They are made from the metals of old. My grandfather, he was a master of smithing with sunsteel and moonstone. He died because of it."

"What did you say his name was?"

"Hm?" Ermo tilts her head to the side. "Maripes. His name was Maripes. And he was killed when he traveled to Esmeraldi in an attempt to form a treaty with your Empress."

"No. No. He assassinated—"

"Oh." Ermo laughs. "My grandfather assassinated your Empress? Who told you that lie?"

"The Inquisition—ah."

"Look, I don't know what happened. All we know is he left one day, never returned, and then a few months later, your armies burned Ut'ome to the ground. Maybe Maripes did assassinate your Empress. I don't know. But all evidence—everything we know about your High Inquisitor—says that story is most likely a lie."

"And how would you have any evidence of what happened in Esmeraldi?" I ask. I try to keep my tone level. I'm actually curious.

"Members of my guard—the humans—were in the city when Maripes visited. They told us about his execution. About what the Empress offered him, and the—"

"Roan, step away from her!"

Koric and Yarwin stride down the steps, blades in hand.

IV

ERMO

Oh look, they've come to collect their lost lamb, says the Lord of Light in my mind. Really? Strange time for sarcasm. Or humor. Or whatever he's attempting in the moment. I shake my head.

As Koric and Yarwin stride down the stairs, I stand, leaving my spear on the ground. Hands raised, I back away from the pair. "Look, we were just talking."

"Seriously, nothing to worry about," Roan says from my side. She's standing too. "If we're going to be stuck with her for quite some time, I figured I might as well talk to her."

"Roan, you can't just sneak away from us like that," Koric says.

His blade points toward me, though his hand is barely gripping the hilt. Yarwin is already sheathing his weapon. I like him—I think. Koric, though—he's going to be a problem. *Oh, I don't know about that. I think all three of them are problems. There will be a way to bring them all into the fold soon enough, though.*

The Lord of Light needs to shove his mind out of mine.

I'm not going to. Not yet. Something you need to see first.

Great.

"—was just telling me about her power," Roan says. In the midst of my argument with the Lord, I missed a few of her words. "Where it comes from. Aren't you just a bit curious?"

"I'm quite curious," says the old man.

"No, not really." Koric finally sheathes his weapon. "Come on. We need to chat."

Roan glances up at me. I nod and motion with my chin for her to join her brother, but she shakes her head. "No," she says. "Koric, she is with us. She's not our enemy. We can't just ignore what's happening here."

I smile, appreciating her quick shift in support. At least, I hope it's support. "Look, I know we fought on the battlefield just a few hours ago, but war is war. You're a soldier. You understand how war works. We *must* put it behind us to figure out what's going on. Those specters . . . I don't know what they were. And I think the answers are here, in this tower."

"Koric, let's hear her out," says Yarwin. "She has a point. Surely you see it."

The younger man places a hand on his hip. "Fine. Yes, fine. We'll hear you out. We'll work with you."

Yarwin chuckles. "Good, because I think your sister and I were going to listen to her anyway. You would have been pretty bored for the next few hours if you sat this out." The old man steps onto the stage, drops his weapons to the ground, and sits down. Roan plops beside him, and with a begrudging huff, Koric joins them both.

Before me, three citizens of the Holy Empire sit waiting. Watching. Wanting me to speak. All the confidence drains from my blood. I've claimed I have answers, but I don't have any. I have no idea what's happened to us.

You have the answers. At least, some of them. Speak. The truth will follow.

Finally, the Lord of Light says something useful. I clasp my hands above the waist. "All right. Where to start . . ."

"Why not pick up where we left off?" Roan says.

"I guess that'll work."

"I heard your last few words," says Yarwin. "You were discussing the assassination of Empress Emelia the Second."

"Yes." I sigh. "Maripes, the one you all know as her assassin, was my grandfather."

They all nod in agreement, though Koric's eyes squint suspiciously.

"Maripes did not murder your Empress. He was sent to you all on a diplomatic mission to establish trade between our peoples.

Specifically, he was offering your Empress his talents as a smith of sunsteel and moonstone."

"Impossible," says Koric. "It's impossible to work those metals."

I raise an eyebrow. "And who told you that?"

"The . . ."

"The Inquisition?" I reach over my shoulder and bring my hammer—Maripes's hammer—into full view. "I wield two weapons. My spear—the *Flame of Maripes*, was used by my father Mono above the Chasm to defeat your armies as they attempted to assault Lethotar. And my hammer—*Thunder*. It's the hammer originally used by my grandfather to smelt sunsteel and moonstone, both for our people . . . and for your Empress."

"Impossible," Koric says. "Utterly impossible. This is nonsense. This is madness. I know the Inquisition lies to us, but to lie about the death of our Empress? The High Inquisitor is her brother!"

"And her son became the heir upon her death, with the Inquisitor as his regent." Not my words, but Yarwin's. "Koric, I wasn't at the final battle of the war when we supposedly defeated Lethotar, but I knew soldiers who were. We—the Slaying Swords—we were stationed at the Gates of Vicor. I saw the faces of the soldiers returning home. The inquisitors leading them . . . no one was allowed to talk. Suspiciously, I never saw many of those soldiers again. The campaign seemed too clean, the war too perfect. We *defeated* her people at the chasm, but no garrison was ever placed in Lethotar. Why? I know men who were stationed at the Gates of Vicor throughout the occupation. I heard stories . . ."

"Stories of demons in the night?" I tense, remembering the slave camp beneath Vicor's walls. "Creatures, undead, stalking the sewers and the caves? Your Inquisition . . . it's doing something to people. Changing them. Corrupting them. And it's a corruption that lasts after death. It affects not just my people, but your people too."

Yarwin nods. "Then it is as I have always feared."

Roan, sitting silently, suddenly perks up. "Ah! The story you told before we encountered Ermo's army! You know, about the Accursed—er, the People of Light—found in that camp during your first campaign. The camp led by the inquisition."

"Exactly," Yarwin says.

I tilt my head. "So you understand. As my troops have moved throughout the Three Valleys, we've been liberating camps all throughout the region. Starved souls—both our people, and your people—inside cages and prisons created by your Inquisition. The High Inquisitor is evil, and we must stop him. For the sake of all nations."

Silence, for just a moment. I remember the fiends, and I mourn River. I've not seen redemption of the dead since that day during the battle before the Gates of Vicor. We've not found many more shadow fiends, either, at least not in the quantities discovered in the sewers beneath the fortress. But Yarwin *knows* of what I speak. He's realizing the truth.

And Koric begins to chuckle. It's a low rumble, but it quickly transforms into a hearty laugh. "This is rich," he eventually says. "Everyone's the same in the end. The Holy Empire condemns your people as Accursed and evil. Our people believe your people assassinated our most beloved ruler in a generation. Your people defend against an invasion. Then, in return, you invade us the moment you have a chance. Now, you accuse our ruler of being evil." He rises and stumbles toward the stairs. "I'm going for a walk." He grabs one of the glowing rocks. "In the end, all that matters is that we protect our own. Roan, best you remember. This witch is trying to deceive us."

Before I can say a word, he sprints up the stairs. Moments later, Roan chases after her brother. Within seconds, I'm alone with Yarwin. He's sitting on the stage with me, staring. Observing.

"Why do you believe me, old man?" I say.

"I've seen a lot of crazy things during my life as a soldier." He rises to his feet. "Never before have I seen a woman shoot fire from her fingertips. I'd call it suicide not to listen to that woman."

Despite myself, I smile. After picking up my weapons and

returning them to their proper places on my body, I approach the man and hold out an arm. "For now, shall we be allies?"

He smirks. "Allies, we shall be." He grabs my forearm. "What do we do now?"

"Well, we're trapped in this tower." I twirl in place, taking in the indoor amphitheater. "We're going to need water sooner rather than later. Food too. I have a feeling the water solution will be easier. If this tower once housed people, it must have a source of water somewhere."

Yarwin, without saying a word, slowly heads toward the room's exit. I follow. He leads us down the spiral ramp. In the distance, arguing voices bounce off the walls. It sounds like Koric and Roan are back in the entrance foyer on the first floor, but Yarwin leads me right past that hallway and down the ramp into the tower's basement. His logic makes sense—if the building has water, the source will be from a spring. But the tower looks centuries—maybe millennia—old. I can't imagine it still has running water.

The ramp ends. Nearby, a bubbling sound rushes to meet us. Past a few strange pillars, Yarwin leads me straight to a pool of clear liquid filling a large metallic basin.

"Did you know this was here?" I say.

"Koric and I found it earlier when we were searching for Roan," he replies.

"You could have just said something."

"The look of surprise on your face was worth it."

With water staring me in the face, my parched lips ache for a taste. I lean over and engorge myself, drowning my throat in a cold wash. It's refreshing. It's the cleanest water I've ever experienced. I sense power emanating from the well, and I recognize the reality of the situation—the water isn't natural. No matter. It tastes like it'll help us survive.

"About finished?" says Yarwin.

I glance up at him, shaking my head. "Just because you already drank some earlier doesn't mean I can't replenish myself. Haven't had a drop to drink since before the battle started."

"A pity." He leans against a pillar. "Tell me, Ermo, daughter of Mono, granddaughter of Maripes. What do you think this place is?"

Are you going to tell him about me?

I swat away the Lord of Light's voice. "It's a place of Power, of the Ancients, of the People Who Time Forgot. Our Lord of Light was a citizen of those people before he founded our nation in the Three Valleys."

"Ah, that's what your legends say, yes?"

"Correct. That's my best guess about this place."

Close, says the Lord in my head. *Close. But not quite accurate.*

"Why do your eyes keep glazing over like that?" Yarwin says. "Every so often. It's like you're somewhere else."

"What are you talking about?" *He's talking about me.*

"Just there, it happened."

"Don't worry about it," I say. "I'm just thinking, that's all."

"Humph. Well, anyway, I like your theory, but it doesn't sit well with the histories of the Church. We speak of Wells of Life spread throughout the world. There's one in the Royal Cathedral of Esmeraldi. I remember hearing about one down near Tethys. They are real places."

"Wells? We have one in—"

"Yarwin!" It's Roan's voice, coming from upstairs. "Ermo! Come quick. I need your help!"

Without thinking, we both sprint up the ramp to find Roan standing at the crossroads.

"It's Koric," she says.

"What's the boy done this time?" Yarwin asks.

"He's not done anything," she retorts. "He's completely fainted." She sprints down the hallway.

I motion for Yarwin to lead, then follow after the man. We reach the entrance foyer, where we first found ourselves inside this strange pillar, and . . .

Koric is floating in the air, back arched, arms outstretched.

"Okay," Roan muttered, "he wasn't like this when I left him, I swear."

Koric's eyes glow. Seconds later, he drops to his feet. From his side, from his wound, faint light seeps.

"Roan?" He shakes his head. "Yarwin? What—"

Blinding brightness smothers the room. I cover my eyes, but the light isn't visible. It's just everywhere.

The shadows return.

Standing beside Koric, a shimmering figure in a golden cloak glows, staring at us.

"Welcome," he says, "to the Pillar of Life and Death and Eternity. I am Orion, your guide. Together, we will uncover your destiny."

INTERJECTION

KYRI

Ah. It's time to return to my story. You call them shadow fiends. Dark wolves. Darkness incarnate.

We call them "Demons-From-Above." Though, we didn't always use that name.

For many years, they were simply "demons."

And as a Vanguard of the Deep, under the tutelage of the Scion of the Vanguard, I was tasked with defending against the demons. In the Far Caverns, in the Near Caverns, in the Root of the World, in the Realm Below. Everywhere. And the demons were always there, lurking in the darkness.

When I was five-and-ten shardcycles old, I was sent on patrol into the Far Caverns. A twisting maze of rocky paths sometimes no wider than two vanguards, the Far Caverns are our most distant realm, hundreds of kilometers of passages interconnected across our western border. Few glowshards grow there, and only a thousand of our people dare live in the region, rather than in Shade or one of the other shadowland fortresses.

On that patrol, I discovered the truth of the demons. Their origin. Their creation.

Vanguards must scout alone; there's too much ground to patrol, otherwise. And from shadow to shadow I slid, using power trained and refined with the Scion. I can bend through light, you see. Create its absence. Shift into a form unseen.

Crouching and creeping, I approached a tunnel recently unearthed by rock fall. Our seismometers detected it a few days prior. With each step, I reached out, seeking any light-signs of nearby demons. Nothing. No—not nothing. There were a few, and they were weak. Almost nonexistent.

And then . . . something else. A new light-sign, one I'd never felt before. I slipped to the next shadow. Approaching my destination, I released a sharp breath, an emerald blade forming in my hand. It never hurt to be on-guard.

I arrived at an outcropping, and past its edge, a much larger, wider cavern expanded upward. Below, a long chamber spread, left to right. And across from me, standing on a ledge, were two men in crimson robes. Over the edge, they lobbed a body. No—not a body. A demon. Beneath their cliff, in our Far Caverns, the brittle and mangled corpses of demons sprawled across rocks and refuse. Except, since they were demons, they weren't all dead. After a few moments, the demon last thrown awoke, and it limped into the shadows.

As quickly as possible, I hurried back to the closest seismo-station. Our outposts in the deepest expanses of the shadowlands, they were my home. My Scion waited, as commander of the Vanguard of the Deep. I arrived. I told him what I'd seen. He laughed, believing my story false. And before I knew it, I was shipped back to Shade.

In that moment, I recognized the truth. The demons weren't a natural reality of our existence. They were thrown to us, by the People-Who-Lived-Above. The Triumvirate taught us those people were afraid of the shadowlands. The Triumvirate taught us they lived in fear on the surface, underneath an endless expanse of "sky" so large, it cast immeasurable fear into their surface-dwelling hearts. The Triumvirate taught us demons constantly accosted their people too, making life a wretched existence.

The Triumvirate was wrong. The People-Who-Lived-Above sent the demons to us. They created the scourge constantly disrupting and ruining lives. And our leaders did nothing about it.

I—who dances amongst the shadows, who bends light to his will—I resolved, upon my return to Shade, that I would begin to make things right.

VI

ERMO

With a flourish, I brandish my spear and point it straight at the chest of the apparition. Yarwin similarly unsheathes his sword, as does Roan. After Koric acquires his bearings and regains focus, he too pulls his blade and points it at the newcomer.

For once, Koric and I agree on something.

"What devilry are you?" I say, observing the glowing man. I step forward. My spear reaches his chest, touches it, and passes through. Nothing happens. It's as if the man doesn't know I'm piercing him.

"I am Orion," he repeats. "I am speaking to you partially from the past, partially from the present, and partially from the future. I am sorry, I will attempt to answer the questions I know you have, but I can only predict so much."

I step back, joining the arc of our little party surrounding him. And—

Ah, here we go, says the Lord of Light inside my head. *I was wondering when this would happen. I've arrived.*

Of course the apparition is the voice inside my head. Not exactly what I expected.

Well what did you expect? A warrior? A god? A handsome dashing politician? I am who I was, and who I was when I sent that message doesn't yet understand everything.

Of course, the voice isn't going to help me understand.

If I help you understand, then what needs to happen will not happen. This might be the last time you hear my voice. At least you made it this far.

I shake my head, confused by his words and unsure what to

think. I refocus on Orion, who has strangely been waiting for me to look at him.

"I don't understand everything," he says once I make eye contact. "I only know a sliver of the future, informed by the past, understood by my actions in the present. But you four . . . of you four, someone will save the world from my mistakes."

"Your mistakes?" says Yarwin. "Who are you really, Orion?"

Orion turns toward Yarwin. "I am exactly the person you believe me to be. I am the Lord of Light—though in my day, that name means nothing. I am also the Saint—the supposed founder of the Church. That one I find the most interesting. History is a fickle thing. Who I really am is less important, though, than how you four will react to what I tell you."

"Then get on with it," Koric scoffed. "Tell us what we must do."

With a pivot—a strange, gliding pivot—Orion faces the other man. "Ah, the stubborn one. Well, let's get to it. Here's the truth. I have made a mistake. My partner, the one I love, he is . . . lost. He has fallen. Together, we tried to create life, but all we have created is death. You, centuries in the future—I'm not actually sure how far in the future you are—must face the consequences of our choices. I am sorry." He pauses, clasping his hands above the belt line. "We dabbled in magic beyond our understanding. The world, and its mysteries, go far beyond anything we can understand. In your day, you will view the artifacts and power of my day with awe and wonder. If only you could see the mystery and majesty of what we can really do. No, you wouldn't want to. You would see the terror we've brought upon the world."

His words have pulled us all in. We're listening. Waiting. I know a little about being told my destiny. I tried to fight it once. I walked right into it. I'm curious to see what the others will do.

Orion's lull continues, as if he is taking time to think and compose his words. His particular magic intrigues me, and it makes me wonder. What power exists beyond the magic connected with sunsteel and moonstone? I have *that* power. What other power can people wield? Of course, there's the sorcery of the Inquisition.

I'll need to think more on the question.

"I need the orb," Orion says. "One of you has the orb." Orion raises a hand to his neck, pulls, and unclips a necklace. Holding it outward in his hand, he shows the same orb. "I created it for this purpose. In my time, it is here, and through one of you, you've been pulled here. And now, we can have this conversation."

I look to my side, and Roan is nodding. She steps forward, holding out the now scarred orb.

Orion's head bobs. Not exactly a nod, but something similar. "Brought together over time and space, we shall see what happens. Come closer, child."

Koric looks like he's going to object, but Roan shushes him with a flutter of her hand. She steps forward, holding the orb, and *moves* through the visage of our visitor.

"As I expected," Orion says. "Its power is gone. To where, I do not know. It's one of the questions I don't know the answer to. But the fact that its power has left ensures you are on the right path. You four will save the world."

I shake my head. More riddles. More non-answers. I point my finger straight at his face. "Look, Orion. Lord of Light. Whoever you are. You've taunted me for years now, taken me on too many journeys of destiny and fate. Speak candidly. What must we do?"

In response, Orion smiles. He looks upward, toward the ceiling, and points. "You must reach the top of the tower. From there, you will have everything you need to rid the world of the shadows plaguing it. But rest assured– this is not an ordinary war. You cannot win by slaying the shadows with the sword. The mistake I made created them, and in our time, they still roam the world, seeking their goal. In your time, their true form has been forgotten, and some seek to recreate them. I can't tell you what I don't know. I don't know what you face, who you must face, who you must defeat, and how. But I do know, at the top of the Pillar of Life and Death and Eternity, the pathway to unlock those answers exists. This is a place of infinite possibility—use it wisely."

And with those final words, Orion vanishes. Roan steps back;

the orb in her hand glows. It, too, vanishes.

"What now?" Koric says. "That was . . . ridiculous, to say the least. If that thing hadn't healed me, I would have thought I was hallucinating from infection sickness."

"We were definitely all seeing the same thing," I reply.

"I don't know about destiny," Koric says, "but at the very least, maybe the top of this pillar will give us a way home." He falls back against a nearby column and sits in the sand. "Ermo. I still don't trust you. But this is all very wild. My sister and Yarwin seem to trust you. I'm willing to move forward."

I close my eyes, almost hoping for the Lord of Light to speak again. Silence. "I'm glad to hear that, Koric," I say.

"Well, I don't know how much of a rush we're supposed to be in," Yarwin adds, "But I think we all might need some sleep."

With that comment, Roan yawns. "I agree," she says, laughing. Yarwin chuckles too, then both Koric and I join in, the smiles refreshing our weary souls.

"I'll take first watch," I say. "I don't think I'd be able to sleep right away." I hold up one of my glowing rocks. "I'll be just down the hall."

VII

ROAN

Before sleeping, Yarwin pointed me in the direction of the spring in the basement. After refreshing and drinking multiple gulps of water, I make my way back to our little campsite. Ermo leans against the wall at the base of the ramp, and down the hallway, Yarwin and Koric chat quietly. I snuggle between two fractured stones.

I struggle to find a comfortable position on the coarse ground. My mind floats in a whirlwind, considering our circumstance. We've uncovered something truly unbelievable.

Losing my strange orb hollows my heart. I was always scared of it, knowing *it* originally made me a fugitive. Without it, I never would have joined my brother and the Slaying Swords, nor would I have fought in a war. And somehow survive. Now, the little magic orb, its visions of the past, and its time-breaking powers . . . gone. Forever. My chest aches. Even when I'd forgotten it, it became a part of me.

The thought of destiny, though, pulling us here. To this pillar. We couldn't have done it without the orb. The orb I stole from the vault of the palace in Esmeraldi. Of all the paths I could have taken, I was led straight to Ermo. And with Ermo, we were brought here. But that transportation—that power to leap across time—it came from me and the orb.

I felt it. In the moment. Ermo helped, yes, but the power surged through me. I've seen what she can do. I know her abilities. I wonder if I have something similar inside me. Yet right now, I merely feel hollow. Like I've lost a loved one to the plague.

"Roan?"

I look up. Koric is nestling against a pillar, eyes drooping.

"Yes?"

"Thank you for staying level. Taking care of me." He tilts his head toward Yarwin, the man asleep against a wall. "He agrees. You've shown composure and balance throughout all of this. You've proved your grit as a member of the Slaying Swords."

"We're all that remains of the company," I say.

"And as I've been saying, we *protect our own*. But I'm not going to say it with as much vehemence as in the past. I think . . . I think we can trust her."

"I do too."

"But I'll still be on my guard. Promise me you'll do the same."

"I will."

And with those words, we both drift to sleep.

* * *

I wake up to the smell of . . . breakfast?

As my eyes open, aches and sores pop into focus. My joints scream, not just from sleeping on rough ground, but from leftover pains caused by yesterday's battle.

Was it really only yesterday that the Slaying Swords charged across a misty battlefield? I can't believe it.

The scent sharpens, and I roll over to face the tiny fire in the middle of our camp. Yarwin is sitting there, stoking small flames. On outstretched sticks, mushrooms roast. Where did he find wood? Doesn't matter. My stomach growls, and I scoot toward the fire.

To my left, Koric still sleeps, leaning against a pillar. Close to the pile of rubble blocking our original entrance to the tower, Ermo rests. With her eyes closed, she looks peaceful, her fiery demeanor taken over by a facade of calm. Of serenity.

As if she can hear my thoughts, her eyes flutter open. A few moments later, Koric awakens as well. We're all sensing the meal Yarwin's concocting.

"I found 'em downstairs, with the water." He lifts one of the kabobs. "I recognize the species, safe to eat. Delicious too, if I remember correctly."

"Yarwin, leave it to you to find edible mushrooms in the middle of an abandoned magic pillar in the middle of the desert." Koric yawns, chuckles, and rolls over onto his elbows. Whatever power healed him yesterday, it definitely helped him feel more chipper.

"Thank you for making a meal," Ermo says, nodding. "It's appreciated. And I've had a lot of time to think overnight. Or whatever time it is. Thank you, all of you, for trusting me."

Koric grunts, but I smile. I say, "To be honest, I think we need to thank you for trusting in us." Glancing at her spear and hammer, resting against the wall, I add, "These two might be great fighters—Yarwin, at least—but they wouldn't have stood a chance against you."

"Hey!" Koric gives me a mock glare. "I'm at least better than Yarwin . . ."

With a raised eyebrow, Ermo sighs. "I wish all of this could have gone another way. Pitted against one another like pawns in some great game? Do you not see how we're laughing here, talking, eating? This is how I lived with my vanguard in our army. We were friends. Humans and orcs, for lack of a better term. The People of Light and the people of the Holy Empire, thriving side-by-side. It's a future we can have if we try."

I steal a glance toward Koric, who's looking across the fire at Yarwin. The two men, motionless, communicate through their eyes. I wish I knew the thoughts dancing between them. Koric says we must protect our own, but I wonder—why *isn't* Ermo one of our own now? She's fought by our side to protect us and keep us safe from the shadows and the snakes. She hasn't threatened us. Why can't she join us?

"Well, mushrooms are finished," Yarwin says, standing. He passes around kabobs stuck with mushrooms then leans against the wall, ready to eat. I look back and forth between our motley crew. No one is willing to take the first bite.

"Well." I sniff the fungus. "I think it smells better than the roasted mushrooms dad served at the bar."

"Hah!" Koric shakes his head. "If that's not an endorsement, I don't know what is." He takes a bite. Swallows. Tilts his head. With a curt pursing of his lips, he nods. "Not your best, but not your worst." He takes another bite.

Yarwin shakes his head before nibbling his own meal. We all dive in, and I think I agree. It's not bad; there's just no flavor. It's a rubbery, chewy mess. But it's food. And we definitely need it. The moment I awoke, my body growled for sustenance. The mushrooms aren't going to satiate my whole appetite, but at least they'll give us energy.

Once we all finish our meals, Yarwin continues stoking the fire, keeping it warm. Ermo stands, donning her chest plate, gauntlets, and grieves. I slept in my leather armor, as did Koric and Yarwin. I'm ready to go.

A question floats in my mind, though—go where?

"So." Yarwin takes a step back from the fire. "Are we really going through with this crazy plan to discover a secret power at the top of the tower?"

"Do we really have any other choice?" Koric twitches his chin toward the ruins blocking the entrance. "Rabid snake creatures outside, or a magic ruin with an old crazy guy who is talking to us from the past? I choose the old crazy guy."

"Hey, be nicer to Yarwin," I say.

Koric stops, stares at me, and laughs. Another hearty laugh. And Yarwin shakes his head too. Ermo, for her part, slightly grins, but with a slight pounding of a fist on her chest, she finishes donning her armor. Without a word, she picks up her spear and hammer, walks past the fire, and heads toward the hallway leading to the spiraling ramp.

"I'm heading up the tower," she says. "I hope the three of you will join me."

"Right to it, then." Yarwin picks up his own bags, strapping them to his back. He slides his sword inside its sheathe between his shoulders and grabs his staff from the wall. I'm impressed he managed to hold onto everything amidst the chaos of yesterday. All I have left is my sword, which I retrieve from its resting place against a downed pillar. After Koric and I strap our swords to our backs, we're ready to go.

Ermo didn't wait, however, so we jog down the hallway, one of her glow rocks in hand. The large woman awaits us, standing on the ramp.

"Glad you're joining me," she quips. "Who knows what we'll find up there."

"I'm a bit excited," I reply. "You know, the other day when we woke up, preparing to fight your army, I thought—if only we were in the middle of the desert exploring a mysterious pillar. That sounds like fun."

As Ermo begins walking up the ramp, she snaps her fingers, and a small orb of light floats above our heads. "I know you joke, but I appreciate the effort," she says. "I suspect, though, we'll need to suffer without humor for a moment. We *do not* know what we will find upstairs, and we must be on our guard. Are the three of you ready for what we might find?"

"We are," Koric says, answering as our captain. "Should our weapons be on the ready?"

"I don't think so," she says. "At least, not yet. I can't imagine anything living has survived in here. Though, I suppose, the entrance was open until we crashed it downward. There could be creatures—or people—living upstairs. Yet, I imagine if any persons lived here, they would have investigated us by now. Or we would have seen signs of them."

"I think that's a fair assessment," Yarwin says. "Of course, I imagine some rodents or other desert critters have found their way in here. With that ample water source downstairs, it's bound to be a popular attraction."

"Makes you think," I muse. "Did we just ruin the lives of a bunch of rats?"

"Somehow, I'm not pitying them." Koric accelerates, passing me to match Ermo's stride. We walk right by amphitheater's doorway. "So we just head straight to the top?"

"Do you have a better plan?" Ermo says. With another step, we begin the next upward spiral, entering unexplored territory.

"Well," Koric says, "We don't exactly know how far we have to go. Might be worth knowing what we're passing."

"I'm not sure we have the time," Ermo replies. "If we want to find a way back to the battlefield—to our soldiers—we need to move as quickly as possible."

"Is that your goal?" I ask from a few feet behind. "To return to your soldiers? What about the greater fate that Orion spoke of? That Lord of Light?"

"I believe it's all connected, yes." She speaks to my question while continuing to face away from me. "He spoke of shadows plaguing the world. Doesn't that describe those things that appeared on the battlefield? If we're to rid the world of the shadows, we need to return as quickly as possible."

"Fair enough," Koric says. "But Roan's orb. It's gone. Seems a bit convenient if there's another magical artifact up there that'll teleport us back."

"Fate is often convenient," Yarwin mutters.

We reach the third level. A hallway, to the left, is covered in cobwebs. Ermo peers in for a second, shakes her head, and motions for us to continue upward.

"How many floors, do you imagine?" asks Koric.

"The spiral is slowly tightening as we head upward," she says. "The base floor was probably a hundred meters wide or so? I'd suspect the top is half that. I tried to get a good look at the pillar when we arrived. I'm guessing at least twenty floors. If not more. And the spiral may shift partway up, we don't know. Who knows what they thought when they built this place. Or maybe physics don't even apply in here."

Continuing onward in relative silence, we reach the fourth floor. The door is shut, with strange markings all over it. We examine it for a moment, but it seems inconspicuous. Merely a shut door. We all agree it's best to continue upward.

The fifth floor. Inky blackness dominates the entryway, and we all shuffle away quickly. It's disturbing and strange, but it doesn't feel threatening.

The sixth floor. Looking through the doorway, we see a completely empty room. Just . . . white floors. White walls. That's it. I'm beginning to suspect each floor had a distinct purpose. Almost like experiments of some sort. Orion's words implied he created something terrible here. The shadows. What else might have been created inside these terrifying rooms?

We reach the seventh floor. Before we can look through the door—a rumble. The floor groans. We turn around, and—

A wall.

The ramp is gone.

We're trapped.

Koric whips around, and swiftly kicks the wall. Nothing happens, other than his boot connecting with stone. He growls, angry, and steps back. "Ermo, fix this!"

Ermo is already facing the wall, spear in one hand, hammer in the other. "Stand back."

We all move behind her.

With a sharp cry, she swings the hammer overhead and slams it against the wall—a flash of light arcs from the spear. It cracks, it sparks, it doesn't mar the smooth wall.

"Devilry," Koric says. "Absolute devilry. We've come here to die."

"Calm down." Yarwin grabs Koric by the collar and pulls him against the side wall of the ramp. "We cannot afford to descend into hysterics."

"Hysterics? I'm not hysterical. I'm being realistic. We're stuck in a magic pillar with no way to escape!"

Ermo pays the two men no attention, opting to storm past them and toward the next part of the spiral. She pauses. She listens. She glances at the seventh floor's door.

She holds up a hand. "Quiet. Both of you."

They stop talking.

"Listen," she hisses.

As we all go silent, I try to sense what she senses. I hear nothing. No sound. My eyes continue drifting toward the mysterious wall. A trap? Certainly triggered by us, but what is its intention? Who placed it here? Or is it old magic, long forgotten? My chest burns. My arms ache. I can't—

There's the sound.

A distant gurgle, a sputter, a whoosh of air. Growls. Groans.

"Ermo," I whisper. "What are we—"

She places a foot on the upward ramp, motioning for us to follow.

I don't think. I just trust. I step forward, joining her. A second later, Koric and Yarwin stand beside us. We backpedal up the ramp, slowly. I don't know when I unsheathed my blade, but the sword now rests in my hand.

The seventh floor landing stands empty, but its shadows grow, creeping toward the ramp. And then, like a nightmare, a monstrous creature slithers through the doorway.

And not only one. Another. And another. Three, four, five, six—they fall upon each other in a grotesque dog pile, hissing and growling and groveling at the base of the ramp.

"No," Ermo says. "Not again. Not here."

"What are those things?" Koric bends his knees, ready to fight.

"Fiends. Dark wolves. Demons. Creatures of darkness and shadow. I defeated them once, but . . . these look different. Stronger."

The creatures' eyes twitch, glowing red. They eye the ramp. They spot us. The first one, the largest, it snarls and rears.

Ermo exhales sharply. "Run."

VIII

ERMO

How do I tell them I don't know how to save them?

"Run." I repeat the word, noticing none of us have started running. I summon all the power welling in my soul. Channeling it through *Flame of Maripes*, a white beam of energy lashes toward the fiends. It strikes the first one straight in the face, vaporizing its head.

With a howl, its compatriots scream. And a half-second later, my target's head regrows.

"Seriously, run!" I turn and sprint up the ramp. I don't look back, our footfalls echoing off the surrounding sunsteel. The creatures are uniquely vicious in their form, unlike the facsimiles we've discovered in Inquisition prisons and camps scattered throughout the Three Valleys.

Other. Unknown. Unimaginably deadly.

Up the ramp we sprint, muscles burning, bones aching. We pass floor after floor, but we can't stop to investigate or learn their secrets. I lose count as we climb, my mind focused on the ever-present snarls close behind.

The ramp continues spiraling, though the spirals shorten. The pillar is narrowing. At some point, we will reach the top. The summit. And then we'll have no choice but to fight. My mind boils with possibilities, imagining what terrain we might discover. Will we have cover? Does the pillar's peak have walls? Can I immediately blast these creatures right off the side and into the desert below?

I need to be ready. I hope everyone else is too. We'll only have—

A wall. The ramp ends. There's no door.

Wait, not a wall. It's a sliding panel, blocking our path. "Cover me!" I rush to the edge connecting the panel to the wall, sheathing my weapons in the process. "Roan, help me—Koric and Yarwin, cover us."

I don't wait to see if they follow my orders. There's enough space for my fingers to slip between the wall and the panel, and I pull. *Pull.* I don't care if my biceps tear from the exertion. We must break through. But I can't do it alone.

A second later, Roan crouches at my side, her hands sliding into place. Together, we pull, and the wall begins to creep. It's incredibly heavy. Probably hasn't moved in decades or centuries. But it moves. Slowly, but it moves into a crevice in the wall.

The snarls grow closer. My mind, momentarily, flashes to the battle before the gates of Vicor, when I fought side-by-side with fiends somehow ignoring their bestial nature. River led them. They were different than these things. Their souls were raw, fresh from the People of Light and the Holy Empire. How long had these things been trapped inside this pillar? What magic strengthens their skin, regenerating it upon destruction?

Slashes. Cries. Bellows. Yarwin and Koric, trained swordsman, will hopefully hold their own against the unimaginable monsters.

The panel budges, now providing almost a half-meter of space. I slide into the gap, pushing my back against the wall. My hands and legs brace the panel. "Go through. Now. Prepare to close it."

Roan complies, crawling under my legs and through the gap.

"Koric, Yarwin, now!"

Unintelligible yelling. Arguing? They're fighting somewhere around the curve. I can't see them, though shadows flicker. Then, Koric sprints up the ramp. Yarwin is backpedaling, using his long quarter-staff to smack the crouching creatures in a flurry of blows.

He's moving too slowly.

"What's he doing?" I say, not wanting to face the obvious truth.

Tears glisten on Koric's cheeks, visible as he dives beneath my legs. Once on the other side, he stands, ready to hold the panel for myself and Yarwin.

"Old man!" I shout.

He turns, only for a second. His eyes, clouded with determination, meet mine. He faces his enemies again.

"We'll hold it open for you!"

"No," he says, his voice steady. "They'll get too close. I see my purpose now. To get you all this far. You're the one that matters. You, and Roan, and Koric. Koric, don't be mad at me."

"No!" Koric's fist slams into the panel. Visceral hatred seeps from his glare. "Save him, Ermo!"

I look toward Yarwin.

The man spares a glance over his shoulder. He shakes his head. "Go!" And he barrels down the ramp into the group of fiends.

Not all of them follow. Two see us, and they pounce over Yarwin's head.

Koric growls, but I push him aside and leave the gap. "Close it!" Without waiting for Roan to respond, I lean against the panel and thrust it toward the open gap.

Fortunately, it slides easily into its original position. The space shrinks. A fiend's grotesque claws reaches through the gap.

Koric hacks it with his blade—and alongside a sickening crunch, the panel clicks into the wall. A writhing, violet hand twitches in the dim light from the glow rocks dropped on the ground by Roan. I step back, grab my spear, and blast the hand into oblivion. Only ash remains.

Before I can say a word or take another action, a fist connects with my chin, knocking me into the panel.

"You could have saved him!" Koric roars. He takes a step away, turns, and points his blade at me. "What type of coward flees a battle in the first seconds, leading us toward a dead-end? That should be you or me out there, sacrificing themselves for the survival of—"

I rise to my full height, surrounding myself in a white light drawn through *Flame of Maripes*. "Koric. Do not ruin Yarwin's sacrifice."

"It was a needless sacrifice!"

"Koric . . ." His sister approaches, placing a hand on his shoulder. "You know the truth. You saw what happened when Ermo attacked. I still can't believe it. Yarwin made—"

"You don't get it, do you?" Koric backs away from both of us. "Yarwin was more of a father to me than father was. That man practically raised me into the man I am today. Because of you"—he points a finger at me—"I've lost him. Forever." He looks around us, analyzing our new surroundings.

My eyes follow his, and I now notice the next door heading into the center of the pillar, like many others we've already discovered. The ramp, otherwise, continues upward.

"I'm done with your little adventure of fate," he adds. "Roan, coming with me?"

His sister shakes her head. "Koric, I—"

"Fine. Join the demon. Whatever."

He drops his sword to the ground and strides through the open doorway into darkness.

IX

KORIC

Seconds pass inside the darkness. I turn, facing the entrance—nothing. It's a wall. I place my hands on the smooth rock, finding it coarse and solid. *Impossible.* My anger simmers. I should be surprised, but with every turn, we've discovered something else impossible inside the tower.

As I contemplate my new predicament, I realize—I left Roan with Ermo. That Accursed monster. She's falling under her spell, and I left them alone. Bad move. Rash move. Father would be furious. Yarwin would chastise the mistake, even while trusting the woman.

Yarwin.

My heart throbs.

"Roan!" I shout. "Can you hear me?"

Silence.

I shift in the darkness, trying to acquire my bearings. A damp smell lingers in the air. "Hello?"

Silence.

I take a few steps forward, hands raised. I can't see a damn thing. Blast my failure to grab one of those glow rocks. Ermo might be an enemy, but she has her uses.

Slowly, I stumble forward, one foot at a time. The ever-present darkness swallows me, threatening to consume my senses. It's an inexplicable darkness, less an absence of light and more an absence of existence. I gingerly step into its daunting embrace.

My foot doesn't find a footing.

I fall forward, face first toward the floor. Except there is no floor. Vertigo sweeps my body, I'm tumbling through the air. So this is how I end.

I accelerate. Strangely, there's no wind, no rushing air bellowing my hair and skin. I know I'm falling, an unseen, shadowy ground pulls me downward. I want to scream, yet no sound escapes my lips.

My end. Death by magical pit. If it's like the stories, I'll fall for days on end, never finding a bottom. I'll die of starvation, or thirst, or madness. Or all three at once.

DARKNESS.

I stand on a battlefield, two armies facing one another. Grassy plains spread all around. I'm in the middle, between the two forces. To my right, golden armor adorned with streaks of red cloth. To my left, silver plate accompanied by blue silk. A trumpet blares. Cavalry charges.

I realize my predicament immediately. Trapped between two stampedes, I'll certainly die. All I can do is *run*.

And thus I run.

A rocky outcropping rises in the middle of the field. Either charge will need to navigate around it, otherwise their horses will trip, injuring themselves or worse. I'll be safe. Then, I can figure out what the hell is going on.

I push my legs, quads burning with a ferocity I've not felt in ages. My arms pump, reminding me of the sprints with Tylor in the fields outside Esmeraldi as a child. The memory reminds me of a distant day, without death or war.

The bittersweet memory sweeps away as I realize I'm not going to make it. My destination's a good hundred meters distant, and I can practically feel the ground shake with the stampede of both armies. I try to pick up my pace, but my breath cascades into wheezing. My heart aches.

Fifty meters. The armies are veering around the outcropping. Perhaps their column will avoid it more than I expect.

Thirty meters. I glance to the left, noting the four horsemen shifting toward me. Of course I'm a target. Of course.

Ten meters. Their almost on me. I have no choice—I turn, holding up my arms. "I surrender!"

They don't respond. A second passes, I scream, their horses barrel toward me, I—

DARKNESS.

My memory recalls the present. I am falling. Falling. Falling. Forever.

DARKNESS.

I stand in an alleyway. The rooftops I immediately recognize—Esmeraldi. Skulking behind barrels, three men brandish clubs. They're whispering. I sneak toward them.

"What're we looking at?" I say.

They don't respond. Instead, their leader—I assume he's the leader, since he's taken point—motions for them to leave the alley. The group rises, exiting onto a main causeway through our city. From other hiding places, another half dozen men appear. Their target?

Two guards, escorting a large man. No—not a man. An Accursed. His clothes bear similar markings to . . . someone. My mind is foggy, I can't remember everything. An elegant hammer loops through an ornate belt. It, too, triggers my mind. A memory. I should understand. I don't.

The leader turns to face his partners, his mouth and nose shrouded by a dark cloth. Before he speaks, he lowers the mask.

I recognize his face. It's too similar to my own. My father, in his youth.

"There's our target, right where the inquisitor said he would be. Remember. Take down the guards, let the big man escape. And no murders. We're not here to kill them. This is good coin." He raises the covering back over his nose.

My eyes widen in recognition. The Accursed before me—he's Maripes. The assassin of Empress Emelia. How did I never hear this story from my father?

The crowd of vagabonds charges. The guards scream. Maripes runs.

DARKNESS.

For a moment, I believe death has fully enveloped me. But before long, shadows coalesce around the outlines of a cavern. Subtle, simple light emanates from red mushrooms dotting rocky walls. I hear voices.

"Trallius, I'm telling you, we will continue to fail because we do not understand the origin of these creatures. Their true purpose. Their original intent."

Trallius. High Inquisitor Trallius. In a cave?

"Garis, we *must* understand what they are. If we understand what they are, we can ensure a proper pathway toward transforming the Accursed into their real form."

"But that's the problem! Every time we attempt to do so, we create those things!"

I've heard enough to know I must learn more. I creep deeper into the cave and around a corner. Standing above a cliff, torch in hand, Trallius lulls beside another inquisitor. The ruler of the Holy Empire looks significantly younger. A chiseled jaw, dark hair.

"Look at them," Trallius says. "Look at what they become. Compare it to what we become."

I walk up beside the two men, confident they can't notice me. Peering over the edge from my position, I see two pits. In one, a rabid fiend growls. It reminds me . . . of something. Of Yarwin. Yarwin's dead isn't he? No. Can't be. I'm misremembering. I turn to the second pit.

It holds a shimmering shadow, its outline glowing in the torch-light. It floats, an ethereal darkness pulsing inside.

"Not every time," says the other man—Garis. "More often than not, they both become the monster."

Yet true humans can never become this purely corrupted form. This docile shadow. From it, we can learn much. So very much."

"And what of the third shadow? The one we cannot create?"

DARKNESS.

I stand in a candle-lit room. Two men sit across the table from one another, deep in a heated discussion. Words bounce between their lips in a strange language, but somehow, my mind understands the tongue.

"Lucius, you *do not* need to go through with this experiment. Yes, the theory is sound, but that doesn't mean we should actually do it."

"You must trust me, brother. I believe in what you've discovered. We have the opportunity to ascend to a new form—why not take it?"

Each man leans back in their chair, sipping from what I surmise are cups of tea. I walk closer, noting gray robes emblazoned with a tree and cross reminiscent of the Inquisition's own symbols. It's more rigid in design.

"You could die." The unnamed speaker sets down his mug. "Or much worse."

"Yet this is what we've worked toward, is it not? It's why we built this place. Why we built all of them. To discover the secrets of the universe. To unlock immortality, unlimited power, and more."

"Certainly."

"Then we must move forward. We must put me through the test, and see what I become on the other side."

"And if you become a monster?"

"Then I become a monster. And you will move forward, learning what you can to ensure our world never faces monsters. Orion, this is our destiny."

I stumble backward at the sound of the word. Orion. The name of the supposed Lord of Light. My memories are fading in and out, but right now, I remember everything. I'm not an idiot—I see what's happening. These two men are discussing the creation of the monstrous, Yarwin-killing beasts. And though my memories fuzz, I know I've seen other related scenes. I'm being shown truth.

Before I know what's happening, I bump into the wall. It's physical, at least for me, and my tumble causes a glass vase to my left to crash from its perch. Into a million pieces it shatters, and with the sound of the crash, the two men look toward me.

"Who are you?" says Orion. "And what—hm, oh, he's a specter. Looks like the Time Tunnel caught another one."

Lucius stands. He approaches. "Indeed, a fascinating one. Look at his garb—it's of a very antiquated style."

"Who are you?" Orion also leaves his seat at the table.

"You're the real monsters here," I say. "Creating things you don't understand, condemning the future of everyone around you."

"This one speaks?" Lucius grins. "We've never had one speak before."

"What are you talking about?" I point a finger at him. "Aren't you listening to me? You must stop what you're doing, you're—"

DARKNESS.

The sun, shining high in the sky, burns with an intensity unlike any I've felt before. I raise my arm reflexively to block the blazing heat.

"What are you doing soldier?" A woman's voice, sharp and crisp. I look around, finding her standing a few meters away. Behind her, a column of soldiers marches onward.

They're not human. They're Accursed. Ermo's people.

At least, some of them. This woman—she's human. She's like me. She stands in full plate armor, a massive sword in her hands.

"I . . ." I don't know what to say.

"Get in line."

My battle instincts kick in, and I merge with the advancing column. We march, in formation, eventually reaching a flat ridge overlooking a massive gorge. The unit I've suddenly joined veers to the left, entering formation upon a bluff above a slight downward slope.

Hundreds of meters away stands a horde.

No other words describe what prepares to assault us. A massive army of shadowy creatures wielding blades and axes and shields. They whoop and howl, but they look human in form. Just merely . . . wispy. And I think their skin mixes with vibrant colors of purple, cyan, and ocean blue. Among them, larger shadows float. A memory of demons surfaces, as if I should make a connection.

Yet here I am, on a battlefield, facing down an unknown enemy.

The soldiers around me speak in hushed tones in a dialect I can't understand, unlike the words of the commander from earlier. As snippets of previous visions shift inside my mind, I recognize, unlike the dreams, the substance of this particular perspective. I'm here, physically, and others can see me. I'm a soldier in an ancient conflict, whether I like it or not.

The warriors around me suddenly roar, unsheathing swords. I follow suit, finding a well-crafted silvery blade ready for use. It's beautiful—better craftsmanship than I've ever seen before in a weapon. Swords rise in a war cry, a charge begins, and we rumble across the plain, forest to our left, gorge to our right.

My heart throbs with the thrill of the chase. I relish the moment to dive into battle again. We close the gap, near the horde. As we reach their line, they lower shields, spears pointed toward us. Our closed flank roars, and we crash into the front.

All hell breaks loose.

It all happens quickly. Shadows dart about the battlefield, striking with unholy grace. Soldiers around me fall as they attempt to parry impossible attacks. A dark blade flies over my head, and I narrowly dodge it by sliding to my knees. Above, the sun disappears, clouds darkening and blackening like ashy smoke.

A trumpet. Our line pulls back in retreat, and our enemy pursues. Another roar, and I steal a glance toward the forest. Thousands of shadows rush from the tree line, targeting our position. We're doomed. We're all doomed.

My unit runs across the field, pushed toward the gorge. Other battalions divert their paths in haphazard directions—the entire army fractures almost as quickly as the battle began. In the distance, beside the gorge, flashes of lightning strike back and forth between two figures. I've seen the lightning before. From the fingers of Ermo. Without caution, I divert my course away from the ragtag remnants of my unit and run solo toward the two opponents.

Time blurs. The vision shifts. A half-kilometer becomes a kilometer becomes ten meters. I stand before two clashing titans, their magnificent blades descending upon one another with ferocity unmatched. I am witnessing a battle unlike any I ever could have imagined. These two are heroes, fighting in a war beyond my comprehension.

Then they speak, and I recognize the full scale of the conflict.

"Give it up," says the shadowy man. "You've lost. The world is mine for the taking."

A blast of white light emits from the gray-cloaked figure. "I have a few tricks left up my sleeve, Lucius. You will not win. You exist only because of my mistake. I am sorry for what happened to you."

There it is. Lucius and Orion again, staring one another down. Fighting. And Lucius became the monster predicted during teatime. Truth snaps into focus. I am the vessel for relaying history to the present.

Orion takes a few steps back, pausing. "And now we reach the climax of our story, my brother. All pieces have led to today. For all time."

"You speak lies. I have become death. I will remake the world."

"You will live again, because I will do everything I must to ensure you find peace." Orion drops his blade and falls to his knees. Swiftly, he uncovers a strange artifact from beneath his robe, similar to the tiny orb destroyed in my sister's hand. He holds it above him, speaks unknown words, and stares into the eyes of the shadow, his former partner.

"You think a party trick will stop me?" Lucius strides forward.

Orion glances toward me and smiles. "I've done everything I need to do to win the war."

Lucius swings his blade. It connects with the orb, slicing straight through it. Its arc continues, meeting Orion's shoulder and slicing him in half.

With a thunderclap, the dark clouds disappear. White light pulses in waves from the orb. With a sharp screech of unfathomable pain, Lucius roars toward the sky—and disappears.

Not the subtle fade of an extinguished flame. No, he disappears into the ground. It's as if his soul is sucked downward, through the broken rocks and dead grass, amidst the soil and uneven sand. I look around, seeing the other shadows similarly distort and shift into a world below like their supposed master, banished from this realm by the man who created them in the first place.

And with that, my mind flips and evaporates.

DARKNESS.

INTERJECTION

KYRI

The Triumvirate lies.

They've always lied.

Our history. Where we come from. What the world-above is like. They've always lied. And now, the world-above has reared its ugly head, dropping their dead upon us.

I dove into the libraries of Shade. I discovered the inklings of the truth. We did not always live here. Once, we resided on the surface, where food, air, and water exist in abundance.

The Triumvirate knows the truth. They have hidden it from us. They must pay. And then, we will take the fight to our real enemy.

Today, my followers join me, on the steps of the Holy Place.

"My friends!" I say, standing beneath violet light. "My brothers and sisters. They have lied to us. We, who worked to defend our lands, we have been lied to! There is a place above where we can live, safe from the dangers of the deep. We must claim it for our own."

They cheer, egging me on.

"And why can't we take it?" I point toward the massive obsidian tower behind me. "Because they will not let us. They believe, for our safety, we must remain in Shade, in our tunnels, away from the People-Who-Live-Above. I say no! They wish to keep us here. They believe—"

With a mighty howl, a stampede echoes from somewhere else in Shade's massive cavern. The crowd quiets. It murmurs. A shout resounds in the distance.

"Demons!"

I look toward my shadows, ready to invade the Holy Place. I

must act fast, to hold my spot as their leader. It all hangs on a thread.

With a weave of light and sound, I send a command throughout the cavern. "Shadow of War and Shadow of Night, redirect to fight the demons. Everyone else, with me. We destroy the Triumvirate."

With a guttural cry, I turn and charge toward the open gates, trying not to consider the horde of demons assaulting our rear. I recognize the significance—something has caused hundreds of the creatures to invade our cavern. Where could so many of them have come from? We only ever see a few at a time. But a whole horde? The world-above must have discovered us. They're attempting to snuff us out.

More reason to take the fight to them.

Through the gate I charge, quickly crossing the outer sanctum and entering the next foyer. Around a corner, we flow into the forum, home of the council and the Triumvirate. In the middle, they all stand, waiting. Watching. Their dark eyes observe me and the shadows at my back.

"Kyri, Vanguard of our people," says my former Scion, now a member of the council. "Tell us, why do you do what you do?"

"I know the truth. We were once from above. We belong up there. Our destiny is up there. Our stories of Lucius, the first of our kind? You have written them as falsehoods. He calls for us to seek revenge against the People-Who-Live-Above."

The Scion nods. More of my shadows enter the room, but I pay them no mind. The council is not resisting. The Triumvirate, standing beyond in dark, billowing cloaks, accepts their fate.

"Tell me why you lied to us." I step into the middle of the room and leap onto their large, moonstone-weaved table.

"We did not lie." The words emanate not from the Scion but from the Triumvirate. The trio speaks in unison. "We hid the truth, preparing our people for a moment like this one. And now, we are ready."

"We?" I stride toward the Triumvirate. "You did nothing. We

prepared ourselves. You will play no part in the world we will create. *We* will rend judgment upon the world-above, and you will rot in your graves."

I pull power from darkness, releasing my mind and entering a battle-fugue. Like a viper, I dash, sword in hand, and it thrusts into the stomach of the tallest of our leaders. "And I will lead them by myself."

Our former leaders die, one-by-one, willingly giving themselves to our blades. It's almost too easy. I feel no pity. They failed us. We will create our own world, forgetting them in the deepest holes of our caverns. Strangely, the Triumvirate, and its council, does not resist.

I slowly lead my army out of the Holy Place. Shouts of confusion echo throughout Shade, the demons continuing their own assault. My heart sinks, knowing I've inexorably changed the path of our people. It doesn't matter. We are ready. The world must transform alongside us.

My epiphany signals truth, and white light begins to glow throughout the cavern. As I walk down the steps of the Holy Place, three of my shadows engage two demons. Except the monsters are glowing white. For a moment, I see a face—a being—inside the demon, as if a trapped soul has been revealed for the first time. The essence disperses into tiny beads of gold, pulling and stretching until the creatures disappear from our city.

It's as if the demons recognize who I am. They fall at my touch. And now, we prepare for the much longer war.

X

ROAN

Two seconds after my brother steps through the door, it solidifies into rock.

I rush forward, banging on the wall. "Koric! No. No-no-no. You can't abandon me!"

Almost immediately, I hear my brother reply. "Roan! Can you hear me?"

"Yes! I'm here. Come back. We can get you back."

"Hello?"

"Koric? Can you hear me?"

I place my ear against the wall. No more words break through its rough, grainy surface. "Koric?"

"I don't know what magic fuels this place," says Ermo, "but he's gone. He's on his own."

"Don't you dare make it sound simple." I step back, pointing at the door. "Use your magic. Blast it open."

"I don't think I can."

"You won't even try?"

Ermo sighs, but she steps toward the door and places her hands on its surface. Visibly, nothing changes, but I feel it.

Not just feel—my mind embraces and understands the power the larger woman pulls from the world around her. She channels it into the door, attempting to crack it, but likewise, I feel the energy dissipate into the tower itself, as if it's draining Ermo of any ability to crack its secrets.

She steps away, shaking. "Impossible."

For a moment, I open my mouth, preparing to reveal what I sensed. But I close it. Not yet. I need to remember my brother's advice, even if he's abandoned me. I must protect my family. And if Koric is still alive, and Ermo becomes a foe, having hidden the ability to detect her power presented benefits.

"Were you about to say something?" Ermo asks.

"No, and we should get moving. You may not be able to break through that door, but we could open this one." I point at the sliding panel leading toward Yarwin and the murdering demons. "Our hunters might be able to, as well."

"Fair enough." But she doesn't move. She stares down at me, squinting. "Are you all right?"

The question startles me. Why is she asking if I'm all right? Of course I'm fine. I'm strong.

"In the span of a minute, I lost both a mentor and my brother," I say. The words waterfall from my mouth. "I-I-I don't . . . what's going to happen? Orion said the four of us were the heroes he expected to arrive. Our adventure will dictate the fate of the world. And now, two of our number, gone. Dead. Probably both dead. Oh, Koric!"

Tears, stream down my cheeks, salty and sweet and soaked in anguish. I fall into Ermo's arms, fists pounding her chestplate. I'm sure it's annoying, but she embraces me, holding me tight in a hug.

"It's all right," she says. "I know it's scary, but it's all right. We are still alive. We will find a way out of this. And your brother—if he's as brave as he seems to be—he'll find a way out too."

Her words cloud my mind, telling me truths I know are real, yet I don't feel the hope needed to understand them. I lean into her embrace, the tears continuing to flow. I sob, her armor muffling my cries.

Sniffling, I escape her arms. I shake my head. "We need to go. We need to reach the summit."

Ermo nods, pointing toward the ramp with her spear. "You take the lead, I'll watch our backs."

I don't respond, instead stepping onto the ramp to continue our climb. The chase over, my legs burn from our upward sprint. Before long, I'm winded, but I keep us moving. I need water, but it's at the bottom of the tower, beyond the demons.

"So what are those things?" I eventually say.

"I have my theories," Ermo replies. Her voices is filled with subtle melancholy.

"Care to share?" I look over my shoulder.

"Did you ever hear about the Battle of Vicor?"

"One of the final battles of the invasion, yes?"

"Wrong one. The second battle of Vicor."

"No."

"I thought not. It felt like it was something the Inquisition would hide from all of you, and everyone we freed or captured hadn't heard of it."

I scratch my head. "What about it?"

Ermo clicks her spear twice against the outer wall of the tower. "That battle ended when a horde of creatures—we called them fiends and dark wolves, at the time—rushed out of nearby caves and sewers, overrunning the Holy Empire's troops."

I narrow my eyes. "And they didn't attack you?"

"No, they did initially. I was terrified of them. But a friend became one of the dark wolves. And together, we rode into battle against the Holy Empire's army. At the end of the battle, all of the fiends—well, they turned into light and disappeared."

"That doesn't make any sense."

"I know. None at all. Yet they disappeared, fading into nothingness. Or they ascended into something greater. Or maybe those phrases mean the same thing. Regardless, souls trapped on this planet left after achieving some greater purpose."

"Not sure I'm following."

"Well, my theory about the shadow creatures, ever since that day? They aren't actually evil. They're just malformed souls, stuck in this world in a form we perceive as evil because they're aggressive and territorial and violent. But they're not evil. Because we—and I mean both the People of Light and the Holy Empire—create them."

"Create them?"

"I'm not positive about how it happens, but I think the endless violence between our people has become a breeding ground for the creation of these fiends. Yet I think the Inquisition is simultaneously trying to harness them as an asset. Use them—or even consciously create them. It's fuzzy. Most Inquisition records are burned whenever we capture one of their camps."

"What about these ones, trapped here?"

"I'm not sure, but here's the thing—they're completely different than any we've witnessed before. More feral. More violent. More aggressive. It makes me think there are different forms. Or more ancient."

I'm about to say more, but I sniff the air, suddenly noticing the shift. The air no longer feels stale. There's a breeze. And ahead, light looms. We've reached the summit.

"You said the Inquisition was attempting to create the shadows?" I say. "Given everything I've witnessed over the past few weeks, I believe it." I remember the red light from the inquisitor in General Wellor's camp before the battle started. It was an evil power, distorting the magics of the world. And then there were those strange images in the palace's vault. I'll never forget the epic battles portrayed. All of it connects. "I don't think Koric would believe it."

"I know," says Ermo. "And as I said, whether inquisitors are trying to create the creatures or not, that fact doesn't really tell me much about what those things are."

We step through a vaulted archway, Ermo a few meters behind me. We're standing on a smooth, shining surface, midday sun reflecting sharply. It's nearly blinding. After a moment, my eyes adjust, and I welcome the natural light following hours upon hours in the dim of Ermo's glow rocks. The edge of the pillar is probably twenty meters from us in any direction, and beyond waits an ocean of sand, though a few mountains rise in the distance. In front of us, the pillar is completely empty, but a large shadow tilts to our left. Taking a few steps forward, I pivot, turning to face the object creating the shade.

Rising above us, a twisting crystalline network spirals and arcs, forming a beautiful mess of shining splendor.

"It's magnificent," I whisper.

"It is," Ermo says. "And I think it's what we've been sent to find. As for what it is—and what it does—we'll need to ascertain."

"And how do we do that?" I ask.

"No idea."

We both drift aimlessly around the summit, searching for anything else of import. After spending the past day inside the pillar, I almost forgot about the desert's overbearing heat, but within minutes, the scorch sears my skin. If I'm not careful, I'll burn.

I approach the edge. Leaning over, I try to see the desert below, and my stomach drops. The pillar's sheer face plummets. I can't fathom the distance. I stumble backward, and before I know what's happening, I fall into Ermo's arms.

"Slow down," she says. "Wouldn't want to fall."

I chuckle, though the serious way she said the phrase creeps me out a little. Might be the accent. "Yeah, definitely. So—"

"Get your hands off my sister."

We turn. Staggering down from the crystalline contraption, Koric walks, sword in hand. He's sweating, he's bleeding, he looks beaten to a pulp.

"Koric!" I say, sprinting toward him.

"Is this real?" he says. "Are you both real? Where are we? What day is this?"

"What are you talking about?" I say. "Yes, this is us. We're real."

"Good." He collapses as he reaches the bottom step, crumpling into a pile atop the pillar.

XI

ERMO

We pull Koric into the shade of the summit's entrance archway, careful not to let his head lull to the side. We prop him up against the wall. He breathes, but barely.

"What the hell is going on?" Roan says. "This is wild. This is impossible. I'm glad he's back, but—where? Where did he come from? What is happening?"

I shake my head. "I'm as lost as you."

"Orion—he healed my brother earlier. Can you heal? Does your power allow you to heal?"

"No."

Roan turns away, I assume to hide tears. "Then he'll die here. Look at his wounds."

I pace away from the siblings, trying to find the right words to say. This young woman wants an answer to her brother's predicament. I have power, I have knowledge about that power, yet I lack the ability to save him. I am failing, one-by-one, the three people destined to help me restore the world.

Reaching the edge of the tower, I kneel and bow my head. I breathe deeply, letting the dry desert air fill my lungs. Years ago, when I leapt from the Bridge of our Lord into the Chasm and the river far below, I leapt on faith. Blind faith. I believed the path forward, guided by voices in my mind, was there for me to grasp. And when I charged into battle alongside an army of dark wolves, faith guided me. I knew I was safe. I simply *knew*. I didn't need another reason for my actions.

Here, on a magical pillar in the middle of an unknown desert, I have no internal assurances. My mind cannot comprehend a way for us to succeed. I need guidance. I've always had guidance, whether from Father Ero, from a specter of Father Mono, or from the voice of the Lord of Light.

If you were going to say a few more words to me from the void, now would be the time. I don't expect an answer, and none arrives. I shake my head, close my eyes, and clench my fist. I must discover my own path, redefining what it means to have faith in a future where we win.

Patience. I must have patience. I slow my heart-rate, entering a meditative state. Since I first uncovered my abilities, I've honed my knowledge of what I can and cannot do. I can mostly channel energy to assault my enemies. Sunsteel and moonstone amplify that power. But I can also still my mind and use my connection to the unseen force surrounding all life to understand more about the world, recognizing threats, both visible and invisible. I confess, I utilize it too infrequently. I always find peace when meditating.

I count. My pulse reaches forty-five beats per minute, and two seconds later, I enter a fugue state. Opening my eyes, I perceive my kneeling body, though my perspective floats a meter above my head. Shifting—more hovering, rather than walking—I turn and face the center of the pillar's summit.

The strange crystalline structure above us takes a new form. From its spindles, glowing lines arc outward in a thousand directions, heading toward unknown destinations. I wonder. Did the pillar itself call us from the battlefield when I activated the orb through Roan? If it brought us to it, could we use those lines to leave? It might explain what happened to Koric, too, if he was drawn elsewhere and then drawn back to this origin point.

The lines trigger another question—what is this place, truly? Its power is beyond all conceptual understanding, somehow giving control over both time and space to those who master it. That conclusion explained Orion's presence downstairs. Terrifying, yet it makes me wonder. It's abandoned. Why?

My gaze shifts from the top of the pillar to the archway leading downstairs. There waits Koric, leaning against the wall. And Roan.

Roan. The girl glows like a bright star, with tiny, wispy strands reaching toward the crystal fractals above her head.

Roan. The girl who discovered the teleporting, time-defying orb.

Roan. A human citizen of the Holy Empire, the first person in my life to exhibit anything related to my powers.

More than the orb transported us across space. The orb didn't give Roan visions. Roan herself contained a power like mine.

The revelation itself knocks my meditation out of focus. Good. I jump to my feet and rush toward the other two living beings on this accursed pillar. "You." I stutter, my breath haggard. "You have power. You might be able to heal him!"

The girl furrows her brows and wipes tears from her eyes. "What?"

"You have power. I sensed it. And fate has drawn us here. Fate has brought the three of us together. We saw Orion heal Koric earlier—what if he was showing you it was possible? Because you can do it too."

"That doesn't make any—"

"None of this makes any sense," I retort. "Trust me. Center yourself. Reach out with your mind. Will your desires into existence, and imagine Koric's wounds mending and healing. You *can* do this."

Unprompted, Koric moans. He coughs. Red droplets stain the otherwise grey ramp.

Roan shakes her head. "I can't believe I'm going to try this." Closing her eyes, she focuses on her brother and reaches out with her hand. Not necessary, but if it helps her believe she can save him, then all the better.

"You can do this," I say. "I believe in you."

She breathes again. And again. Her fingertips emit light.

XII

ROAN

I stare in awe.

Power. I have power.

My fingers glow, a shimmering silver sheen vibrating slightly between my digits. Energy pushes and pulls from my soul, a wave aching to reach toward my brother and save him. I open the floodgates.

Resting my hand on Koric's arm, first a trickle then a downpour of healing rays ripple across his body. Wounds stitch closed. His breathing levels. Blood cakes skin, but his eyes flutter open.

"Roan?"

"Koric, I'm here," I say, spoiling my tear-soaked cheeks with a tiny smile. "You're going to live."

He twitches upon noticing my hand. His mouth opens as if to object, but instead, he sighs. "Don't fall under her spell, sister."

At those words, Ermo shuffles behind me. I resist the urge to look over my shoulder. "This is all me. I'm doing this. Not Ermo. I'm saving you. This is good." With those words, I step back, releasing my connection to the unseen energy. That's the best way to describe the sensation, at least. It's all too instinctual to put properly into words. I lean back onto my haunches and rest against the wall opposite Koric.

"I'm glad you're alive," Ermo says. "We're going to need you."

Koric shakes his head. "I'm not going to help you."

Involuntarily, my eyes widen. "Koric, stop it! After everything, do you still not understand?"

"Oh, I understand all too well what's happening. You don't know what I saw."

"Then tell us," Ermo snaps. "If you've learned a truth we all need to know, then tell us!"

Koric growls and stands. He pushes past Ermo, striding into the open sunlight atop the pillar. The giant woman follows, and I trail close behind. When he reaches the edge, he turns, hatred seeping from his eyes.

"Truth?" Koric's arms flail. "What is truth? I don't know anymore. I've been raised my entire life to believe one thing: the Accursed are evil. The Inquisition might be evil too; I know that from my own experience of them. But that doesn't change what the Accursed have done. And their Lord of Light? You know what their Lord of Light did?"

He's addressing me, though the message clearly targets Ermo. Regardless, I shake my head.

"I saw the end of his war with my own eyes. He created the evil shadow fiends down below. He created the shadowy creatures that attacked us on the battlefield. We're helping an evil—"

Wind. A rush of wind. It knocks Koric onto his stomach and away from the edge of the pillar. A ray of light blasts from above, and an apparition—Orion returned—appears between us.

"And here he is!" Koric rises to his knees. "The man himself, here to tell us—"

"You're right," Orion says. The words hang in the scorched air, cutting Koric off in mid-sentence.

"You created the dark wolves?" Ermo says. Her hands clench into fists. "You created those demons downstairs? Come out with the truth!"

"I don't know exactly how your story will play out," Orion says. "As we attempt to speak across time, I barely know the words you're saying to me. But by now, you should have discovered the truth. Yes, I created the dark creatures you fought. Created them with Lucius. I paid dearly for my mistake; Lucius paid a greater price. In our quest for immortality, we doomed the world in chaos. And I lost my life's love."

Ermo took a few steps back. "You created them? This whole

time, I've been listening to the voice of the man who created the creatures distorting the dead corpses of my fallen soldiers?"

"Yes. I am truly sorry for my mistakes. But you four are the only ones capable of saving us. You have followed the path I've created for you. The first sacrifice has been made. Two more must be paid before the end."

Ermo charges the visage, but her body flies straight through his ghostly figure. "Orion, you bastard! You've forced us down a fateful path against our consent because of a mistake you made a thousand years ago? I've made my own path, to save my people, to save the world. And you're claiming it's all part of some grand plan?"

"I know what you must think," continues the ghost. "I'm a terrible person for thrusting fate upon you. But the world depends on you."

"It's like he's not even listening to us," I say to no one in particular. "It's like it's a recorded message."

"I think it is," Ermo says, her shoulders loosening. "He's attempting to predict our questions, and he gets some right, some wrong."

Koric shakes his head. "I don't understand. I watched him banish the dark creatures into the void. How are they coming back?"

Orion's form shifts, facing my brother. "You are right, my friend. Soon, very soon, I *will* banish them. There are two problems you must solve. First: the descendants of the enemy I defeated are returning to the world, believing they deserve restitution for their banishment. Perhaps they do. Their existence, and the greater blight upon the world, is not one of their making. It is mine, and Lucius's. Second: your Inquisition believes it can finish the work I started years ago. You must let neither come to pass. I have seen only glimpses of your future, but your path from here forward is opaque to me. Fortunately, you have everything you need."

Ermo pulls her hair before pointing a finger in the face of her Lord of Light. "Then answer one final question. What are they?

Are they evil? What are the different forms? How do we defeat them?"

Orion sighs. "I can't answer it all. There are three forms—the monstrous, the shadow, and the visage. A visage is sapient, and the first were transformed from humans. Lucius was the original. Monstrous and shadow forms are shallow representations of the visage. Many would call them failed experiments. All are corruptions of life, their minds twisted. But they do not deserve blame for their actions. They are trapped souls, deserving freedom from their pain."

Ermo lowered her finger. "What—"

Orion disappeared.

"I can't believe any of this." Ermo storms away, presumably heading toward the tower's doors.

"I'm incredibly confused," I say. "I don't understand what any of this means."

Koric stands, watching Ermo stride away. "That man . . . he admitted his mistake. He owned what he did. I . . . I didn't expect that."

I glance over my shoulder. To my surprise, Ermo isn't in the tower entrance. She approached the large crystalline lattice ever-present above our heads.

"Can you not fight her for two seconds?" I say. "We need her."

"Do we?" Koric looks away. "You have her power, you claim. You healed me. Can you help us escape?"

"I don't know," I say. It's an interesting question he poses, though. I can heal, a power unknown to Ermo. And I used the orb which brought us here.

"Anyway, I'm starting to understand that man. My mind is clearing. I'm remember the flashes I saw—"

"What happened to you?"

"I stepped through the door and into the past," he says. "I jumped from memory to memory, some more real than others, where I saw a world long dead. Yet it told me Orion's story, I think. It showed me his mistakes. I thought maybe he wasn't remorseful.

And I'm still confused by how he did it. But he showed me those memories for a reason. But in my last vision, he caused hundreds of monsters—I suppose they're called visages—to disappear. And he said he'd done everything he needed to win the war."

I rush forward, hugging my brother. "I'm just glad you're all right."

He wraps his arms around me. "Remember, we protect our own. Now tell me, do you believe we are supposed to follow through with this whole 'fate' thing? Everything is . . . grey. I don't know what we're supposed to do. The Inquisition exploited us. This Orion exploits us. Ermo, in her own way, is using us too. What is the right thing to do?"

I let go of Koric, and for a second, he doesn't let go. Once he releases me, I step back, finding his eyes. Pain hides beneath his gaze. He's struggling to know what to do.

"Yarwin died because he believed Ermo," I say.

It's almost imperceptible, but Koric nods.

I add, "He sacrificed himself so we could move forward. Orion said one sacrifice, with two more to come. I don't think he's perfect; I don't think he's the savior Ermo believes him to be. I don't think she believes he's a savior anymore, either. I don't know if we'll know the full truth about the past, and what has brought us to the crossroads before us. But Koric . . ." I pause, considering my words. "Something pushed us to meet Ermo on that battlefield. I escaped the vault with a magic orb, walking hundreds of kilometers by your side with it in my pocket, before we showed up on the same battlefield as the person who could help us travel all the way to a pillar in the middle of the desert. That means something, doesn't it? What would Father say?"

Koric scowled. "I don't know. I saw Father in one of the visions, you know. I think he assaulted the supposed killer of Emelia the Second."

I frown. "Strange. When all this is over, you'll need to tell me about all these visions."

"I'll try to remember them all." He shifts, looking out across the desert plain again. "I think Father would tell us to trust our instincts. In this moment, all my instincts are fighting against one another. I don't know what's right or wrong anymore."

"Do you trust me?" I whisper.

He doesn't look back at me. "Yes."

I step forward and loop my arm around his. "Then I think we try to save the world, whatever that means."

"That means two more sacrifices must be made," he says. "And I imagine those sacrifices are equal to or greater than Yarwin's."

"Then we'll make the sacrifices when we must."

Koric nods. "All right. What do we need to do?"

"We use that thing to travel back to civilization."

We both twirl, finding Ermo standing a few meters away with her arms crossed. "What?" I inquire.

She points at the crystal structure rising above us on its pedestal. "It's a transporter. Best name I can give it. I can sense lines exiting and entering it from all different directions. I think it connects to places of magical power across the world. I think it pulled us here, using the orb as a focal point of sorts. Roan, I think you can use it to transport us elsewhere."

I let go of my brother's arm, taking a few steps toward Ermo. "I barely figured out how to heal. How am I supposed to teleport us across an entire continent?"

"I don't know."

"It makes sense though," says Koric. "And I'm sorry, Ermo. I've been reacting out of fear. You deserve better from me." Stepping past me, Koric does a light bow. "I am the Captain of the Slaying Swords, a company of the Army of Wellor. Please accept my formal surrender. As the final two members of the Company, we formally pledge allegiance to your banners." He kneels.

I tilt my head in confusion, but with a motion of his hand, I follow suit, kneeling beside him. I don't break eye-contact with Ermo.

She takes a few steps back before she starts to chuckle. "Koric, I do not deserve your allegiance."

"What do you mean?"

"You have every right to hate me, as the person who struck down your brothers-in-arms. I've lost too many family and friends during this war. I know how your heart breaks. I do not deserve the allegiance of a man fiercely loyal to those he loves."

Koric bows his head. "I do this not because I believe I must, but because I trust Roan, and she trusts you. And Yarwin trusted you. Accept their respect, then respect mine."

Ermo nods. "Then I accept."

"Roan?" Koric says.

"What?"

Instead of words, he responds with a sharp jab to my leg.

"Ow! What?"

"Pledge your allegiance."

"Why are we being formal?"

"If we're going to save the world with her, we need to do it the right way."

I shake my head. "Fine. Ermo, as the ward of Captain Koric of the Slaying Swords, I too pledge my services to you. Do you accept?"

"I accept," she says. "Now please rise, you look foolish."

"That's no way to greet your new soldiers," I say. "All right. What are your orders?"

She motions for us to follow her to the crystal contraption. There isn't a better way to describe it. A complex web of fractals crisscross atop the stone pedestal. It's beautiful. Wonderful. Potentially terrible.

"My theory—the orb may have given you the ability to use this structure," Ermo says. "We just need to figure out how." We reach the top of the platform, the network a meter above our heads. Our leader kneels. "Join me."

I glance at Koric, but he simply nods. I likewise kneel beside Ermo. She holds out her hand, and I interlace my fingers between hers. As our skin touches, electric energy surges.

"You will see what I see," she says. "I hope."

For a moment, I see nothing.

Then . . .

I see everything. Strands of light dance across the sky, an amalgamation of arcing paths and roads. It's a network, a highway transmitting information about the past, present, and future of distant unknowable lands. The crystal lattices intakes the stories and distributes it *into* the tower. My eyes widen, adjusting to the truth.

"Orion saw the past and future using this device," I say. "I can see images. I recognize them. Events from my past. From your past. From Koric's past. They're all here. And the future. And the present. Orion used this place to chart his plan."

"That explains my visions, then," Koric says. "Maybe."

"All right," Ermo says. "We need to find the pathway to take us back to the battlefield, right? I'm not entirely sure we can trust Orion, but even if he's partially to blame for everything, he hasn't truly led us astray thus far. Okay. We need to topple the Holy Empire. That would mean taking out the High Inquisitor, yes? To stop them from continuing Orion's work?"

"In my visions, I saw High Inquisitor Trallius creating demons from the corpses of the dead." Koric sighs. "Including our own people, Roan. Yes, the Inquisition must fall. Never thought I'd say those words."

Ermo grimaces. "I'm sorry. I can't imagine the pain in both of you, knowing you must betray your own nation."

"Eh." I release a tiny laugh. "Most people don't really like the Inquisition deep down. Too many rules."

"Good to know," Ermo says. "And then there's the shadow fiends that attacked us on the banks of the river at the end of the battle. Based on Orion's description, they're probably visages."

"They look like what I saw in my visions, most definitely," Koric replied.

"They're our two targets, would you agree?"

"I don't know," I say. "You know more about this than me. I don't understand what we're supposed—"

My mind shifts without direction. I find a path. It takes me into darkness. I see a man—no, not a man. A visage. A shadowy, distorted figure, walking along roads and paths in an underground cavern alien to my eyes. He wields the power of shadow and death.

And my mind—

Interjection

Kyri

For years we prepared, and now our time to strike arrives. I know you see me. I know you've seen my story. Understand it, and despair.

I stand atop a rocky slope, the sun rising in the east. The sun! To think we didn't know it exists a few months ago. The secrets of the world are now revealed to us. We have found our way to the surface, we have watched the squabbles of those-who-live-above, and we are ready to bring vengeance upon them. It is our time.

Turning, I face westward. A river flows in the distance, surrounded by lush forests and grasslands. We believed the surface-world a harsh mistress, but how wrong were we. The land is plentiful and empty. The people have squandered their resources, choosing to fight meaningless wars. Along the riverbank, two armies face one another, a battle beginning. We will use the confusion to strike. We will ruin the military forces capable of standing against us. Once we destroy them, we can move toward control.

Behind me, a host of a thousand waits. Without speaking, I raise a fist, calling forth the power we've waited to unleash. From high above, clouds fall, drawn to the planet through our collective summons. Mist rolls at our feet, and at my command, fog rushes downhill toward our unsuspecting victims.

And then we begin to walk.

It's a long journey, but the mist covers our approach. We descend from the mountains, blades in hand, ready to reveal ourselves.

Though, we have one last trick up our sleeves. As the sounds of clashing swords reach my ears, I pause, and I know my army halts in anticipation alongside me. Raising both my arms above my head, I breathe inward, sucking in the mist, and my soldiers join me in the ritual we've prepared for the past six months.

With a thunderclap, the mist disappears. We enter our shadow forms, our ghastly images rushing onto the battlefield. We do not look ourselves, but that's the point. With darkness blotting out the sun, we descend upon the unsuspecting soldiers, prepared to strike fear into their hearts.

It begins. Our magic does its trick. I find myself towering over cowering men dropping their blades in fear, eyes widening. They cry in surprise. Tears stream down faces in forever terror. It's as if they're seeing the ever-present glare of death itself.

I know what we look like as shadows. I know the terror we can bring, floating above the ground, gliding in hideous splendor.

Yet . . .

Four individuals do not appear afraid. I float toward them. They shout in their strange language. We've observed the words from afar yet still cannot decipher them. They're reaching for one another, they're—

They disappear. Into thin air, they evaporate.

Impossible. Those-Who-Dwell-Above do not have power. They do not know our ways. How could they disappear into the void?

I scream. It's a bloodcurdling scream, and with it, I shift from shadow to humanoid-form. My army joins me, and with blades in hand, we begin our slaughter. These soldiers will die. I will make certain of it. And then we'll hunt the four who escaped.

I approach a soldier kneeling in the grass, his head staring straight at the sky as if in prayer. "Suffer," I say. "Suffer for the thousand years we lived beneath your feet. No more do we hide in darkness." I know he can't understand me, but he comprehends the weapon in my hand. Raising it overhead, I swing it toward his neck.

* * *

And now you see me. You know my story. I've sensed your presence, across time and space. With new-found knowledge, what will you do?

XIII

KORIC

"Roan?" I sputter her name, watching her frozen in place, eyes glazed. "Roan!"

Before I say another word, my sister shakes her head. "I'm fine. I saw our enemy. I saw his current trajectory. And I saw his past. It's complicated. And tragic. As a child and as an adult."

"What?" I stand there confused, not understanding her words.

"There's been a world beneath our feet this entire time we never knew existed," Roan says. "I saw it all, in its splendor. It's beautiful, in its own way, and it's where . . . what did Orion call them? The visages. It's where the visages live."

"Then it all makes sense," Ermo says. "Orion banished the demons of his time to this underworld realm. They've lived there, unknown to us. And now they're coming back, slowly, and we must stop them." She claps. "That's it. That's all of it. The Holy Empire—well, the Inquisition—they've been attempting to recreate the shadow creatures. Even if we defeat one problem, the other problem persists. We must nip both in the bud preemptively."

Koric nods. "In the visions I saw, I witnessed inquisitors dumping monsters into an underground pit."

"I saw it too," Roan says. "Through the eyes of the visage, I saw inquisitors dumping monsters down below. That's the thing—the visages seem almost normal. A functioning civilization. But the Inquisition has been sending monsters into their realm. They want revenge."

"It's obvious, isn't it?" Ermo says. "We must reconcile both sides. We must—"

A mighty roar echoes across the desert wind. I look away from the two women, unsheathing my sword in the process. Stepping down from the immense pedestal, I search the horizon. My warrior instincts tingle with anticipation.

Another roar. More of a rumble. From the left. Toward the endless expanse. I approach the edge of the pillar, looking at the horizon. The sand groans, as if churned by an earthquake. An immense plume of cloudy dust rushes toward us. And inside the tidal wave of grit, as if floating on the wind, a giant leviathan stares into my soul.

"What in the seven hells?"

It's massive—the size of the royal palace in Esmeraldi, if not larger. It looks like a worm—no, a snake. Like the snakes which assaulted us when we first arrived outside the pillar yesterday. Only yesterday.

A million possibilities flash through my mind. The snakes and the leviathan out there—connected? Maybe it is their mother? Or perhaps we pissed off a giant ancient god in the process of stumbling through the pillar.

Does it matter?

I shake my head as the creature rushes toward us, crossing kilometers in seconds.

"Ermo, you and Roan must figure out a solution," I order over the growing wind. "Now!"

"What about you?" shouts someone—Ermo, I think.

"I will handle *that* thing." *Two sacrifices*, Orion said. Anger tries to bubble in my mind, but I push it all down. I glance back toward Ermo and Roan. My sister. Hatred targeting Ermo, ingrained fury, it tries to overtake my mind. But I've learned. I know the truth. I've seen my sister's power. I must resist the vitriol forming inside my soul and ensure my Roan survives.

I must be the first of the final two sacrifices.

My blade, resting in my sword-hand, waits for the terror to arrive. Roan shouts, but I ignore her words.

"Sister," I scream. "When you see them, tell our family I love them. And remember, we protect our own. I love you, Roan."

I think my fate was ordained the moment I found her in the war camp outside Esmeraldi. A glorious destiny it shall be, a worthy end to the Company of Slaying Swords.

The giant monstrosity dives into the sand a kilometer away. All goes still. The wind dies. The sand settles. My fingers sweat. I look down.

The ground explodes in an inferno of dust and rock, the maw of the giant snake thrusting upward. It curls like a screw around the pillar, rising toward us with frightening speed.

"Koric!"

I must ignore them.

"Koric, you need my spear!"

Wait what?

I turn, and without fail, Ermo throws her weapon. I catch the long spear with both hands, dropping my sword to the ground. What had she called it? *Flame of Maripes?* The cold metal feels refreshing against my sweaty palms. I know the legends. I know the power of moonstone and sunsteel blades. And her spear is both.

I bend my knees and wait. With a rush of hot air, the giant serpent rises above me, its head barring hundreds of fangs each larger than a horse. I can't hesitate. I cannot wait. I must act, I must save my sister and the supposed Daughter of Light. I must delay this creature at all costs.

I sprint toward the edge and fall, sliding onto the serpent's back. Its scales are slippery, but without waiting, I plunge *Flame of Maripes* into the snake's skin, cutting it like butter. The spear becomes my rudder, and it drags behind as I slide down the spiraling mass surrounding the pillar. Will I kill the immense creature? I doubt it. Will I distract it?

Most definitely.

In response, it begins to uncoil, spiraling and spiraling away from the pillar. Its body unravels, flinging me in a million directions, but I grip the spear with iron strength. It's as if the weapon is glued to my fingers.

That doesn't matter, though. When we hit the sand below, I'll die.

Its writhing mass thrashes. A giant maw appears above, bulbous eyes spotting me, the annoying gnat. It dives toward its own body as we fall through the desert sky.

I pull the spear out of the snake's skin. As its mouth encloses around me, I thrust the blade upward, welcoming death's embrace. I've protected Roan, and in my death, I pray for the world's salvation, too. Let my sacrifice, and Yarwin's, be worth something.

XIV

ROAN

"No!" I throw myself from beneath the crystal structure, but Ermo catches me by the arm. My last image of Koric: my brother leaping off the pillar.

The beast dives after him, its hulking form slithering out of view.

"We can't just leave him to die," I say, staring daggers toward Ermo. "He—"

"Roan." Ermo's eyes widen as if embracing my pain. "This is the end. Everything moved much faster than I could have imagined, but this is the end. We must move quickly. Koric made his sacrifice. One sacrifice remains. It'll be one of us. I'd prefer it be me. Don't go throwing yourself off this pillar before you can finish the war."

I shake my head, not able to accept her words. But I stay hanging in her arms, tears trickling from my eyes. "Give me a second."

I exhale as a harsh scream releases through the sky. With a loud thump and a rumble reverberating through the tower, the massive creature hits the desert beneath the pillar. I can only hope Koric somehow killed it. It's nearly impossible he survived the fall.

Shaking my head, I rise. Ermo releases me from her grasp. "What must I do?" I ask.

She holds out her hand again. "Find the paths that will take us to our destiny."

"How am I supposed to do that?"

"I have no idea."

"Great." I stare upward at the crystal lattice.

"Would help if I had more than an hour to learn my abilities," I say. "You've had years."

"Yes, well, nothing we can do about that," Ermo says. She shrugs.

"Helpful." I reach out my hand, resting it on a crystal leaf.

Nothing happens.

"Not sure what I expected," I mutter.

"Sometimes, our power takes time."

"Why didn't Koric just wait a damn minute to see if I could figure this out?" I close my eyes. "He didn't need to die." My heart wrenches. I bury the pain, knowing I will have time to grieve later. It's almost impossible to steel my heart.

But I must.

Ermo sighs. "I know what it's like to lose everything. To feel lost in a moment like this. Just breathe. Listen to the voice inside your head, guiding you to find the path forward. You *will* find it."

I nod. My heart aches to mourn my brother, but I must resist and hold to the present, finding us a path away from the hellscape of a desert surrounding us.

My brother's ever-present words echo in my mind. *We protect our own.* And now I see a greater truth to those words. We've been tasked with saving the world, a world including both the Holy Empire and the People of Light. Ermo and I, together, we can unify our nations and save the truly distorted souls. These visages. Though, a thought flirts with reality. "Ermo, what if this new enemy—the shadows that attacked us—even if we figure out how to save them, what if they don't want to be saved? How are they any more evil than the Holy Empire or your people? We wreak violence upon one another, too."

"That's a great question." Ermo shakes her head. "I don't think I have an answer. They're threatening our lives, they're threatening our world. But I've seen it happen before. To the monsterform, not these sapient creatures of which Orion spoke. When I first fought against your armies, I witnessed trapped souls burst forth from the creatures. I believe it's a tortured existence. They may not believe they need saving, but we are freeing them, in the end. In some ways, we'll be giving them a grace our two peoples may not ever deserve or even experience. We will continue to suffer. They will not."

"Curious. I suppose that makes sense." I turn my focus back to the supposed transporter. "All right. Think. I need a path forward."

I trace the sky, searching for the right line to take us from this place. Not just to save the world, but to take me away from my brother's grave. Koric risked his life and career to ensure I survived after I made the stupidest mistake of my short time as a professional criminal. His sacrifice *must* be worth it.

There. A faint glow. My mind detects a difference between one line and all the others. It means something. I reach out—not with my hands, but with my mind—and I find a rope. No, not a rope. A ladder. It begs to be climbed. "Ermo, are you ready?"

"I am."

"I don't know what's about to happen, or where we're going."

"You trusted me. I trust you."

I begin our climb.

* * *

Unlike yesterday, when we used the orb to transport us across time and space to the pillar, we do not move instantaneously. Each step forward feels like a thousand kilometers. Each step forward burns my skin to the bone. Each step forward feels like I'm going to die a death too painful to comprehend.

The space we travel through, I don't know what it is. A place between life and death? Hell? Heaven? Something else? It's like we're sliding through an ocean made of tar.

All around us, a million pinpricks of light reveal a thousand worlds. Possible realities. Pathways into other places and times. I don't know. I must ignore them.

But they call to me.

I want to look.

I want to see the world.

I want to escape.

I catch glimpses.

Through a window, High Inquisitor Trallius rants and raves, wagging a finger at white-robed men. He points at a map on a table, screaming obscenities. The scene calls to me, urging me to step through and end the man. I resist.

I see a distant past on a bluff, two armies facing each other. Blades and axes clash. And there—Koric? Standing and watching two figures fighting. I recognize one—Orion. The other must be Lucius, of whom Orion spoke. They're fighting. It's the scene Koric witnessed, then. But I have a bird's eye view. A voice whispers. *Watch closely.*

Orion kneels. Lucius attacks. As Orion's life expires, the enemy host vanishes.

The first part of the ritual, complete. You, the Vanguards of Light, must complete the second half.

The second sacrifice?

Another tug toward the present. I climb.

A window opens, showing the figure whose story I witnessed when first touching the transporter. The visage. The one who charged us on the battlefield using mist. We walked right into their trap, and we didn't even know it.

The window closes.

And a window again shows High Inquisitor Trallius. He's presiding over an execution of a man. An Accursed. In an arena in Esmeraldi. He shouts orders to the crowd, and I hear a name. Maripes. Ermo's grandfather. The vision shifts again, returning to Trallius, yelling at his attendants.

Another shift.

The shadowy man leads his visages down a road I recognize. It's the road I traveled with the Company of Slaying Swords to reach the battlefield where fate and destiny collided.

Two leaders.

Two sides of the same coin.

Of course!

Remove the heads of each snake with a single blow.

Our window is closing. I can shrink our path and end it all right now. We've almost reached our destination. With unseen hands and a torrent of power, I reach for Trallius. I reach for our unknown foe. I know his name now. Kyri. I grasp their souls, seeking to drag them with us.

It's not enough. I'm not enough. I'm—

A surge of energy rushes through my heart. I'm bathed in warmth—it's the power I felt when Ermo first helped me transport us to the pillar. For I recognize the truth now. I, with the assistance of the orb, brought us to the pillar. I've been awakening these powers since the moment I was inside the vault in Esmeraldi. When I pulled a spear across time and space.

Her power feeds mine, amplifying and transforming it into something greater than the sum of our parts. In a maelstrom of white fury, we tumble forward, reaching our destination.

XV

ERMO

With a tiny pop, we roll to a stop upon a hard moonstone surface. Light, all around. It's sunny.

I vomit, the gut-wrenching experience obliterating my insides. As my senses resolve into meaning, I remember what I witnessed Roan achieve. Her terrifying power lives in a league of its own.

I roll to my feet.

We've arrived at the Bridge of Our Lord. The Bridge I rebuilt. Above the Chasm. The place where it all began.

I don't know if the legends are completely true, but supposedly, the Lord of Light built the bridge. If Orion was the one who caused its creation through some arcane magic upon his death, then it holds more significance than I could have ever imagined. Maybe, once we finish the fight, Roan and I can discover many mysteries of the past.

Regardless, I rebuilt it. After my father fractured it, I rebuilt it. And now I've returned.

I breathe, turn around, and see Roan, sprawling on the bridge. Beyond her, two other figures stumble to their feet.

A visage sprawls. It's the one from the visions during our trip here. And High Inquisitor Trallius. I've been told enough about him to know it's him. Moreover, he was in one of the visions, too. The one where he executed my grandfather.

The proof we've always desired. He deserves to die.

I grasp the hammer sheathed on my back, brandishing it in my right hand. In his language, I say, "Do you know who I am, High Inquisitor Trallius? Do you know who I am?"

His eyes widen. He stumbles toward Lethotar's side of the

Chasm. With a glance to the left, he sees the visage rising.

It—or he?—is unlike any of the fiends we've found before. The creatures held by the Inquisition are pale imitations of this monstrosity. Its eyes are fiercely intelligent. Its blueish-purple skin ripples and shimmers in waves beneath blackened obsidian armor.

I keep wanting to say it's a man, but I don't know whether I'd be speaking truth with that assessment. Do these creatures—

"You! You are from my dreams!"

Trallius points at the visage, not me.

"I am," it says. Its words are unintelligible, yet we all somehow understand. Ripples of white mist float upward from the bridge. Orion had truly thought of everything. It's not merely a bridge between lands, it's a bridge between peoples. Cultures. Tongues. "And I know who you are. We have watched for years. Prepared. Our time has arrived to rend vengeance upon you and your transgressions."

For the first time, I see the giant moonstone blade on its back. I pause, surprised by the rapid shift in the encounter. I cautiously step forward, helping Roan to her feet. "What did you do?" I whisper.

"We're ending this," she replies. "Right here. They're the only two that matter."

"That can't possibly be true."

"I suppose we'll find out."

The visage turns toward us. "I am Kyri of the City of Shade, within the shadowlands in the Caves of Akonar. My people have come to the surface realm to bring vengeance to the Holy Empire and all who live here who wish to oppose us. Bend the knee, and you shall be spared."

I tilt my head in curiosity. "So, you're just another tyrant, like that one."

Kyri places a hand on the hilt of the sword resting at his hip. "No, we are liberators. We are the Shadow that brings Death to the Scourge plaguing this world."

"No," I say, taking a step forward. "You wish to bring war upon innocent lives, no differently than the Holy Empire that sought to murder and exterminate my people. You are no better. You. The Inquisition. You're all a disease upon this world, a way of thinking that we intend to destroy."

"By killing us," Kyri replies, "how does that make you any better?"

I pause. As much as I hated it, his logic is sound. How does it make me any better? How do we end the cycle of violence?

Kyri grins, as if seeing the hesitation attempting to hide behind my eyes. "Yes, you see the truth. We are all weapons of violence, in the end. Killing me, killing him, you won't end anything. My people will continue their assault upon the world. They will conquer without me. You'll make me a martyr."

He's right. He's absolutely right. How do we defeat an enemy without killing them?

Two sacrifices.

Orion said two more sacrifices remained. And here we stand, upon the Bridge of our Lord. Above the Chasm. Where my journey began, three years ago, when I leapt into the depths below.

I see the path forward. *My* path forward. Koric sacrificed himself, paying half the price. And now, we reach the climax of our destiny.

"Well, no use wasting anyone's time," Kyri says. "We'll start with the Inquisitor, then the two of you." With lightning speed, he unsheathes his sword and darts toward the old man.

Trallius trembles. Standing all alone, the old man is terrified. He may be a monster, but in the end . . .

He's an old man. Probably the same age as Ero, maybe a few years older. Sure, the old man who murdered my grandfather, ordered the genocide of my people, and the exploitation of his own followers.

An old, helpless man.

Who I can save.

My grandfather's hammer in hand, I leap forward, propelled by power and purpose. But I do not intend to block Kyri's blade.

I slide into place between the visage and the High Inquisitor. The ghastly creature's blade finds my chest, cutting through my armor with ease. The sharpened moonstone breaks my skin, but I feel no pain.

Only peace.

The fires of life embrace me. The souls of grandfather Maripes, and Father Mono, they welcome me with open arms.

My eyes connect with Kyri as blood seeps down my armor. Somewhere, Roan screams, but she will understand. I am the final sacrifice.

"You lose," I say. "And the ritual is complete."

I grab his blade, thrusting it deeper into my chest. Stumbling backward, I plummet off the side of the Bridge of our Lord, welcoming the Chasm once again.

* * *

Yet that is not my end. It is an *ending*, but it is also a beginning.

I float in darkness, witnessing a million lives passing by. A billion years condense into a singularity of life and death. Floating, in the shadow, a young girl stands lifeless. At her feet, a spear beckons. I reach out, speaking words I don't understand.

"Ermo, *follow*."

I hear, in my words, the voice of my ancestors.

"Follow."

In my first moments, when I leapt from the Chasm, I heard my own voice. Pushing me toward destiny.

"You are the light. They were the light. They are the light. You are all the light. Will be the light."

The girl. Me. She opens her eyes. She grasps the spear. She reaches for the light.

XVI

ROAN

I watch Ermo's body fall off the bridge, plummeting quickly out of sight. First Yarwin. Then Koric. Now Ermo. I can't take it. I scream, preparing to charge the monster who killed the last of our destiny-driven team, but I pause. I don't think I need to.

Kyri steps back, staring at his hands. They're glowing.

"Ash-kar Taro Bin?" Words in his own language, I presume. Whatever strange power translated his words previously, it's fading. Before he says another word, his body explodes in brightness, a light overwhelmingly vibrant. I close my eyes, the blinding white threatening to burn away my sight. The inferno attempts to crack through my eyelids, but I hold strong.

And then it's gone.

I open my eyes.

A thousand little orbs float into the air, dissipating onto the wind. Kyri, the visage, is gone. We've completed the work Orion started a thousand generations ago.

With the sacrifice of those who came before me, the victory feels hollow.

Standing, trembling, High Inquisitor Trallius watches the lights float away. He's distracted. I see my chance. I can't throw it away now. Yet, I consider the sacrifice Ermo just made. She saved Trallius. Dare I sully her memory by killing the person she chose to save? Could he change, changing the Empire as well? My hand releases the hilt of my blade—I hadn't known I'd been clenching it. It remains in its sheath.

After a long moment of watching the lights slowly disappear, Trallius turns to face me.

"I recognize you," he says. The icy demeanor I know from the visions returns. "You. You are the girl who stole from my vault. I saw you. You have power. Join me. Join the Inquisition. You can be great." He steps toward me, arms spread wide

I shake my head. "Join you?"

"Yes. The Inquisition is always searching for people of power. You are a citizen of the Holy Empire, are you not? Do you think if we had found you, we would have killed you? No. Not at all. You are special. You deserve a future serving the Empire." He steps closer. "You deserve—"

And he attempts to strike, reaching for my shoulders.

But Yarwin's training kicks in. I see his hands, they fly toward me. I duck, sweeping a kick toward his legs. The feeble man instantly falls, his head crashing toward the bridge. His skull hits hard, and with a crack, blood spills onto the moonstone.

Drool and phlegm drain from his mouth, eyes glazing over. In his arrogance, he believed he could still win. Ermo made the ultimate sacrifice for a man who did not deserve a life given for his own.

I fall to my knees. The battle, over. I scream, releasing all the pain built up in my soul over the past day.

Only a day!

Ermo, Yarwin, Koric, and I arrived at the pillar in the desert yesterday morning, and three of the four of us have died.

And I survived.

As Trallius releases his final breath, I fall into a fetal position. Koric. Gone. At the hands of a giant snake. What happened to us? How could fate drive us on such journey? Yarwin, dead fighting demons on a pathway up the pillar. His sacrifice. Was it worth it?

Ermo, laying her life down for a man who didn't deserve it to break a curse afflicting an entire people. Set by the man who created our path a thousand years ago. Did any of it matter?

I rock back and forth, letting the emotions overwhelm. It feels good to just release the tension building since the day I set foot in the palace's vault. I had begun to love Ermo, seeing in her a future

I wished would happen. Together, we could have united our people. Showed them our powers, proving to them we could bridge the divide. Instead, she's dead at the bottom of a giant gorge.

Where am I? Where do I go? How do I move forward after this incredible journey?

I cradle my legs, sobbing. It's all over. And I have broken in the process. I am the one to live while the others die.

EPILOGUE

Ero enters the High Keep of Lethotar, not even bothering to stop at home. He received the message from the Council and the other High Priests the moment he passed through the Gates of Vicor. He had news for them as well, though he knows word from the borderlands traveled ahead of him.

"Welcome, Councilor," an attendant says, nodding as Ero enters. "We've been expecting you. They are already in session."

"Thank you," Ero replies. He knows what to expect. But he doesn't want to believe it.

Striding through the giant bronze doors, Ero enters the High Council of the People of Light. Five men and women await him in grey and black cloaks—and a young human woman. He hadn't expected this development.

"Ero, finally," says Ryik. "You couldn't arrive soon enough."

"I assume you've heard the news?" Ero says. He takes a seat, and as he sits, everyone else takes a chair. The girl follows suit.

"We've heard the rumors, but we also have an eyewitness of an event you must understand. We still don't comprehend its significance ourselves, but you should hear it from her mouth. Are you up-to-date on your Esmeraldian dialects?"

"I am."

In the language of the Holy Empire, Ryik says, "Roan, please tell Ero your story."

Ero turns to face the girl. She grimaces, clearly uncomfortable and fearing the words she was about to say. "I was with your daughter when she died."

Ero nods, confirming the truth he felt in his heart.

"She stood atop the bridge and sacrificed herself for the world. A demon—Orion called it a visage—sought to kill us all. He was the same demon that led a horde against us on the battlefield along the River Wi. Except he wasn't truly a demon. His name was Kyri.

He was a tortured soul, just like all the other corrupt creatures encountered by both your people and my own. And your daughter freed their souls."

Ero nods again, contemplating the girl's words. The reports from across the Three Valleys all rang similarly. In the initial attacks from the fiends, everyone fell, but suddenly, the fiends disappeared into light. The accounts matched Ermo's retelling of the battle before the Gates of Vicor but on a grander scale. When he first heard the tales, he began to suspect the truth of his daughter's fate. Ermo fulfilled prophecies as the Daughter of Light in a way she never knew possible.

"Please, continue," Ero simply says. "Roan, is it? I hope I can hear many tales of my daughter's final hours."

"Your daughter . . . she opened my eyes to the truth of the world," the young girl says. "What we need to do to save it, and bring our peoples together. I wish she could be with us as we reunite the People of Light and the Holy Empire. We're undoing a thousand years of history, after all." She holds up a book. "I've written down my account. I'm still understanding the power I have—a power similar to what your daughter possessed—and I believe it will allow me to tell the whole story."

Ero says, "And what truth will that story tell?"

"It will tell the story of your family, and the sacrifices they made for not just the People of Light, but the entire world." Roan brushes hair back behind her ears. "Ermo, especially, sacrificed herself in a ritual a thousand years in the making. That is my belief. She saved us in a way we won't ever comprehend."

"And Ero," Ryik says, "Trallius is dead, by the hand of Roan. Don't ask me how, I still don't believe it. But he's dead."

Ero exhales. A path forward. It won't be easy. "Then I will help you write this tale, young Roan. So Ermo, Mono, and Maripes achieve immortality."

"Not just them," Roan replies. "Yarwin and Koric. My family. And I think we need to tell Kyri's story, too. The story of the visages. They were a people caught between life and death, and not on their own accord. They weren't evil. And now they've been given peace."

Ero nods. "You have quite the story to tell me."

Author's Note

Thank you for reading **The War of Light: The Compendium Trilogy**. I hope you've enjoyed the adventures Ermo, Roan, and the other characters as much as I liked writing them.

And I hope you'll consider leaving a review for the story on Amazon!

In addition, make sure you stay in touch to hear about opportunities for free books and new releases. You can join my mailing list easily by heading to my website, https://www.twodoctorsmedia.com.

If you're looking for more SciFi and Fantasy, I encourage you to download **Storming the Stairway to the Stars**, a story available for free if you join my mailing list. It's part of my **Shattering Worlds** story collection.

And please, share **The War of Light** with your friends!